AND PROUD OF IT

"You're a rake," she managed to say.

"Why yes, I am," Gabriel almost purred, now fully in command of himself.

Imogen went suddenly still as he leaned over her, rolling more fully onto his side, and sliding one leg over her hips, trapping her on the bed.

Gabriel leaned down further, capturing her mouth with his, and when he felt her quiver, and not—he was positive—with desire, he pulled back and looked her right in the eye. "Don't you dare," he warned sternly, before returning to the eminently enjoyable task of kissing her.

Also by Kalen Hughes

LORD SIN

Published by Zebra Books

LORD SCANDAL

KALEN HUGHES

ZEBRA BOOKS
Kensington Publishing Corp.
http://www.kensingtonbooks.com

ZEBRA BOOKS are published by

Kensington Publishing Corp.
850 Third Avenue
New York, NY 10022

All Kensington titles, imprints, and distributed lines are available at special quantity discounts for bulk purchases for sales promotion, premiums, fund-raising, educational, or institutional use.

Special book excerpts or customized printings can also be created to fit specific needs. For details, write or phone the office of the Kensington Special Sales Manager: Attn. Special Sales Department. Kensington Publishing Corp., 850 Third Avenue, New York, NY 10022. Phone: 1-800-221-2647.

ISBN-13: 978-0-8217-8150-0
ISBN-10: 0-8217-8150-2

First Printing: June 2008
10 9 8 7 6 5 4 3 2 1

Printed in the United States of America

For all my girlfriends, who've read this book over and over, made suggestions, loaned me books, cooked me dinner, got me drunk, and in all ways been the best friends I could ever hope for. I love you guys.

ACKNOWLEDGMENTS

First and foremost the late Georgette Heyer, without whom I would never have written a romance novel. Julia Ross, whose books taught me that lyricism isn't dead in modern fiction. Candice Hern, whose insight into publishing has helped me immensely, and whose amazing collection of Georgian antiques literally inspires me (she knows exactly which scene I'm talking about!). The members of the San Francisco Bay Area RWA chapter, especially Monica, Jami, Nyree, and Doreen. The members of the Beau Monde RWA chapter, who share their knowledge and resources so generously—especially Nancy Mayer and Dee Hendrickson, fonts of knowledge, both of them. The Wild Cards, for their endless support and unflagging optimism. My agent, Paige Wheeler, and huge thanks to my editor, Hilary Sares, who makes everything seem effortless.

Chapter 1

The Angelstone Turk would appear to have given his opera dancer her congé. We eagerly await the impending melee amongst those desirous of taking his place . . .

Tête-à-Tête, 11 August 1789

He had her.

Gabriel Angelstone slid his hands around the countess's waist and pulled her back against him. God he'd missed her. Childhood friend, first love, best friend. She'd been the cynosure of his world and the sad truth was that without her, he was bored.

Bored with drinking. Bored with gaming. Bored with whoring. Bored with London. And when one was bored with London, one was bored with life. No truer words had ever been spoken.

She gasped and went stiff, sent her basket tumbling to the ground, and rammed him hard in the ribs with one sharp elbow. Gabriel let go of her immediately.

What in hell was wrong with her?

He was early, by a full day, but that was hardly unusual. What was a day or two between friends?

She spun around, skirts flying out, gravel churning underfoot, and backed away from him. She stopped only when her heels hit the edge of the fountain and threw out a hand to steady herself, tense as a cornered doe.

Staring up at him from under the most ridiculous portrait hat he'd ever seen was a face that clearly wasn't Georgianna's. Not George's, but oddly familiar all the same. Like a melody once heard in passing. Memory stirred, but refused to wake.

Little audible pops accompanied the greedy frenzy of the carp as they sucked up the bread crumbs she'd just scattered over the water, loud even over the merry splash of the fountain. Gabriel smiled, swept off his hat, and bowed.

His unknown victim watched him warily through large blue-grey eyes, thickly rimmed with sooty lashes the same color as her mass of spiral curls. She had a wide mouth; the top lip fuller than the bottom one. It should have looked luscious, well kissed, seductive, but at that exact moment her lips were pursed. Disapproving. A little downward curl marred their edges. As she studied him, she straightened, shoulders back, chest thrust out. Her eyes took on a decidedly flinty edge.

His garden nymph had a temper . . . how delightful.

Imogen stared at the man who'd just accosted her, struggling to keep her mouth from dropping open. He was undoubtedly one of the countess's friends. It was common knowledge Lady Somercote came from a wild set. But guests weren't due to arrive for at least another day or two.

As the countess's titular companion she'd been busy assisting with all the tasks no one had time for in the rush to finish the party preparations. Simple things: feeding the fish in the maze, taking the countess's dog for a walk, delivering a jar of pig's feet jelly to the parsonage. Servant-stuff really, but they were busy too. Helping out with such tasks was little enough considering all the Somercotes had done for her.

She stared at the smiling man before her, smoothed suddenly damp hands over her skirts. If only she'd brought the countess's mastiff with her on this errand. The elegant beau smiling predatorily down at her wouldn't look nearly so attractive with Caesar pinning him to the ground. It would serve him right to have the immaculate folds of his cravat disordered, his beautiful coat covered in dog drool, smeared with mud.

She could picture it as clearly as if it was actually happening.

He wouldn't be smiling at her in that impudent way, either, the jack-a-napes. She really should go, but it would be too undignified to scramble around him like some ninny of a girl. His had been the offense. It was for him to make reparations, not for her to run away. He certainly wouldn't hurt her—not if he was a guest of the Somercotes—and it had been a long time since anyone had looked at her with such open admiration. With such clear intent.

Had a man such as this one ever looked at her? It seemed unlikely. He was magnificent. Tall, with an odd cast to his features that put her strongly in mind of the foreign princes and Italian counts who littered the pages of the popular novels. Especially his eyes.

Those were *not* English eyes.

Gabriel smiled down at his nymph. She was undoubtedly another early arrival.

George would skin him alive if she caught him trifling with any of her friends, but he couldn't resist the challenge in the lady's snapping eyes. Anger brought out the best in some women. Firing the blood, raising a flush beneath their delicate skin, making their bosom rise and fall with entrancing rapidity. Yes. Angry, proud, and undeniably a wee bit intrigued.

He knew the signs.

Delicate lace mitts obscured her hands, but no tell-tale flash of gold warned him off.

Besides, what could a little flirtation hurt? Wasn't this what country house parties were for? He rose from his bow, eyes locked with hers, his free hand held to his still smarting ribs in theatrical display.

"'She that makes me sin awards me pain.'"

The lady cocked her head, sparrow-like. The corners of her lips betrayed her, quirking up into the slightest of smiles.

Oh yes, he had her.

She dropped him a rather frosty curtsy, barely more than a dip of the knees accompanied by the slightest inclination of her head. "'Nothing emboldens sin so much as mercy,' and so sir, I shall show you none."

Gabriel's smile widened. Beautiful, well read, and witty? What were the odds? "'And for this sin there is no remedy'—much like the wound you've done me, my fair Daphne."

Her brows drew together as she considered him, the winged shape flattening. She crossed her arms, breasts rising another degree like an incoming tide. She really did look familiar. Why couldn't he remember? How could he have forgotten such a woman?

Gabriel took one small step to the right, placing himself between her and the courtyard's only exit. Her gaze left his, darted over his shoulder and back again. His strategy hadn't escaped her notice. Her moment of panic had dissipated, leaving her calm, and—he grinned again—condescending in a queenly way.

She stared him down, batting her eyes at him the way his cousin did when she thought him deliberately obtuse. "'Tis a sin to flatter,' sir, and you'd do well to remember your Greek; Apollo lost his nymph."

Gabriel gave a bark of laughter, startling the thrushes in the hedge into flight. They escaped in a loud, chattering swarm, spiraling upwards and away.

"The sun god must have been a bit slow, but we were quoting Shakespeare, not the classics, let us return to whence we came . . ." He smiled his most beguiling smile, the one that set young ladies fluttering, scandalized dowagers, and always made his cousin rap him with her fan. He took a deliberate step towards the lady in the monstrous hat. She held her ground, merely raking her glance up and down him appraisingly. "'Some rise by sin, and some by virtue fall.'"

"'Man-like it is to fall into sin, Fiend-like to dwell therein.'"

"That's not Shakespeare." His smile widened. It was beyond his control. He was going to have to kiss her. There was simply no help for it. "You're wandering afield again."

"It's from a German poet, but apt all the same."

"Now, now. Let's stick to our parameters . . ." He took another step towards her, getting within arms-length. "'Repent you, fair one, of the sin you carry.'"

"The sin I carry?" One arched brow rose. "I thought we were speaking of your sin?"

"My sin? 'Love is my sin.'"

She snorted.

There was no other word for it. It wasn't a giggle; couldn't even vaguely be construed a titter. It was a snort, and a rather derisive one at that. Gabriel closed the last step between them, casting his hat aside as he did so. His hands closed on crisply glazed cotton, and for the second time that day, he pulled her into his arms.

He leaned in, ducking his head beneath the brim of her hat, so close her curls tickled his face, fine hairs catching in the slight burr of his cheek. "'Shall we continue in this sin?'"

"Now who's wandering?" One side of her mouth crinkled upwards. A dimple winked in her cheek, unabashed and unintimidated. "Unless I'm mistaken, that's biblical. Better to have said, 'but sin had his reward.'"

Mirth flooded through him, warming him from the inside out, making him want to taste her even more. He tipped back her hat. "Shall I wander further? 'To sin in secret is no sin at all.'"

He lowered his head and captured her lips with his own. He kissed her softly, teasingly. Testing the waters. Giving her every chance to pull away, to slap him . . . to kiss him back.

She did none of them. She just stood there, cool and stiff as the laurel tree Apollo's nymph had become.

After a moment she sighed, boredom oozing from every pore, hands trapped limply against his chest. If only he could pretend such disaffection. She was soft and rounded in all the right places. High breasts full above a small waist, what he was sure would prove to be a perfectly heart-shaped bottom hidden beneath layers of petticoats held out by pads. She smelled ever so faintly of soap and rose water. Not the musky ambergris that opera dancers and paphians always seemed to be drenched in, but something that spoke of sunlight, of practicality . . . of virtue.

He ran the tip of his tongue along her lower lip, trying to provoke a response. No lady had a right to look as she did and smell of virtue. She pressed closer, sliding her arms around his neck, her body softening against his in unmistakable capitulation. He chuckled and adjusted his grip, sliding one hand down to press her hips against his.

With a deceptive twist of her body she stomped down on his instep, hard enough to make his eyes water.

He yelped and let go of her. She stepped back, her gaze scathing, her lips curled into a mocking little smile. She raised her chin another notch, and looking altogether pleased with herself, swept past him as composed as a dowager at court. She didn't even have the decency to hurry.

Gabriel gathered up his hat and the basket she'd left behind and limped back towards the house, smiling all the while at the temerity of his garden nymph. George's house party was going to be amusing on several counts, and the presence of his assailant promised to contribute mightily to his enjoyment of the next fortnight.

Still swinging the basket in one hand Gabriel let himself into the house via the French doors that had been left wide-open to capture the sea breeze. Just inside he found George sitting at the small desk, a blank sheet of foolscap spread out before her. She was staring off into space, caught up in thought, rhythmically running the soft end of her quill along one cheek.

"George?" he said from the doorway, smiling as she jumped in surprise. She tossed aside her quill and leapt up to welcome him, amid the deep baying that erupted as her dog was roused from his nap.

"Gabriel. You're early, you scoundrel." She hurried across the room, hands extended, then stopped, a look of perplextion crossing her face when she spied the basket.

The mastiff wooffled a few more times, sniffed Gabriel's boots, then settled back down on the carpet with a thump that made the floorboards protest.

Gabriel took both George's hands in his, gave them a quick squeeze and dropped a brotherly kiss on her cheek. "You're looking well. Married life obviously agrees with you."

"Ivo agrees with me at any rate," she responded, with what he thought was just a hint of a blush.

"Much more so than widowhood did." He let the blush go; there'd be plenty of time for teasing her about the joys of marital bliss when reinforcements arrived. And she did look happy. Almost sickeningly so. Was it wrong that he'd hoped to find her moped? It suddenly felt wrong. Like a shameful secret.

Love ruins everything. His motto. His one truth. A fact he'd been aware of nearly all his life, damn his parents, but George's having succumbed to the malady didn't appear to have ruined hers.

As he studied her, taking in the glow that lit her cheeks, the tumble of auburn curls and the slightly scandalous chemise dress, she eyed the basket he was carrying and raised one brow. "Taking up gardening? Or is that the latest rage in portmanteaus?"

"Neither, as well you know. This was abandoned by the lovely termagant I caught feeding your fish. Not only did she ruthlessly abandon the basket, but she left me to find my own way out of the maze after luring me into it, and she stomped on my foot in the bargain. And I think she's scuffed my boot." He extended his damaged footwear for George's inspection.

George looked skeptical. "And what, my tulip, did you do to make her abandon her basket and stomp on your foot?"

"Do?" Gabriel responded, all mock innocence. "Nothing, I assure you."

"Nothing indeed. No sooner did the lady lay eyes on you than she was overwhelmed with the need to assault your boots?"

"Something like that." Gabriel pressed his lips together to keep from grinning. George was likely to slap him if he did.

"I'm sure," George replied acerbically. "Shall we see if we can get through the rest of my house party without any of my other guests being overcome by a similar need?"

"I believe I can confine myself to the one guest. Unless your friend has a large, and perhaps, watchful husband in tow?"

"I'm warning you, Brimstone." George eyed him sternly. "You're to leave Miss Mowbray alone."

"Oh? And why is that?" He picked a bit of lint off his sleeve. She never called him Brimstone, except when she was annoyed. Never.

"Don't be childish." She took hold of him by the arm and led him back outside. "Come and take a walk with me. I've been inside too long today."

"George," he growled, tossing the basket aside and allowing her to lead him off all the same.

"Don't take that tone with me. I'm well aware of your

style of dalliance—having been witness to it for years—and believe me, she's not it. The last thing Imogen needs is her name coupled with yours."

"Imogen . . . I like the name Imogen."

George glared up at him. "You're going to be difficult about this, aren't you?"

"Difficult? Me? When have I ever been difficult?"

Her fingers dug into his arm as she propelled him across the terrace. "When haven't you been? You can survive two weeks without setting up a flirt, I know you can."

"Are you going to tell me why I'm to forego the considerable enjoyment of flirting with Miss Imogen Mowbray?"

George sighed and looked up at him, her gaze serious. "Because you don't flirt, you seduce. Because she used to be Mrs. William Perrin. Because I asked you not to."

"William Perrin . . ." Gabriel removed George's claw-like grip on his arm and steered her down the brick path towards the large formal herb garden laid out on the second terrace.

He turned the name over in his head. There was a scandal. Years ago now . . . it had all been over a painting.

That's why she looked so familiar.

He'd seen those eyes gazing down at him every day for the past year. Ever since he'd added the most infamous portrait in England to his collection. Those amazing eyes, a wicked come-hither smile, and the creamy skin of her shoulder where her gown had slipped, seemingly unnoticed . . .

His blood heated. His cock twitched, rude and demanding. How could he have not recognized her? "You've got the Portrait Divorcée staying with you?"

George nodded, her mischievous smile peeping out. "I met her at Helen Perripoint's last season. She's been living in the most dreadful boarding house imaginable, and we have all this room." She waved one hand around, taking in the house, the gardens and park. "She's currently occupying our dowager house, and I like her very much."

George stopped and turned to face him. She took his lapels in her hands, holding him in place. "So, you see why you should leave her alone."

"I do?"

"You do," she replied firmly, giving his coat a little yank, then smoothing the fabric. "Your cousin and I have plans for her social resurrection—at least on a small scale—but we'll never pull it off with you sniffing around. She has to reek of respectability and repentance."

"Does Miss Mowbray know about your little scheme?"

George looked at him as if he'd broken out in purple spots. "Of course not."

"My God!" Gabriel's jaw dropped slightly, icy fingers crawled up his spine. "You're getting to be as bad as Torrie."

"Aren't I?" George agreed, stooping to sniff one of her roses, trailing curls spilling over her shoulder.

Beautiful, graceful, dear as a sister. She scared the hell out of him. He'd survived his cousin's machinations all these years, but if Torrie and George were to unite forces? There wouldn't be a man in England who could stand against them.

Chapter 2

Lady S—— is set to host her first country house party, dare we hope for a bit of the old Lady Corinthian to appear and provide us with something like the entertainments we once enjoyed?

Tête-à-Tête, 11 August 1789

She shouldn't be amused. She shouldn't be repressing laughter. Being accosted by a stranger was supposed to overset a lady's delicate sensibilities, or at the very least, enrage her. So why couldn't she stop smiling?

Her foot twisted in the loose gravel of the walk and she forced herself to stop, take a deep breath, and continue more slowly. The countess's friend was clearly used to getting his way with women. He had the unmistakable air of a rake. There was always something cynical about the eyes. Something a tad humorless about the mouth, no matter how they smiled. They were a breed apart. The fox hiding within the dog pack.

He'd been genuinely surprised when she'd stomped on

his foot. Apparently that was not the response he was used to receiving to his overtures. She put one hand up to hide a grin. She sincerely hoped she'd left a scuff on his boot for him to remember her by.

Barton Court's dowager house was a neat, three story manor house set off to one side at the far end of the gardens. Compared to the great house it was little more than a cottage. It was pure heaven compared to the boarding house she'd been living in only a few months before.

When William had divorced her, her parents had simply wanted the scandal to go away by whatever means necessary. And if that meant leaving her nearly destitute, well, her father had plainly informed her that was her own damned fault. He wasn't about to have a ruined daughter hanging on his sleeve.

So she'd scraped by on the pittance an aunt had left her, unhappily purse pinched and well aware that she would remain so until her dying day. No matter how many watercolor lessons, French lessons, or music lessons she gave to the daughters of wealthy cits and shopkeepers, she was never going to be able to command more than the basic necessities of life. The elegancies she'd been raised with were completely beyond her means.

Then this past spring she'd encountered the new Countess of Somercote at a small party given by a mutual friend. Within a month the countess and her husband had extended an offer of the use of their dowager house. Imogen wasn't fool enough to look a gift horse in the mouth.

After more than four years of less than genteel poverty, her new circumstances were a relief. There were horses in the stable for her to ride, and there was always an ample supply of coal and wood in the house. There were real wax candles and oil lamps in every room—not sooty tallow ones that sputtered, stank and smoked—good quality tea, and a lovely pianoforte which had been sent down from the main house for her use.

For the first time since William had walked into their home and literally thrown her out the front door and down the steps, her life didn't seem to be an endless, bleak burden. There was air to breathe.

Imogen came to the end of the gardens and slipped off her hat as she entered the house. Several hairpins pinged on the wooden floor. She stooped to collect them before hanging her hat on a peg near the door and retreating to the parlor.

She really should go up to the house and see if the countess had any further need of her, but she wasn't up to another encounter with the countess's friend just yet. She could feel him lurking up at the house, just waiting to catch her out again.

She repositioned her slipping hair and maneuvered the pins back in, twisting them through the curls until they felt secure.

No, best to wait for more guests to arrive before she encountered him again. She sighed and picked up her work basket; the last thing she needed was another scandal attached to her name, and her new acquaintance had trouble written all over him.

The next morning Imogen was comfortably ensconced in the parlor, habit on, booted feet extended to the fire, embarking on her second cup of tea when the countess arrived for their morning ride.

"George." She rose to greet her friend. "And Caesar,

too." She bent to scratch the mastiff and pull softly on his floppy ears, not caring that the dog was likely to wipe his drool-covered chin on her skirts. "Are we ready to go? I'm pining for a good gallop."

"I'll be ready just as soon as I get a cup of tea or two into me, and eat some of the scones cook made this morning. And I have to return your basket as well," George added slyly, "since you didn't come to the house for dinner last night and retrieve it yourself."

Imogen blushed hotly and George raised one brow. Why had she never learned to control her blushes? It was mortifying. "Yes. I-I dropped it yesterday . . . in the garden." Why had she left it behind? Why?

"You needn't dissemble." George poured herself a cup of tea, steaming liquid flowing in a graceful arc from pot to cup. "When Gabriel Angelstone arrived with your basket over one arm, a sadly scuffed boot, and wearing a sheepish smile, I was quickly able to put two and two together. He's always been a rogue. I didn't expect him until Monday at the earliest, or I'd have warned you."

"Warned me?" Imogen's stomach lurched, twisting like a fish caught on a line.

"Don't look so stricken. I didn't mean to startle you. Though I'm sure Angelstone did, dreadful, provoking beast that he is."

"Angelstone. So he is English? I thought perhaps—"

"That some foreign devil had leapt from the pages of a horrid novel and invaded my garden?" The countess laughed, shoulders curling inward with pure amusement. "His father was old Edymion Angelstone, diplomat, world traveler, and in the end, one of the great scandals of his day."

Imogen took a bite of her scone and nodded, wanting the countess to continue. "What did he do?"

"Nothing so very terrible, unless you're English and anything foreign threatens to shake the foundation of your world." George set her cup down, and tossed the crumbs of her scone into the fire. "He married the daughter of a Turkish Pasha, lived happily with her in the shadow of Galata Tower for more than a decade by all accounts. When she died he brought his eight-year-old son home to England."

"Ah, a great misalliance as my grandmother would say."

"As she probably did say. Mine certainly did. It's one thing for poor Englishmen in India to take a native wife. Something else entirely when the wealthy grandson of a duke does the same. Don't mind him, though. He'll do everything in his power to make you blush—especially considering you do so so prettily—but he's not a danger to you."

"He's already succeeded in making me blush." Imogen tried to keep the amusement from her voice. Her response was yet another symptom of what her father referred to as "her fatal flaw." Humor was not, in his opinion, a trait one looked for in females; let alone a healthy sense of the ridiculous.

"Really?" The countess sipped her tea, eyes dancing. The silence stretched, making Imogen's throat tighten. Her pulse raced with the slightest beginnings of panic, heart fluttering like a caged song bird.

"I think he thought I was you, and he-he-he grabbed me from behind." Laughter, totally inappropriate laughter, bubbled up, nearly choking her.

"And that's when you stomped on his foot?"

"Not exactly." Imogen bit her lip, trying to hold the laughter back. George quirked a brow and waited for her to continue. "He started quoting Shakespeare, and trying to be . . . flirtatious," she considered her words, "seductive. It was really quite funny."

George smiled, nodding her head. "I don't think I've ever heard any woman who's been the object of that particular Angelstone's attentions laugh at him. They're usually too busy fainting or fawning."

"Oh?" Imogen replied, doing her best to present a picture of casual interest. It was easy to imagine either response, she'd swung between them both before anger had burned them away. "He clearly thinks himself quite something, but really, *Shakespeare?*"

"Too cliché?"

"Well, not the way he employed it, but—"

"So it was the Shakespeare that got his foot stomped on?"

Imogen shook her head. "He kissed me. More to shut me up than anything else, I think. That's what got his boot scuffed."

"He got less than he deserved, then." George said with an edge to her voice that Imogen was hard put to interpret. The countess rose from her chair and shook out her skirts. "Shall we get underway? Some of the guests are due later today, and I want to be back in time to greet them."

Their return to the house coincided with the arrival of the Earl and Countess of Morpeth, along with their three boys. The middle boy, who looked to be ten or eleven threw himself upon the countess, cries of "Aunt George! Aunt George!" echoing in the great hall.

Imogen stood quietly to one side as the family swirled

about. The eldest boy bowed credibly before George laughed and hugged him, neatly disposing of his bid for manhood. The commotion drew Mr. Angelstone and the earl out of the billiard room, boot heels ringing sharply on the marble floor.

He looked even more out of place—more foreign—here than he had in the garden. Golden skinned and almond eyed: a Sultan masquerading as an English Gentleman.

"Torrie." He grinned widely at Lady Morpeth as he scooped up her youngest son. He slung the rambunctious child over his shoulder, the boy erupting into squeals and giggles. "Morpeth," he added, nodding at her husband. He caught her eye and smiled. It was a very intimate smile. A lover's smile. She twisted her crop in her hands and raised her chin. He was not going to fluster her, no matter how hard he tried.

George broke the moment, waving Imogen over to her. "Victoria, you remember Miss Mowbray? You met her at Helen Perripoint's last spring. Imogen, I'm sure you remember the Countess of Morpeth, and this is her husband."

Imogen dropped a curtsy. She had been too young to mingle freely with their circle when she'd been married, and she sincerely hoped they didn't recognize her. Please? Just this once, let her scandal go unremarked upon?

Lady Morpeth gave her a friendly smile, without a hint of scorn or condensation. "Of course I remember Miss Mowbray. Morpeth, you remember my mentioning her, don't you?" The earl chuckled and assured her that he remembered both his wife and George mentioning their delightful new friend.

"And this," George said, indicating the man who'd

kissed her the day before, "is Mr. Gabriel Angelstone, the countess's cousin, and a very old friend of mine. Gabe, Miss Mowbray. I think the two of you have already had the pleasure?"

"The pleasure was entirely mine," he said, somehow managing to sound disreputable and seductive even while being climbed upon by a small boy.

Imogen nodded, then excused herself to go and change. His look of warm appraisal was far too forward. Especially in front of the other guests; his own family no less. He looked at her as if she were a sugared bun at a frost fair. She wouldn't allow it. Couldn't. She should have inquired how his footwear was fairing today, but under the assembled guests' curious gazes, she'd faltered.

After luncheon the guests began to arrive in droves, carriages rolling in one after another. Dust rose in the stable yard. The sound of iron-rimmed wheels on gravel became a constant hum of background noise. By late afternoon the garden was filled with ladies in colorful robes, their hair piled high in massive curled coiffures, mingling with gentlemen in equally magnificent coats, some in wigs, some with their own hair pulled back into casual queues. Laughter and conversation filled the garden as the guests swirled about like so many bees and butterflies.

Imogen sat in her favorite perch in the dowager house, idly working her tambour frame, watching them. The countess might think it no matter for her to be present, but she could feel a knot of uncertainty coiling in her belly. She recognized many of the people strolling past her window—she was one of them by birth—but she couldn't get up the courage to go out and join them. It would take an amount of brazen confidence that she was far from feeling.

As the light failed and the garden emptied Imogen reluctantly called her maid to help her dress. She chose one of her simplest gowns, a pale blue silk robe with a matching quilted petticoat. Striving for demure, she filled in the neckline with a fichu, the sheer fabric swathing her bosom, hiding her entire décolletage from view.

She sat down in front of her mirror and watched as Nancy carefully pinned up her curls. Her hair had always been a trial. It was a thick mass of tiny, spiraling curls, so darkly brown it almost appeared black. No amount of curling papers or hot tongs had ever been able to tame it.

When Nancy had achieved something they both thought passably attractive, she secured the whole with a dozen more pins. Imogen studied herself in the mirror, praying the pins would hold, and then took a deep breath. It was time to go up. She'd only a half-hour or so before dinner would be announced. She pulled on a pair of slightly darker blue gloves, grabbed her shawl, and made her way up to the house.

In the drawing room she quickly found herself lost among all the happily chatting guests. There was a knot of immaculately dressed men gathered around the fireplace, and two ladies gossiping in one corner. There were also, inevitably, several people Imogen had known previously when she'd been Mrs. Perrin, such as the elderly Earl of Carr and the even older Duke of Alençon.

Chest tight with panic she looked about for George. If she could just find the countess, she'd make it through the evening, and if she made it through the evening, then she'd likely make it through the next two weeks.

The countess had her back to the door, and over the din didn't appear to have noticed her arrival, but Alençon noticed her right away. He rose and quickly crossed the room, as immaculate and frightening as ever.

"We reprobates have to stick together, Miss Mowbray," he said with what would have been a flirtatious twinkle in a man half his age. He had to be over eighty, but was still trim and spry, with boyish dimples in his cheeks. He was a flirt and a roué. Someone her husband had loathed. That alone made her want to like him.

With a grateful smile she allowed him to lead her over to where Carr was seated, Lady Beverley—herself well past middle-age—beside him. Carr had changed little since she'd seen him last. Not so well-preserved as the duke, he was beginning to shrink. Wisps of his own hair peeked out from under his wig.

The duke placed her in the seat beside his and then fell easily back into conversation with his friends, one hand playing idly with the gold-headed cane he didn't appear to need.

This wasn't nearly as bad as she'd feared it would be. So long as she remembered to breathe everything would be fine. It was even beginning to feel familiar. She'd done this thousands of times before. Perhaps if she acted as though tonight were no different from any of those occasions, it wouldn't be.

Across the room she could now see the countess, surrounded by a tight knot of men, including Mr. Angelstone. His dark hair gleamed in the candlelight. As she studied them, he caught her eye and winked. Imogen fought to keep from blushing. She heard Carr chuckle and yanked her attention away from the group by the fireplace.

"The rogue making up to the countess is Angelstone," the earl said. "He's about the only one who can get within ten feet of our George without setting off poor Somercote. The earl has, on occasion, even taken exception to poor Alençon here. The lanky copper-top beside them is her brother. He's been up in Scotland for the summer, so I don't suppose you've met him yet; delightful boy. The handsome devil kicking at the fender just now is St. Audley, and the sandy-haired gentleman on the other side of him with the dashing scar is Colonel Staunton."

Imogen smiled at her elderly comrades and sat back to listen to them gossip. When dinner was finally announced, the duke led her in, breaking every rule of etiquette Imogen had ever learned. As the highest ranking man present he should have taken the countess in, leaving her to one of the misters. George had warned her that they rarely paid any attention to such rules, but she'd been wondering if she'd be left to partner Mr. Angelstone into dinner all the same.

She spent the first several courses mentally sorting all the details she'd been given. There were a smattering of guests who were merely friends, but most of them were related in one way or another. Once upon a time she'd been quite absorbed with such things. As the wife of a rising political star, she'd had to be.

She'd tried to make William see reason, but he had been unable to see anything but what he'd been told he'd see: a love letter written in oils; a declaration of her indiscretion—his betrayal—put up for the world to see.

He'd ranted and raved. He'd even thrown things. She'd

never imagined that he was capable of such violence. That had been an awakening. She'd thought her husband loved her. He'd never given her any reason to doubt it. At least not before he'd come home, still tousled and untidy from his fight with poor Mr. Firth, and thrown her down the steps of their town house.

Lying there on the sidewalk, with their butler, two footmen, her maid, and the boy who swept the street crossing, all staring at her she'd realized that it didn't matter what she said. William didn't love her.

Like Caesar's wife, she was no longer above reproach, nor ever could be again, and that made her worse than useless to her husband. It made her an embarrassment, a liability. To save himself, William had needed to be rid of her in a way that painted him the victim, and he'd done so. Quite thoroughly, as a matter of fact.

Down the table there was a sudden burst of laughter. She turned toward it, shaking off her gloomy reminiscences, only to find Angelstone watching her with soft, dark eyes. Desire sparked through her. An almost painful stab of awareness running from nipple to womb.

She looked away, turning her attention back to the filet of turbot in a dill cream sauce on her plate. She picked the fish apart with her fork, not eating it so much as playing with it. A footman leaned over, silent, practiced, and filled her wine glass. Imogen reached for it, grateful for the distraction.

How long had it been since a man had made love to her? Years by anyone's count.

Gabriel had been closely observing his garden nymph all evening. She'd slipped into the drawing room quietly, and Alençon—the old spoil sport—had made off with her before he'd had a chance to intercept her. He'd been waiting for her arrival for what seemed like hours.

She looked warm and inviting. Her hair begging to be disarranged. Just the sight of her had his breath tight in his chest. She was just so damnably pretty. Not a diamond like his cousin, nor an out-and-out dasher like George, she simply drew the eye and kept it. Perrin was a fool; only a complete nod-cock would have divested himself of such a woman, scandal or no.

He'd seen the relief that washed over her when Alençon claimed her, but still found himself irritated that the duke had absconded with her, and again when the old roué had escorted her into dinner. He'd have to see what he could manage after dinner. George couldn't fault him for flirting.

Alençon caught him watching them and raised his brows challengingly. Damn the old man. He was in on it. Another slave to George's machinations. Gabriel stared right back. Age and treachery couldn't win out every time.

After dinner, when the gentlemen rejoined the ladies in the drawing room, Gabriel casually wandered over to stand behind the sofa Miss Mowbray and George were seated on. His nymph needed to be reminded that he was not interchangeable with St. Audley, or, god forbid, Alençon. He leaned forward, placing his hands on the back of the sofa. While George droned on about the preparations for her ball, he traced small circles on the back of Miss Mowbray's shoulder with his index finger. He wished he were touching bare skin rather than the fine silk of her fichu, but the thin fabric did nothing to obscure the delicate heat of her skin.

She stiffened ever so slightly, but didn't move away. He smiled and leaned forward further, resting his forearms on the sofa back, putting his head on level with the seated ladies. The soft rose scent she wore enveloped him. His stomach clenched with repressed desire. The euphoric feeling of being near her washed away, replaced by a deep well of frustration.

He wanted to lean in, place his lips on the pulse point at her throat, catch the lobe of her ear between his teeth, press a hot, openmouthed kiss to the sensitive skin where her neck and shoulder met.

Before he could do anything so insanely stupid Viscount Layton interrupted them, suggesting a hand of cards. Gabriel agreed, making sure his fingers trailed her shoulders as he walked away. He drifted off across the room to pour himself a drink. Drinking, fleecing his friends at cards, and plotting Miss Mowbray's seduction seemed the perfect way to spend the next hour or so. Idle dreams of the flesh . . .

While he was still occupied at the card table, Miss Mowbray slipped out of the room. His senses cracked, urging him up. Urging him after her. He shoved the impulse down. Running after her was pure folly.

She'd timed that well. Another hand or two and he'd have been free to pursue her. As it was, he was well and truly stuck.

Once out of the drawing room Imogen drew a deep breath of relief. Angelstone had stared at her all through dinner. She'd hardly been able to eat a thing. Her mouth was too dry. Her stomach too unsettled. She was tipsy from the wine she'd washed her scanty meal down with and the port the countess had given her after dinner. No one else seemed to notice the amount of attention their friend paid her, but it seemed excessive to her. Oppressive even.

He'd been touching her all day. Driving her to distraction. Nothing overt, just a little unnecessary brush here and there. His foot rubbing hers under the breakfast table. His hand brushing her shoulder when he leaned forward to speak to George. He was like a cat stalking a bird.

She hurried through the garden, her skirts beheading flowers, making a mess of the beds she'd worked all summer to perfect. Her nipples were peaked inside her stays, abraded and tender. Her whole body was throbbing in time with her heart, flushed with the almost forgotten sensation of lust.

Chapter 3

The on dit of the week is the news that Lady R—— has eloped with her footman. This is the sad outcome of the recent penchant for handsome, strapping footmen.

Tête-à-Tête, 13 August 1789

Imogen stood on the terrace with a basket over one arm and watched the gentlemen disappear towards the lake. Angelstone glanced back over his shoulder, the distinct curl of his smile making her stomach flutter.

It was a beautiful, sunny morning. A perfect day for a ramble. The garden full of the low hum of bees and the chirping of birds.

Colonel Staunton had returned this morning from his neighboring estate with his very pregnant wife and several dogs in tow. Lurchers. Tall, rangy dogs that reminded her of grey hounds. Or at least of the severally bastardized descendents of grey hounds. They were scruffy and disreputable looking, with wildly mottled coats and long, narrow heads. Whatever their parentage, the colonel clearly doted on them.

He had settled his already wilting wife onto a sofa overlooking the garden, dropped a fond kiss upon her brow and then raced down the steps, his dogs loping along beside him.

George sent a maid running to fetch the suffering woman a glass of lemonade, and tucked a pillow in behind her to make her more comfortable.

"Eleanor," the countess said, "he didn't make you ride with the dogs?"

"Oh, didn't he?" Mrs. Staunton brushed a loose curl back from her face. "I'm big as a house, and being carted about like a prize heifer. Don't you dare laugh," she added darkly, "I'm sure you'd rather be out with the boys than here with us."

"Not at all," George assured her ruffled friend. "If I wanted to go coursing I would; Julius, Hay and Simone are tagging along, and the men were practically begging me to come along to watch them, and Imogen here is more than capable of giving you all a tour of the gardens; she certainly knows more about what's been planted out there than I do."

Imogen laughed, a blush rushing to her cheeks. "The children have gone with the men? I'm sure they were delighted," she added dryly, clearly able to picture the havoc the children were capable of creating.

"Julius is too old to leave behind," George said, "and they're too wise to think they're going to get out without Hay and Simone."

"Because mischief without George's changeling and my step-daughter is impossible; inconceivable even," Mrs. Staunton interjected with mock severity. When she'd finished her lemonade Mrs. Staunton pronounced herself ready for the tour, and George helped her up off the sofa.

"Lead on Imogen," the countess commanded. "Lead on."

Imogen took them all slowly through the gardens, pointing out any special touches they'd added, clipping flowers for the house as they went. She led them through the maze, and showed them the conservatory and then the wilderness.

Inside the artfully overgrown walled garden they found the Morpeths' youngest son rambling about with Caesar, both of them covered in a combination of dirt, spider webs, and a variety of stickers and seed pods. When his mother asked him where his nurse was, he shot her a smile and yelled, "No time now, got to be going." Then he dashed past them all, the dog hard upon his heels.

Lady Morpeth pursed her lips and swore under her breath, which simply made the other ladies laugh all the harder.

"What harm can he possibly come to?" George asked, gazing after his rapidly retreating form. "It must be very boring for him being left behind."

Rolling her eyes Lady Morpeth conceded the point, shaking her head ruefully.

When they had finished with the tour Lady Beverley pronounced their improvements first rate. "How are you with town gardens, my dear?" she asked Imogen as they strolled back up towards the house. "Mine's become rather stale of late, and you display a definite talent for garden design. When you come up to town next, George shall have to loan you to me."

"Oh, but I didn't do it all myself," Imogen dissembled,

not wanting to take all the credit, it wasn't her house after all. "George—"

"Stood on the terrace and said 'That looks very nice, Imogen.' Imogen did it all. No, that's not right . . ." she bit her lip, obviously racking her brain. "I think I was responsible for directing Hatcher to have the maze trimmed up . . ."

"And for deciding we should have punts on the lake," Imogen added when the countess seemed unable to come up with anything else.

"And for deciding we should have punts on the lake," George concurred with a laugh.

Noticing that Mrs. Staunton seemed to be tiring, Imogen caught George's eye and nodded ever so slightly in her direction. Quick on the uptake as usual, George suggested they all retire to the terrace for refreshments, and offered her arm to her pregnant friend.

"It really is ridiculous how quickly I wear out," Eleanor grumbled as George assisted her up the stairs. "You'd think I was in my dotage."

"The last couple of months are like that," Lady Morpeth said. "You'll feel more the thing when we've got you settled on the sofa with a cool drink. I basically didn't move for the last month or so," she added. "I slept and lounged around my boudoir, and snapped at poor Rupert anytime he came near. It's no wonder the polite world refers to pregnancies as *confinements*. God knows that's how it feels sometimes."

The gathered ladies all began to laugh, while Eleanor squinted up her eyes and glared. "Just you wait George. When you're big as a house, and haven't slept properly in months, and you can't do the most basic things, like tie your own shoes, or go for a ride . . . or, a whole host of other horrible things I won't even bother bringing up, then we'll see how you feel."

"When I'm big as a house and dying for a good gallop I promise to visit you so you can rub it in," George agreed solemnly, slightly marring her performance with a smile.

Eleanor harrumphed and shifted about on the sofa, obviously trying to find a more comfortable position. Imogen felt for her. Pregnancy always looked decidedly unpleasant.

Mrs. Gable came out to check on them, accompanied by several maids loaded down with lemonade, ratafia, and a selection of tea cakes and finger sandwiches. She arranged all of them on the low table the ladies were seated around, then marched off into the house, the maids trailing behind her like ducklings.

George served everyone, and they all set into gossip, chatting about a host of people Imogen knew nothing about. It was amazing how a few years away from the thick of things could affect the list of players.

When Simone's governess peaked out Mrs. Staunton called her over to join them. The countess seconded the invitation, insisting that Miss Nutley come out and help to swell their ranks, asking her to fill them all in on how Simone was coming along with her studies.

"Quite well," she said, accepting a glass of ratafia. "I think you'll be quite impressed with the improvement of her playing on the pianoforte."

"She's astounding really," Eleanor said of her step-daughter. "Her painting is improving in leaps and bounds as well. She's going to need a real painting master soon. I think once this one arrives," she added, patting her stomach lightly, "I'll have to see about that."

"I think you'll find my cousin could take care of that for you," Victoria said. "He's well acquainted with many of the leading artists. I'm sure he could find one of them willing to take Simone on; even young as she is."

"Mr. Angelstone?" Eleanor bit her lip.

"Yes," George said with a chuckle. "You'd never know it to look at him, town beau that he is, but he has a very discerning eye. His London house holds quite a collection of fine art, and he's friends with quite a few of our leading artists: Reynolds, Stubbs, Sandby, Cozens."

"Well then," Eleanor said, "I suppose I can safely leave it in your hands. I wouldn't feel comfortable asking a man I barely know for such a favor, but he'll gladly do it for you."

Listening to them Imogen was amazed. Much like Mrs. Staunton she could no more imagine Mr. Angelstone hobnobbing with a bunch of painters than she could picture him squiring a young debutante about the dance floor at Almack's. He exuded man-about-town, and she had no trouble at all picturing him haunting the opera house—or more particularly the opera dancers' dressing rooms—or socializing with the rougher element that frequented the gin parlors around St. James. But then he was obviously very well read. She flushed ever so faintly, remembering their first encounter.

Mr. Gabriel Angelstone was more than a rake with the face of a Medici Prince. Her face grew warmer and she dug her hand into her pocket for her fan.

Chapter 4

We wish to extend our most sincere felicitations to a certain MP who has bravely taken a second plunge into matrimony. Our advice? Keep this wife far away from artists and footmen of all kinds.

Tête-à-Tête, 13 August 1789

Wandering along behind the coursing party, Gabriel kept one eye on his cousin's sons and little Simone Staunton. They were keeping up rather well, but the younger ones would soon tire, or lose interest, and when they did he was more than ready to escort them back to the house. Back to where Miss Mowbray was waiting. George had clearly warned him off, but it wasn't a warning he could take to heart.

The lure of the Portrait Divorcée, the illicit tug of scandal and beauty . . . it was too strong to ignore. George and Torrie could have all the plans they wanted. He had plans of his own, which ran entirely counter to theirs. He just had to figure out how to get the delicious

Miss Mowbray into his bed without George killing him afterwards. Had to make it seem her idea, not his.

The children held out until after the first run of the day, but when the excitement wore off, they were ready to head back; the promise of lemonade and cakes a powerful inducement. Waving their fathers off, Gabriel turned back with the younger ones, leaving the young Lord Lovet to fully enjoy this foray into his father's world. The boy would have a better time of it without his younger brother underfoot.

As they ambled back towards the house the children searched about for stones for their slingshots, ran off in pursuit of butterflies and birds, chatted happily about their plans for the coming weeks. Circling past the lake they encountered Aubrey, accompanied by George's massive dog. The boy quickly claimed Gabriel's hand, allowing himself to be led up to the house. By now he was wet from falling in the water, and muddy from climbing back out, not to mention covered in dog slobber and all manner of twigs and stickers. His appearance was thoroughly disreputable, and perfectly normal.

Making their way up through the garden, Gabriel spotted the ladies out on the terrace and quickened his pace. Finally, a chance to catch his nymph. He smiled to himself as he and the children hurried up the stairs and he caught Miss Mowbray watching him.

She might be avoiding him, but she was definitely aware of him. It shouldn't be too hard to bring her round. After years on the town he could tell when a woman was ripe to fall and when she wasn't. Miss Mowbray had already fallen. She was just lying there, waiting for somebody to come along and pick her up.

His elusive nymph eyed him warily as he approached,

children dancing around him as though he were the Pied Piper. His cousin took one quick look and announced that she'd have nothing to do with her little gutter birds. "Aubrey's filthy as usual," she sighed wearily.

Feeling very much like a fox let loose in a chicken coop, Gabriel suppressed a chuckle. George was watching him appraisingly, while his cousin smiled warmly and made room for him beside her. Miss Mowbray was trying to look uninterested, but succeeded only in appearing slightly dazed.

It was delicious; she was delicious. She had on another modest, simple gown, again with a fichu covering her shoulders, almost totally obscuring the swell of her breasts. Who did she think she was kidding with that ridiculous garment? He curled his lip disdainfully and tried not to dwell on how badly his fingers itched to remove that offending wisp of fabric. At least she wasn't wearing a cap over that magnificent hair.

The nursery maid appeared to collect the children and Miss Mowbray leapt up with the excuse of arranging for refreshments. George flicked him a mocking glance and assured her friend that was an excellent idea; resulting in his nymph's quick departure. Gabriel grimaced at the amused glances being shared all around him.

Two days later Gabriel's temper was starting to fray. His nymph was proving far more adept at avoiding him than he'd thought possible, and instead of enjoying the warm glow of a seduction, he was feeling decidedly piqued. He'd barely been able to get near her, and he'd yet to manage to cut her from the herd. She was always firmly planted beside George or Alençon, surrounded by the children, or bustling off to consult with Mrs. Gable about something or other. They were frequently in the same room, but she might as well have been at another party entirely.

After dinner she would flirt and gossip with the other men—especially St. Audley, who would roundly quiz Gabriel with his eyes whenever she did so—even join them for a game of billiards, or a hand of whist, but he could barely get a nod out of her.

She'd set her pickets, and he wasn't going to get past them without a plan, without a bold maneuver.

This morning, as they were preparing to go down to the lake for an *al fresco* luncheon in the summerhouse and an afternoon of lawn games, she was busily organizing things with the housekeeper: making sure the pall mall set had already been sent down and set up, going over last minute alterations to the menu, and generally doing all the other things that should have fallen to George. And George, damn her, encouraged Miss Mowbray to do so. "It's so pleasant to have someone to rely on," the countess had said to him yesterday, feigning innocence, as Imogen slipped away from them just as they were setting out for a ramble.

The entire situation was maddening.

Once they were all assembled on the terrace—guests, children, Simone's governess, Miss Nutley, George's great lump of a dog, and Simone's little pug, Bella—they set out through the gardens. Strolling along towards the rear of the pack, Gabriel watched Miss Mowbray walking up ahead, her arm tucked neatly into Alençon's. Her petticoats flirted with the skirts of the duke's coat, muslin and wool clinging to one another.

Gabriel jerked his eyes away.

The duke was clearly a part of George's scheme to reintroduce her to Society. Alençon could always be counted on to further George's goals, and if by doing so he tweaked the noses of society's grand dames, well, he usually liked that, too.

Letting out an exasperated breath, Gabriel scooped up Aubrey and tossed the boy up onto his shoulders. It was a ways out to the lake, and while he didn't think the boy would wear himself out, he was certainly slowing them all down.

Sitting in the summerhouse, Imogen sipped her lemonade and listened to the two countesses heckle the cricket players. The men had divided up into two teams, and were busy yelling, arguing, running back and forth between the wickets. Mrs. Staunton was catnapping on a chaise, with Miss Nutley seated beside her, skillfully employing her embroidery needle on what looked like some sort of table runner.

The men had tossed their coats aside, forming a mound of poplin, buckskin, and stuff on one of the chairs. They presented a magnificent sight stripped down to waistcoats, shirtsleeves and breeches. Imogen bit her lip and met Lady Morpeth's comprehending gaze.

"I do so love the great outdoors," the countess drawled. "Such magnificent . . . views."

Imogen laughed, nearly choking and turned her attention back to the game.

Angelstone rubbed his hands down his thighs, preparing to bowl against Colonel Staunton. Imogen bit the inside of her bottom lip and swallowed hard, trying not to stare. She'd had those hands on her, and she could almost feel them now: strong, sure, knowledgeable.

Her mouth watered, forcing her to swallow again.

After he knocked down the wicket, without the colonel so much as coming near the ball, Lord Somercote came up to bat, and George yelled, "Gabe, I'll lay you pony my lord and master hits."

Angelstone stood up straight, turned to face them, and bowed deeply, his empty hand sweeping over the grass. He turned on his heel, returning his attention to the earl. He looked him up and down, and bowled. When the earl hit the ball with a thunderous crack Angelstone's face slipped into something which looked very much like a pout, his full lower lip thrust out in a way that made her want to suck on it.

Imogen ran a hand over the back of her neck, forcing herself to breathe. He wasn't going to have to make the slightest effort to seduce her at this rate, she was going to end up on her knees, begging.

The game continued in much the same vein, with bets being laid, frequent appeals to the ladies for their opinions about the fairness of the play, and friendly arguments breaking out. George finally wandered out onto the sidelines to pronounce judgment, causing both sides to announce that she was biased: her husband and St. Audley playing on one team, Angelstone and her godson, Hayden, on the other.

The game broke up when the food arrived, carried down from the house by an army of servants. The men dropped their bat and ball and joined the ladies at the table in the summerhouse, each team grumbling about the other while they piled their plates high.

When the meal was over Lady Morpeth eyed her husband and asked slyly, "Do you know what we all need, Rupert dear? A nice cooling trip out onto the lake." She sighed, and fanned herself with one hand for emphasis. Her husband smiled back indulgently, rising and extending one hand to his wife.

Somercote turned his gaze to George, raising his brows inquiringly, and without a word she allowed him to tug her up and sweep her off towards the punts.

Lady Morpeth, her arm resting securely in the crook of her husband's, paused for a moment, and looking back, said almost offhandedly, "Miss Mowbray, you should join us." She glanced around, seemingly without purpose. "Now let me see . . . Gabe, Miss Mowbray is in need of a companion for a little trip about the lake. Do be a gentleman and oblige her."

Angelstone grinned before schooling his face into a more somber expression and offering his arm. Imogen hesitated momentarily, glancing about for help, but there was obviously none forthcoming. The Somercotes had already pushed off, and the duke was off playing with the children. If she wanted to avoid him—and the temptation he presented—she was going to end up causing just the sort of scene she'd been working to avoid. Always being busy elsewhere was one thing, but flat out refusing to accompany him on something so mild as a trip out onto the lake was something else entirely.

"Shall we, Miss Mowbray?" he prompted, just the slightest hint of a purr in his voice.

"Certainly," Imogen replied, swallowing hard and trying to appear calm. She placed her hand on his arm, a slight shiver running through her as they made contact. She hated the fact that she reacted to him so; that his arrival in a room caused her breath to hitch, and made her fingers tingle. Hated the fact that she was disturbingly aware that only thin layers of kidskin and linen separated her hand and the bare skin of his arm. She could feel the muscles flex and move as he steered her towards the lake.

When they reached the end of the small dock he carefully handed her into one of the three remaining punts. He untied the small boat from its mooring, and leapt lightly down into it, causing her to gasp as the little boat swayed and sloshed. Grinning at her openly, he grabbed the pole and pushed off, heading in the opposite direction taken by the others. Imogen swiveled about, rocking the small boat. They were headed for the willow-shrouded right shore.

Overtly aware of her rapid pulse, and equally aware of its cause, Imogen settled back against the feather-stuffed sailcloth pad that occupied the front half of the punt and tried to concentrate on the light breeze blowing across the water, the warmth of the sun on her skin, the sound of the water lapping against the little boat's sides.

She was certainly not going to allow her attention to rest too long on Angelstone. This outing was ridiculous. He looked like a pirate king, or a freebooter. It didn't help that he was looming over her, his shadow flitting across her with each sweep of the pole, sun glinting off the gold buttons and bullion trimming of his chamois waistcoat.

He planted the pole hard and used his hip to propel the boat through the curtain provided by the enormous weeping willows that grew along a goodly portion of the lakeshore. Imogen gasped when the trailing branches swept damply over her, and the temperature suddenly dropped as they slid into the shade.

She took several deep breaths. The air was damp here in the shade, almost like that of a cave. She glanced questioningly up at Angelstone. He was smiling down at her, his face alight with pure mischief, very much like a little boy caught in a prank. He had a smattering of yellow leaves caught in his hair, a fairy king's diadem.

Another push and they moved through another veil of leaves, becoming almost completely screened from view; there were just occasional glimpses of the world outside the willows' branches as the breeze blew the trees about.

He pulled the pole from the water and propped it inside the punt, lowering himself to sit beside her once the pole was secure. The boat spun lazily about as he scooted a bit closer to her, his hip pushing against hers as he displaced her from the center of the pad. Still smiling he leaned in. "'Tis no sin love's fruit to steal'. . ."

His arms closed about her, and he pulled her over so that she was half draped across him, his mouth met hers in a sure, demanding kiss. She'd been expecting flirtation, teasing, seduction, not action. She'd been certain he'd get around to kissing her—or at least attempting to—but this was more decisive than she'd been prepared for.

Caught, beyond denial or prevarication, she kissed him back. Slipped her arms up and around his neck. Slid her fingers into his hair, dislodging his queue and his crown of leaves.

She'd be damned if she was going to act like some meek girl, a conquest to be claimed. She opened her mouth, taking his bottom lip between hers, sucking on it gently. He went perfectly rigid. She nipped one last time at his lip, before pulling her head back. She'd thrown him off-kilter. Good.

"'Repentance is but want of power to sin.'"

"Dryden," he replied with a chuckle, tightening his grip, pulling her fully into his lap, skirts riding up her legs until her calves were bared. "'Ah, how sweet it is to love! Ah, how gay is young desire!'" he quoted back before taking possession of her mouth again, lips firm, mouth open, tongue sweeping inside like a marauder.

One arm wrapped around his neck, Imogen sent the other slipping down his chest, exploring. Gabriel hissed as her thumb found his nipple and began to circle it, slowly. Even through his waistcoat and shirt the sensation was distinct.

Where was at least a cursory show of resistance? Where the demure dismissal? What a deceptive little minx.

Stomach tight with the effort to control himself he took hold of her distracting hand and moved it up and away from his chest. If she slid that hand any lower he simply wouldn't be held responsible for his actions.

She giggled, but she didn't move her hand back to taunt him further. She'd made her point, and she knew it. Gabriel deepened the kiss, teeth clashing as he sought to overwhelm her. To shake her. He slid one hand slowly down to cup her bottom, delighting in the shiver that elicited, not to mention the lush feel of her. He groaned into her mouth, picturing her hair unbound in a wild halo, her lips and eyes smiling in welcome, her body clothed in nothing but dappled sunlight.

They were screened from the party taking place on the lawn, but he could hear the children's laughter, mingled with snatches of conversation. All it would take was a lost ball or an arrow gone astray . . . Much as he wanted her, this was hardly the time or the place. Ignoring the very real urgings of his body, he broke off their kiss and pushed her off his lap so she was seated beside him. Even so, nestled against him as she was, it was nearly impossible to get his thoughts in order; not to simply roll her underneath him and pick up where they'd just left off.

Imogen sighed and laid her head back against the hollow of his shoulder. She caught one side of her lower lip between her teeth and glanced over at the stranger she'd just allowed to maul her. He was staring up at the branches overhead, seemingly lost in thought, but his body was taught beside hers, his awareness of her evident.

She watched the leaves dance overhead. She didn't have another ounce of resistance left in her, and there was a distinct possibility that she wouldn't like the outcome of whatever it was they'd just started, whatever it turned out to be.

There were other considerations as well.

While her family was content to ignore her now, if she was to set herself up as some man's bird of paradise she was fairly certain they wouldn't ignore that. Her brother's threats had always been vague, but there was no doubt her situation could well go from bad to worse if Richard took a hand.

Beside him his nymph sighed again. An entirely different sigh than the last one. Registering her unrest, Gabriel blinked several times and forced himself to sit up, putting Imogen away from him as he did so. His nymph was unsatisfied, and he didn't need any further reminders that so was he. He stood up carefully, reclaiming the pole as he did so.

"You've lost half your hairpins."

"So I have," she agreed, in quite the friendliest voice she'd ever employed with him. He gripped the pole, gritting his teeth, willing his erection not to return. It would be entirely too evident in his current position.

Imogen pushed her skirts about, hunting for her stray hairpins, giving him a far too thorough glimpse of delicate ankles and rounded calves. She found the ribbon that had held his hair and passed it to him. She made quick work of rearranging her curls, twisting them up and jamming the pins in to hold them in place.

Gabriel watched, totally absorbed.

"Is it all up?" she asked, turning her head about.

"Yes," he choked out, hoping he didn't sound as constrained as he felt. "Not a hair out of place."

"They're all out of place." She thrust her skirts down and lounged back. "One of the few perquisites of curly hair: It always looks a mess, so who can tell when it actually is?"

Gabriel gave a bark of laughter at her temerity and then applied himself to the pole. He pushed them out into the open again and headed directly for the dock.

It had to be now.

If he didn't do it now, he wouldn't do it anytime soon.

George tapped Victoria on the arm and directed her gaze out towards the pier where Gabriel was assisting Imogen out of the punt.

Everyone else had rejoined the party nearly a quarter of an hour ago. When George had noticed that both Imogen and Gabriel had gone missing, she had not been pleased. She had thought that she and Victoria had understood one another, and had in fact, set themselves the same goal. But apparently Victoria had other ideas. The countess was suddenly enthralled with the idea of her naughty cousin tamed at last.

"Are you sure, Victoria?"

"Absolutely," Lady Morpeth replied. "I've never seen Gabe in such a state. Just look at him. Rattled."

George narrowed her eyes and studied the pair who were currently walking along arm in arm. Gabriel looked up suddenly and accidentally met her gaze, and with what she could only call a start, he abruptly turned and lead Imogen off towards where the children were practicing their archery.

"They've only just met," she protested.

"Pooh," the countess responded. "I knew the day I met Rupert, and though you were loath to admit it when you met Somercote, you did too."

Chapter 5

We wish to reiterate that the rumor concerning Mrs. F——'s having presented the Prince with squalling, illegitimate proof of their love is just that . . . a rumor. Delicious and distracting as it may be.

Tête-à-Tête, 17 August 1789

Imogen handed her fowling piece over to Lord Somercote and grinned as he shook his head. She'd completely missed her mark and had blown a spectacularly large chunk out of one of his oaks. She felt more than a little foolish, but they'd all insisted she come along, even when she'd protested that she'd never so much as held a gun in her life. George had even said, "You poor dear," as though she couldn't imagine any worse neglect.

So here she was, tramping across the fields behind the dogs and their keepers, entirely out of place. She'd nearly hit herself in the face with the gun the first time she'd fired it, and she could only be glad she hadn't accidentally shot anyone. The Viscount St. Audley had assured her that he had done just that when he was a boy, filling one of his father's gamekeeper's legs with shot.

She took a deep breath, wrinkling her nose at the lingering scent of sulfur that overlaid the damp, earthy smell of the woods. She would have much rather simply gone for a walk, but such tame excursions weren't to the Somercotes' taste.

As the next round of shooters wandered forward Imogen watched the earl go through the process of reloading. She tried to pay close attention to the steps, only to be overwhelmed by wadding, shot and powder. Lord Somercote finished, tapping the butt on the ground, and presented the gun with a little flourish and wink.

Imogen rested the gun across her arm and the earl tipped the barrel up. "Careful, you'll scatter your shot all over the ground."

Imogen blew her breath out and smiled at him again. He really was amazingly patient. At the fore, George took aim and neatly took down her third bird. Imogen flinched as the gun went off. She was never going to get used to that sound. Gun shy, just like the pointer she'd had as a child.

The countess's brother clapped her on the shoulder—as though she were one of his boon companions rather than his sister—then stood chatting animatedly while she skillfully reloaded. Imogen sighed. Her own brother had never been anything like that. He'd dismissed her as useless as casually as he had her dog.

No amount of practice was going to make her an even vaguely competent marksman, though everyone else seemed quite sure she'd be up to snuff in no time. They couldn't seem to imagine any other option.

Lady Morpeth clearly knew how to handle a firearm as well, but her aim was sorely lacking. She had yet to hit anything either, though she hadn't gone quite as astray as Imogen had with her shots. After merely winging a grouse, the countess wandered back to Imogen and linked arms with her.

"Just think of it as a noisy walk," Lady Morpeth said with a laugh. "We'll only go on for another hour or so, and then we can head back to the house."

Rambling along with the countess, Imogen tried to keep her eyes—and her thoughts—off of Gabriel. Much easier said than done. He was ranged up ahead with his friends, helping George and Lord Morpeth with the children. All of them patiently showing the youngsters over and over the skills and little tricks it took to become a top marksman.

"It's amazing how devoted they are to the children. My own father would never have taken me out with him, let alone foisted me on his friends."

Lady Morpeth chuckled silently, her hand gripping Imogen's arm reassuringly. "No coercion or foisting in our circle. Most of us were raised the same way—cosseted and indulged—so I suppose it simply seems normal to us to train them up by hand."

"They have no idea how lucky they are, do they?" The countess shook her head, eyes brimming with maternal pride.

Little Simone Staunton fired her own small gun, and the countess's middle boy hooted at her. The girl glared, her small frame rigid, then she burst out laughing as Hayden's father cuffed him lightly on the head.

She watched the children wistfully. If she'd run about

with her brother like a hoyden, she'd have been summarily packed off to some extremely proper, and strict boarding school; not encouraged with promises of new riding habits, and ponies.

Alençon broke into her musings, calling her up to take another shot. Imogen raised her gun, waiting patiently for the dogs to flush another partridge from the undergrowth. When a bird erupted from only a few yards away she amazed herself by actually hitting it. The bird squawked as she blew off a large section of its tail feathers, and awkwardly made its escape into the trees. The dog ran after it until the gamekeeper called it back with a sharp whistle.

"You see," George said, practically shouting, as she was well across the field. "We'll make a marksman out of you yet."

Imogen smiled by way of reply and glanced around, looking for assistance with reloading. Gabriel caught her eye and marched over towards her, one hand extended and a smirk quirking up his mouth. He had powder streaks on his face, and his gloves were sooty, the fingers blackened. She restrained the urge to reach up and brush away the streaks marring his cheek. Touching him would be a mistake.

"You're going to have to be careful," he warned, digging into the satchel he wore over one shoulder. "You'll end up addicted to sport, rattling about town in a dangerous carriage like Lady Lade with a nasty little tiger perched behind you."

"Not a chance." Her hand tingled where his fingers brushed hers as he took the gun. She brushed them over the skirts of her jacket, letting the one sensation replace the other. "I'd look ridiculous with a tiger. Besides, if I could afford to flaunt myself about behind the kind of cattle you're talking about, do you think for a moment I'd be crazy enough to entrust them to some scrawny child? Well," she added, her gaze drawn back to the guests' children, "other than one of those little imps over there, that is."

Gabriel gave a bark of laughter and returned her gun. "I take it back," he said, still laughing. "It's too late for you. Once you admit you'd hand your team over to George's changeling, there's no hope for you. No hope at all." Shaking his head he pulled her free arm through his and they quickly moved to catch up with the rest of the party.

Imogen stiffened for a moment, then allowed herself to be pulled along. Beneath her hand she could feel the hard play of muscle over bone, all of it sliding beneath linen and buckskin. She stared at the embossed leather of his coat, the buttonholes adorning the cuff worked in gold, embroidered tassels jaunty.

A blush began to work its way up her neck, her skin burning as though she'd been out in the sun far too long. He steered her around a fallen tree, and her mouth went dry as his hand momentarily rested on her lower back; strong, sure, possessive.

It had been two days since he'd kissed her on the lake, since she'd touched him far more intimately than she was doing now, and in those two days her awareness of him had grown in leaps and bounds.

How did a lady signal more overtly than she already had that she was interested in something more than flirtation? Some women seemed born with that kind of knowledge, but she wasn't one of them, damn it all.

Her friend Helen would know exactly how to pursue

the course Imogen had decided upon and would be a font of ideas and advice. If only she were here. It was almost depressing to have finally decided to be wicked, and to have no idea how to go about it. Or at least no idea of how to go about it in even a semi-dignified manner.

Imogen's hand tightened about his biceps, and Gabriel turned his head away so she wouldn't see his grin. He couldn't help it. She wouldn't be happily tripping along beside him if she had the vaguest idea what he'd like to be doing to her, with her. It had been all he was worth not to pounce on her every chance he got, and she was suddenly given to presenting him with all too many opportunities to do just that. She'd gone from being entirely wary, to far too trusting, and for the life of him he couldn't figure out why. Nor could he decide what to do about it.

His body had very certain opinions, but a man who let his cock lead him was asking for trouble. Just now she was clinging to his arm, her breast rubbing against him with every step, her skirts threatening to tangle his legs, to send them both crashing to the ground—if only!—It was enough to drive him mad.

She dangled herself in front of him, but what to do about it? Let her go on in blissful ignorance, or make a more blatant advance? The only problem was that if he'd completely misread the situation, George would flay him alive, and Somercote, for all that they'd become friends over the past year, would delight in his fall from grace.

He was still pondering the various paths open to him when Somercote called a halt to the afternoon's shooting and the party turned about to stroll back to the house. He had almost finished formulating a plan to whisk Imogen away from the rest of the guests and escort her down to the conveniently secluded Dowager house when George suddenly sprung up at their side and stole Imogen away from him with such an arch look that he could only stare as the two of them disappeared up the stairs in search of—or so George claimed—a fan Imogen wanted for the upcoming ball.

Chapter 6

Life in Town seems rather flat just now, what with all the choicest object of scandal gathered together at a certain earl's house. Oh, to be among those privileged with an invitation.

Tête-à-Tête, 19 August 1789

Imogen covered her face with a large paper cone as her maid began to powder her hair. She held her breath, trying not to choke as the air filled with pale blue powder. When the job was done she stripped off the dressing gown and studied herself in the mirror. Her gown left a huge portion of her chest and shoulders exposed. Moiré silk spread wide across hoops, paste jewels sparkled on the gown's stomacher and winked in her hair.

She looked every inch the elegant ton matron that she should have been. The gown was conspicuous, flamboyant. A heady sense of power pulsed through her. When combined with the tingling state of awareness that Gabriel had engendered in her over the past few days, it made the whole night seem unreal.

Like a play with the footlights casting a glow all about her.

She was still contemplating herself in the mirror when there was a knock at the door and Helen Perripoint burst in.

"Don't you dare change," Helen said, circling around to get the full effect of Imogen's toilette. "That gown is perfect, and I won't let you talk yourself out of wearing it. Come to my room and help me with my hair, I can't seem to do a thing with it tonight."

Helen dragged her out of her room, chattering all the while about how difficult her hair was being, and by the time the two of them had achieved something they both found satisfactory, Nancy had come bustling in with Imogen's gloves in hand to announce that there were gentlemen waiting in the parlor to escort them up to the house. Imogen looked quizzically at Helen, who shrugged as she pulled on her own gloves.

She had yet to work up the courage to ask her friend for advice about how to make her desires clear to Gabriel. It was one thing to think about asking for advice, but it was hard to put the question into words. Every time she opened her mouth to do so her brain simply went blank.

Down in the parlor they found St. Audley and Carr, both elegantly attired in lavishly embroidered *habits à la française,* the curled wigs on their heads shedding bits of powder onto their coats. "Lady Somercote sent us down for you," St. Audley announced with a bow, offering his arm to Imogen.

"With instructions to retrieve you post haste," Carr added, taking Helen's hand and leading her off. "The musicians have already struck up, and there are too many gentlemen drifting about unable to find a partner. It looks more like a meeting at Tattersalls than a ball."

Gabriel wove his way through the crowd in Barton Court's enormous ballroom, impatient for a glimpse of Imogen. He leaned back against the wall and looked out over the room. Not being able to locate her in the throng was becoming irksome.

The party would break up after tonight. Everyone would return to their estates, to London, to Bath, to Brighton, or to wherever else they chose to spend the summer months.

Who knew when he would encounter his nymph again. The likelihood of them being thrown together in the near future was dim, and the prospect of leaving things as they stood was unappealing at best. Damn it all, he wanted her. And she'd given every indication that she was receptive. But first he had to find her . . .

George had outdone herself. Candles blazed in the chandeliers overhead, the light glinted off a fortune in diamonds and paste. Half the ton had descended upon them the preceding day, and the other half appeared to have arrived tonight. The room overflowed: guests spilling out into the top two terraces of the garden which had been lit throughout with lanterns. The first story gallery, running all the way around the edge of the ballroom, was crammed with elderly matrons. Women who were content to wander about and gaze down at the dancers, or to sit and gossip about the other guests.

The dance floor was a sea of couples, each moving in the stately, precise steps of the minuet. As the music washed over the room, filled it, and spilled out into the night, pairs formed, altered, broke apart and reconverged. George was dancing with his cousin Julian. As she turned into the next figure he spied Imogen, partnered by St. Audley.

He had her for the supper dance, but it rankled that she was so patently enjoying another man's company, even if that man was one of his best friends. With a grumble of disgust he took himself off to the billiard room. The supper dance wasn't for hours yet, and if he simply stood and watched her dance all evening, he'd drive himself mad, and likely cause just the sort of scandal George had warned him to avoid.

The first notes floated out across the assembled dancers, raising the hairs on the back of his neck. Gabriel turned to face Imogen, claimed her right hand with his, and led her to their place in the queue. Her breathing gave a little hitch, and he sternly repressed a tell-tale smile.

They made it halfway through the complicated steps of the minuet in total silence. Gabriel leaned in as they turned, artfully circling one another.

"You're awfully quiet."

Imogen laughed, glancing up to meet his eyes, a bit of blue powder catching the light, liming her hair.

"Just enjoying the dance." She slid past him, shoulder to shoulder, head turning to bare her neck as she held his glance.

She completed the cross-over, turned in place, reached out to take his hand for the next figure. Gabriel pulled her towards him, overtly aware of the play of bones in her hand as she gripped his hand in return and allowed him to steer her to the next place in line.

They exchanged places again, opposite shoulders brushing ever so slightly as they passed. The silk of her gown clinging to that of his suit. Couples swirled past, crossed over, changed places, circled through a hay. Gabriel moved by rote, by memory. His attention entirely on his partner. The dance more hunt than seduction, more an overt expression of passion than it should have been. When the dance was over, the soft whine of the violins washing over the room as the musicians slid the bows away from the strings, he led her off the floor, steering her towards the doors to the already crowded terrace.

"Hungry?" Angelstone inquired, looking down at her, mischief clearly sparking in his eyes.

"No, just thirsty." Imogen fanned herself, flushed and nearly panting. What was he thinking? He looked perfectly bored if one missed those eyes, the upturned corners lending him an even more devilish air. "And glad to be out in the air a bit," she added, taking a deep breath of the cool night air. She hadn't realized just how warm it was in the ballroom until they'd stepped outside. The sweat on her face and chest dried almost instantly, leaving her skin tight and tingling.

"Then might I suggest," he said, plucking two glasses of champagne from a passing footman and handing one to her with a grace that made her long to touch him, "that we skip supper, and instead commandeer a quiet corner? You've been dancing for hours, and you've hours more to go."

Resting for the supper hour was quite obviously the last thing Gabriel actually intended to do. If she really wanted to find out what it was like to take a lover, this was her opportunity. And he was leaving the decision up to her. He was suggesting, offering, but not demanding. To decline all she had to do was say she was hungry after all, and he'd tamely accompany her to supper, where they would be safely chaperoned.

She took a sip of champagne, gazing up at him, pretending she was considering her answer carefully. She'd known from the moment she'd said she wasn't hungry what her answer would be.

"I think a quiet hour would be absolutely divine," she replied softly, with what she hoped was a seductive smile. "Perhaps we could escape the crowd by heading down towards the maze?"

Angelstone quirked a brow, his smile almost mocking, but he allowed her to lead him off down the steps and into the garden, where many like-minded couples were strolling about, drinking and flirting. Imogen glanced over her shoulder as they slipped past a couple half-hidden inside an alcove of jasmine. The supper room must be wall to wall gentlemen, so many of the ladies being otherwise occupied at the moment. She smiled and hurried her steps, trying to match her stride to Angelstone's. As they passed the dowager house he paused.

"Do you think, perhaps . . ."

"My maid will be waiting up for Helen and me, and the children have all been moved there for the night." She smiled sadly at the rueful expression on his face. She felt the tug of disappointment herself. Resolute, she wrapped both hands about his upper arm and pulled him along into the darkened paths of the lowest terrace.

The maze was lit with lanterns, splashes of red and yellow light bobbing in the breeze like giant fireflies. So nervous she could barely breathe, Imogen led him quickly through the maze to the courtyard where she'd first encountered him.

She strained her eyes and ears. Was there anyone else playing in the maze? Not so much as a hushed giggle came back to her. The only sounds were the bubbling of the fountain, the crunch of their shoes on the gravel, the sweet, lonesome song of a nightingale.

"If a truly private assignation is denied us, let us take full advantage of this secluded spot," he scooped her up and carried her over to one of the stone benches that surrounded the fountain. Imogen gave a little squeal of surprise when her feet left the ground, but she didn't protest. Soon he'd be gone, and her pleasant life at Barton Court was likely to seem rather flat in the ensuing weeks.

Angelstone lowered them both onto the bench, Imogen balanced in his lap.

"We're going to have to do what we can without destroying the pearly façade you've worn tonight."

He sounded pleased with the prospect. Amused even. One hand at her waist, fingers splayed over her ribs, he tugged the glove from his free hand with his teeth. He slid her round so that her hips were wedged between his thighs, her back to his chest.

"Wha—"

"Hush." His gloved hand held her to him, his erection evident where it pressed against her. His naked hand slid into her bodice, lifted one breast free. He glanced down. "Of all the nights not to have a full moon," he complained, tipping her back and to one side, lowering his head to take the peaked nipple into his mouth.

Imogen froze. Her breath hitched strangely. Her nipples had tightened as soon as he'd touched her, and now her breasts felt full and hard. He bit down lightly, flicking his tongue over the tight peak of her nipple. She bucked in his lap, causing him to chuckle.

She could easily make out the glint of his smile. He looked like some wicked demon lover half-hidden in shadows. The way he was touching her only added to the illusion. He took her nipple back between his teeth while his hand slipped down to her ankle, and up under her skirts.

Imogen resisted the urge to squeeze her legs together, to bat his hand away as it slid up over her knee, past her garter, over top of her stocking, onto the bare flesh of her thigh. She swallowed hard and took a deep, panting breath, cold night air nearly drowning her. He released her nipple and blew softly across it, causing it to ruche almost painfully.

He sat her up, her back once more to his chest. His hand moved further up her thigh, the soft scrape of the whorls of his fingertips electric. She couldn't seem to get enough air, couldn't think straight. The slightly roughed texture of his cheek against hers was exciting in ways she'd entirely forgotten.

His thumb caressed the tendon that joined her thigh to her body, fingers slipped past the curls at the apex of her thighs caressing, probing, seeking.

His gloved hand curled around her knee, lifted her leg so that it hooked over his, opening her to him, opening her to the night and the air. Imogen was past caring. It had been far too long since a man had touched her. And William had certainly never bothered flattering her, seducing her in such a manner.

She'd had no idea what she'd been missing.

He leaned forward, his chin ever so slightly abrasive against her ear, his hand—naked and sinful—between her thighs. "These are the wings, like the wings of an angel. Delicate. Sensitive." His fingers traced the slick inner folds of flesh. "And here," his palm rested on her mons, one finger touching the sensitive bud normally hidden between her thighs, "is what the Greeks call the little hill, but I prefer Aristotle's name for it," he pressed down, rubbing, teasing, "the throne of lust."

Imogen gasped and arched, embarrassed to be responding like a cat in heat, to be pressing her hips forward, rocking in harmony to the rhythm he established.

His tongue traced the curve of her ear. "Do you think anyone else might find their way into the maze?"

Imogen froze, but his fingers continued their dance, sliding down to swirl about the entrance to her body, gliding back up, wet and slick to reclaim their place upon her throne.

"The maze is lit, the true path is red, false ways yellow. Did you notice."

She hadn't . . .

One finger slid into her. Her body clenched around it, hollow and wanting. She bit her lip to keep from crying out, from begging him to take her back up to the dowager house. Her maid and children be damned.

"Anyone could stumble in. Find us here. Your legs spread. My hands where they shouldn't be. My fingers inside you."

He slid a second finger in with the first, curving them to press against a spot she hadn't even known existed. He worked them deeper, his thumb finding its way back to the throne.

The sound of her panting was loud in her own ears. She shuddered, so close to climax her fingers and toes had gone numb. Nothing existed except his hand between her thighs, his chin against her ear. The tight feeling building low in her belly, her womb twitching like a butterfly in a net.

She leaned back, hands gripping his thighs for leverage, silk slipping under kidskin, muscles hard as the marble bench beneath them. His straining erection pressed to her bottom. God how she wanted to turn, open the fall of his breeches and take him inside her. On the verge of climax she desperately wanted him to be inside her when she found it. This was wicked. Dangerous. Perfect. His mouth, hot and wet pressed an open kiss to the tender spot just below her ear. She mumbled his name, gripped his thighs harder, fingers digging in as she tried not to scream.

"Yes, Daphne?" he inquired softly, choosing that moment to cup her still bared breast with his gloved hand, pressing the nipple between his thumb and side of his hand. She bucked, tightening around his finger.

She was so close. So close.

"Gabriel?" she said his name again, half protesting, half begging.

He shushed her, reestablishing a rhythm. She gave a high pitched little whimper, much louder than she'd intended.

"Eh-eh-eh." His breath stirred the fine hairs that curled next to her ear, sent a shiver through her. "You're going to give us away."

Her toes curled. Back arched. Legs went ridged, shaking, clamped around his one thigh and the bench. The coloured lights swirled as her vision blurred.

"God I love the way it feels when a woman comes apart in my hands."

She throbbed as he flexed his fingers, clenching and unclenching around him, her whole body shaking. She could feel the fullness of his fingers inside her—wonderful, yet not enough—the pressure of his hand against what he'd called her little hill, her throne. She hadn't known there was a word for it. It was just "that spot." She tipped back her head, trying to see his face, wanting desperately to see his expression. It was too dark. All she could make out was the glitter of eyes, the quick flash of teeth as he smiled. Just that little glimpse made her want to drag him up to the dowager house and start all over.

He bent his head and kissed her, lip to lip, the slightest flick of his tongue tracing the seam, slid his thumb over her one last time, causing her to jump. His chuckle, soft and wicked, rumbled from his chest to hers, rattled through her sternum, made her lungs seize. He withdrew his hand, leaving her empty, bereft. His cock, impossible to ignore, rode her bottom. The hard length mocked her. Reminded her that the act had only just begun. That there was so much more she wanted.

"Take a couple deep breaths, my darling nymph." He lifted her leg and swung them both round so that she was again in his lap, her skirts decorously covering her once more. "Cinderella has to go back up to the ball, and yours truly turns back into a pumpkin a few minutes hence."

Imogen smiled into the dark and shook her head. "The pumpkin was a coach."

"Was it?" Gabriel asked, standing her up, his hands lifting her and setting her down on her own unsteady legs. She wobbled and he rose, his arm steadying her. He kissed her again, his hands tugging at her bodice, rearranging layers of corsetry and silk. "I shall have to read it again. I knew there was a pumpkin in there somewhere." He pulled his glove from his pocket and promptly tugged it back on. Imogen cocked her head and looked up at him consideringly. She reached one hand out and dusted off his shoulder. Even in the dark she could make out the slightly light patch on his coat where her head had rested.

She didn't want to go back up to the house. She wanted to find a far more private place and see what else she might tempt him into, but she was promised to the earl for the next dance, and her absence—their absence—would be far too conspicuous. With a discontented sigh, she allowed Gabriel to lead her back into the maze and up to the house.

Lord and Lady Somercote took their place in the foyer to say their good-byes to their guests who were staying elsewhere. Helen Perripoint paused to watch the subtle machinations taking place as the guests who were staying retired for the night, some of them obviously making illicit assignations for the hours to come. Mr. Nye, for example, was hovering around Lady Hardy, and several of the men were busy trying to detain Mrs. Lade. But even as Helen watched, the lovely widow curtsied to her court, and made her escape. Helen spotted Imogen across the room and hurried to join her. Thus ending Gabriel Angelstone's tête-à-tête with her friend. Completely ignoring the scowl Angelstone directed at her, Helen slipped her arm through Imogen's, and stole her friend away from him.

The evening was over, and now it became a matter of escaping the gentlemen unscathed. Helen rather liked several of the men who'd been vying with one another for a few more hours of her time, but she wasn't going to get caught making such a public display of herself.

Better to gather up her obviously besotted friend and make their way back to the safety of the dowager house together. Imogen, she was afraid, was really not at all up to snuff when it came to the intrigues required to carry on a discreet ton affair. She'd been glowing throughout her dances with the disreputable, and damnably handsome Brimstone, and Helen was not about to abandon her oldest friend to his scandalous care.

Really, she didn't know what George was thinking. Not to have warned poor Imogen about the reputations of some of the gentlemen present. Between the attentions of Gabriel Angelstone, Ste. Huntington, and Lord Reevesby, all of whom Helen had seen her dance with, Imogen could rapidly become the talk of the town if she didn't look out.

All it took was for one of the tabbies here tonight to take umbrage, and tongues would be wagging all over London within the week. It didn't even require one of the stiff-rumped sticklers to have noticed. The Duchess of Devonshire could unwittingly do just as much damage with a few careless conversations.

The plan had been to bring Imogen back into favor, not to blacken her reputation further, and Helen was determined to reclaim her friend. She was simply enraged every time she bumped into William Perrin and his oh-so-superior new wife. She'd given them both the cut direct recently, and she'd enjoyed doing so immensely.

Laughing loud enough to attract attention, she pulled Imogen out of the ballroom and onto the terrace. This was a moment to make oneself conspicuous. A moment to be noticed.

Chapter 7

It would appear that London's most amusing divorcée has resurfaced . . . Could it be that Lord S—— has grown tired of his wife already?

Tête-à-Tête, 20 August 1789

Imogen buttered a bite of scone and chewed it slowly while all around her the breakfast parlor churned: Maids and footmen delivering crockery, ale, laden trays straight from the kitchen. The guests milled about, filled their plates, found places to settle at the table to eat before returning to their rooms to finish dressing.

Those not leaving were heading down to the beach for the morning; an outing which was excitedly, and loudly, anticipated by the children.

"For after all, what's the point of owning an estate right on the sea, if one never goes down to the water? I'm longing for a nice, restful morning." George covered her mouth while she yawned, blinking her eyes sleepily.

"We'll have to put it off for another or hour or so,

though. I don't think the Morpeths have risen yet, and Alençon hasn't put in an appearance either."

An hour later everyone was gathered near the marble steps leading down to the drive, ready to follow the earl and countess down to the water. Carriages, loaded with bags and trunks, were already filling the drive.

Carr, Alençon and Lady Beverley were already gone, and the Glendowers were in the process of getting underway. Colonel Staunton passed them, helping his wife out to their carriage. He paused to tug on his daughter's long hair, recommending to her that she be a good girl, and listen to her Aunt George.

"Papa," Simone said, a note of reproof in her voice. "I'm not a baby."

The colonel merely chuckled and climbed into his carriage.

The beach combing party was small, compared to what Imogen had grown used to in the past weeks, consisting of only a dozen or so guests, the children, and, of course, Gabriel Angelstone. He hadn't been at breakfast, but he'd appeared just as they were all setting out, obviously prepared to join them.

The group had suddenly transformed into a family party, the more formal air of the house party evaporating along with the more formal guests. Gabriel, his cousin's youngest child once again perched on his shoulders, was seemingly prepared to do nothing but watch her.

Imogen adjusted the ribbon holding her hat in place and caught one side of her lower lip between her teeth, unsure how to proceed. Helen would have gone on as if nothing had happened, and she couldn't imagine the countess allowing a little thing like last night to put her out of her usual cheer. But it would be so much easier if

Gabriel would take the initiative and give her a hint as to what he was expecting.

She was rescued from her dilemma by the countess's brother. Mr. Glenelg suddenly appeared at her side, and smiled down at her, his merry grey eyes twinkling. He put out one hand. "Can I carry that for you, Miss Mowbray?" He reached for the blanket she had draped over one arm.

"Of course." Imogen relinquished the blanket. "Thank you."

"Shall we?" He draped the blanket over his shoulder and extended his arm. Imogen smiled, feeling her shoulders relax. Sometimes it was simply so much easier to take the path of least resistance.

Gabriel pressed his lips together as his friend absconded with Imogen, repressing a grin. It didn't matter whose arm she went down to the beach on, and while he would have preferred to have Imogen all to himself, he had a much better view from where he was.

Besides, she couldn't be constantly chaperoned, especially since Mrs. Perripoint was still abed, and would be gone by the time they returned to the house. Helen had quite effectively played duenna last night and he didn't want her doing so again tonight.

George and her besotted husband led them down to the beach, George abandoning the effort to keep her hat on long before they reached their destination. There was a strong sea breeze. It tore several people's hats away, molded the ladies' gowns to them, making their casual *Chemise a la Reine* all the more scandalous.

The twisting, rambling foot path followed a narrow stream across the back lawn from the lake to the ocean, eventually leading to a rather steep set of stairs cut into the bluff. The children and dogs scrambled down the stairs in a rush, but the adults took it a bit more slowly.

When they reached the beach, the gentlemen spread out the blankets, while the ladies took George's example and removed their hats. All three ladies seated themselves on the blankets, fully prepared to lounge there and relax for a good, long while.

The boys quickly stripped to their drawers, and ran out into the surf, splashing one another and giggling loudly. Simone, in nothing but her shift, joined them a few moments later, running out and dunking Hay under with all her might. He came up sputtering, and dunked Simone in return. Caesar was busy splashing in the waves, leaping about and periodically knocking the children down, while Simone's small pug ran up and down the surf line, barking hysterically.

George shook her head. "Silly beast." She leaned forward and kicked off her shoes, then carefully rolled off her stockings, stuffed them into one shoe, and with a sigh, buried her toes in the sand.

Imogen quickly did the same, utterly loving the feeling of the warm sand between her toes. She'd never been barefoot on the beach before. Her mother would be horrified if she could see her now.

St. Audley wandered over, and joined them in their barefoot hedonism. He sank down just behind George, and the countess immediately settled on her back, her head pillowed on his thigh. She stretched and glanced up at her friend. "Marcus," she said, reaching to poke him in the side, "are you coming to the races?"

"First October?" he asked, not looking down at the countess, but continuing to watch the children play. "I wasn't planning on it, but I'll be up for the later races after Lord Glendower's shooting party."

George pulled a face. "I guess that will do."

"It will have to," St. Audley replied with a chuckle.

"I suppose." She sat up again, the breeze pulling her hair across her face. "I hate it when a party breaks up. Let's go for a walk. There's a lovely little cove just up the beach with a waterfall and everything. I don't think Imogen has seen it yet, though she's been here all summer. I've been remiss in my duties as hostess."

St. Audley helped George to her feet and led her over to where her husband stood watching the children play. Imogen ran her toes through the sand, watching the grains roll down her feet.

How to steal a moment alone. That was the question. The challenge.

A pair of shod feet stepped into view, wet sand clinging to the shiny leather. Imogen followed them up, tracing a path over stockings, breeches, waistcoat, cravat, all the way to Angelstone's politely bland face.

How did he do that? Look so cool, so disinterested?

"Coming?" Imogen's head snapped around to where George and the earl stood, waiting beside the outcropping of rock that hid the waterfall from their view.

Imogen reached up and Angelstone pulled her to her feet in one neat motion. She took a couple deep breaths, willing her nerves to calm down. The last thing she wanted was for George to notice her reaction. She was sure the countess would guess instantly what its source was. And she didn't want George to know about her encounter with Gabriel, at least not yet.

Not until she knew what it meant. What his intentions were. What her own were.

Gabriel placed his free hand over hers, trapping it in the crook of his arm. His fingers slid across the back of her hand, making her shiver. Imogen fought to repress any sign of awareness or embarrassment.

Around the bend they found the others gathered near a small pond at the base of a lively little waterfall. A crab scuttled away, snapping its claws at them.

"It would be lovely captured in water colors, wouldn't it?" Lady Morpeth said.

A loud shriek caused Lady Morpeth to wince. "We'd best get back to the children. Lord knows what they'd get up to with only Glenelg and St. Audley to watch them."

George agreed and pulled her husband along after the Morpeths. Left suddenly alone, Imogen flushed hotly, and focused her attention on the scenery, trying hard to ignore the sensation of Gabriel's thumb lightly stroking her hand.

It really was a lovely spot. Tiny plants grew out of the rock wall. A twisting stream meandered its way through the sand to pour itself into the ocean. Several large trees grew at the top of the low cliffs, providing ample shade for the shallow pool. Down the beach gulls fought over something washed up on the sand, raucous cries loud and harsh.

Imogen's head snapped up when his amusement at his friends' and family's blatant tactics overcame him. "So much for subtlety."

She stared up at him, doe-eyed, reticent.

Torrie clearly thought his infatuation with her new friend ought to be encouraged, it hadn't been his imagination, and she'd even apparently brought George round. What could they be thinking? Could Torrie possibly be dreaming of bridals? He was positive George knew better.

He was not the marrying kind . . . though if he was, his nymph would be a tempting option. But Gabriel sincerely couldn't picture himself becoming a tenant for life. Not with Imogen. Not with anyone. The confines of marriage would turn something which was a delight to duty and ashes inside of a month.

He'd yet to encounter a woman who'd held his interest for more than a few months, and rarely even that. It was always relief he felt at the end of an affair, and sometimes something almost akin to joy when a mistress announced she'd found a new protector, or a lover drifted off to try her luck with someone else. But that flush of emotion was nothing when compared to the excitement he felt upon setting up a new flirt; commencing a new seduction. And just now, he was very much engaged with the lady standing so demurely beside him.

"I don't believe there's a subtle bone in the countess's body."

"Very likely not." It was impossible to defend George on this particular occasion. "George is many things: kind, loving, reliable, trustworthy, but not subtle." Not feeling particularly subtle himself, he tipped Imogen's head back, his hand under her chin, and kissed her, letting his mouth explore hers, slowly deepening the kiss. She tensed in his arms, and then slowly relaxed against him, leaning into him, hands spread out against his chest.

Imogen was not surprised when Gabriel kissed her, she'd known it was his intent as soon as he'd joined them that morning. When he looked at her, she could feel it, and it made her nervous and slightly sick to her stomach, in a dreadfully excited way.

It was quite a lowering thought to be forced to recognize just how eager she was for him to kiss her. Having him finally touch her was a relief. She'd been struggling all morning to figure out how to treat him, how to respond to him; to know what to expect from him, what he expected from her. It was different than anything she'd ever experienced before. It wasn't courtship, and it didn't follow the same rules, but parts of it felt familiar.

She hadn't been embarrassed by what they'd done last night. Not when they were doing it, and not afterward, but now . . . now she was feeling decidedly embarrassed and unsure. Today, last night seemed unreal. Unreal and impossible. She'd lain awake last night, slightly horrified by what she'd done; by what they'd done. Slightly horrified, and terribly excited. It had been glorious; positively the most decadent, delightful, wicked thing she'd ever done. She'd taken a step forward into a new life. One in which she felt beautiful, desirable, and oddly free. She wasn't sure where she might end up, but she was positive that it had to be better than where she'd been for the past few years.

Anything had to be better. She was already ruined, could being someone's mistress really be all that much worse? Well, not really even mistress.

Lover.

That was the proper word: Lover.

She shivered and pressed closer. His lips were parted over hers, his tongue leisurely exploring her mouth, twining with hers. He broke of their kiss, moved up along her jaw to the extremely sensitive spot just below her ear.

"Gabriel." She was suddenly flustered, barely able to stand.

He stopped, pulled his head back far enough to look her in the eye. "I like the sound of my name on your lips," he said, his eyes warm and teasing, "Say it again," he urged her, his lips returning to her neck.

"Gabriel?" she managed to hiss out, amazed at how breathless she sounded.

"Yes, my beautiful nymph?" he replied, taking her earlobe between his teeth.

"We—I mean . . . it's . . . Oh!" Imogen squeaked as his tongue circled the rim of her ear.

Gabriel stopped what he was doing, drawing back from her with a sigh. "You mean this is not wise?" he queried.

"I . . ." Imogen took a shaky breath, not exactly sure what she had meant to say. She was unsure if she'd been asking him to stop, or begging him for more. He'd clearly assumed it was the former, and for the moment, she was willing to let him. She needed a minute to catch her breath; to think. It was, after all, mid-morning on a very public beach.

"Perhaps you're right," he said with a wry smile. He took her by the hand and led her to the edge of the pool, drawing her down to sit beside him. He tugged off his shoes, removed his socks, and they both sat there silently, dangling their feet in the water.

Tomorrow he would be gone, and perhaps it was best that they take this no further. Wanting what one should not have was damnably harder than wanting what one could not have.

He moved the foot nearest to her, bringing it over to rub hers. It was a small thing, but she was glad of it. Glad he couldn't seem to escape the urge to touch her.

Imogen watched their feet, studying his ankles, and the oddly elegant lines of his feet. She'd never really noticed a man's feet before. She was sure she must have seen William's on numerous occasions, but she had no clear memory of them. She was fairly certain she'd be able to sketch Gabriel's when she was eighty. This particular moment: the sand cool under her thighs, rough against her palms, Gabriel's foot caressing hers, the breeze blowing her hair into her face, was turning into one of those moments where everything froze, and you could recall it exactly as it had happened forever. Why this moment instead of a hundred others she couldn't say, she just recognized the signs.

She opened her mouth to speak, only to shut it again. What was she going to say? What was there to say? They'd shared a delightful flirtation, and a little, light dalliance, and that was really how it should be left . . . light.

While she was still struggling for the right words, Aubrey came pelting around the corner, calling, "Uncle Gabe! Uncle Gabe!"

Imogen jumped.

Gabriel smiled down at her, a smile she recognized by now as the one he wore when he was thinking particularly naughty thoughts. He stood up, and turned his attention to his cousin's son. "Yes, brat?"

"Aunt George says it's time for lunch," the boy announced.

Gabriel stood up with the easy grace Imogen had quickly come to associate with him. Long limbed, sure of himself, solid, like a stag hound.

He dusted the sand from his breeches and helped her up. There was a world of things unsaid between them, but she was more than a little relieved at having been interrupted before saying any of them.

Lunch passed in a blur, everyone discussing plans

for the coming months: The races at Newmarket, Lord Glendower's shooting party, the Devonshire rout which would start off the Little Season. Imogen listened absently.

She wouldn't be attending any of the events they were all looking forward to with such uninhibited glee. Most of it didn't sound like all that much fun to her anyway. She'd never been to a horse race, and couldn't imagine what the attraction was, and she hadn't gotten a great amount of satisfaction out of going grouse hunting either.

She missed balls and routs, but since there was no chance of her attending something as fashionable as a ball thrown by the Devonshires, it was better not to think of it at all. Perhaps Helen would host a small party in the coming months? That would be nice . . . give her a reason to go up to town.

After lunch they returned to the house, and went their separate ways to change out of their sandy, salt-water stiffened clothes. Imogen could feel Gabriel's eyes watching her as she left them all on the terrace. She glanced back over her shoulder, and sure enough, he was standing alone on the terrace, one hand gripping the balustrade, watching her.

She spent the afternoon on tenterhooks. Would he seek her out? She was half-relieved, half-piqued when she heard the clock chime five, and realized she'd frittered away most of the day alone at the dowager house practicing on the pianoforte, and he hadn't come.

She dressed unusually carefully for dinner, wanting to look her best on this, their last evening, and joined the others in the drawing room.

Once there she found the room in an uproar.

"He's done it." George's eyes gleamed, her whole

body quaking with repressed energy. She put out a hand and Imogen hurried over to her.

"Who? Done what? Not the king?"

"No, not another episode of greeting the foliage. I'm talking about the Marquis de La Fayette. He's done it. Passed his declaration in the French Assembly. There was a letter waiting for me this afternoon from Foxglove in Paris. First the Bastille, and now this."

The remainder of the evening sped by, everyone discussing the events raging across the channel. No other topic seemed worthy of broaching.

The meal was cleared, and the port brought out. They all lingered over it, George making no move to leave the gentlemen alone now that the party had grown so small. They talked until several of the candles guttered in their sockets, and the noise made them all suddenly aware of how late it had become.

"Come, Georgie. Let's have one more stroll through the gardens." Mr. Glenelg stretched in his seat and hid a yawn behind his hand. "We can escort Miss Mowbray down to the dowager house."

Imogen's eyes flew to Gabriel's. This was it. Their last chance for a quiet moment alone, and it had just been yanked out from under them.

There was to be no casual conversations in the drawing room over tea, no chance to excuse herself and slip away for a moonlit walk. Nothing. Not even a chance to say good-bye, for he'd plainly stated earlier that he was going to be rising early and setting out for London at first light.

Gabriel smiled back at her a little ruefully. He gave an almost imperceptible shrug. Her eyes burned, tears making her vision blurry. She blinked them away. She took in the resigned slump of his shoulders. He didn't like this any more than she did.

"Shall we, George? Miss Mowbray?" Mr. Glenelg rose and offered them each an arm. With no chance of escape, Imogen stood and wished everyone a good night and a safe journey home on the morrow.

Gabriel grimaced, bracing his boot against the footboard of his curricle as he rounded a corner coming on towards Chelmsford. He was sure George would bring Imogen to the races, which meant it would only be a few weeks until he saw her again. Her being mired out at Barton Court was damnably inconvenient. If she lived in town, with her friend Helen, for example, things would be so much simpler. Hell, if she'd just been staying in the main house things would have been simpler.

He'd tossed and turned the night through, subject to disturbingly erotic and explicit dreams. Even now he could feel himself stirring to attention as he remembered them.

This was ridiculous.

He shook out the reins and increased his speed, flying down the turnpike. Wind ripped his hair from his queue. His horses' sweat began to turn to foam where the traces touched them.

It was a game. A delightful and often times rewarding game, but nothing more.

Chapter 8

If Lord S—— has indeed set up the former Mrs. P—— as his mistress, can we look forward to the unheard-of sight of a female duel? One can only hope . . .

Tête-à-Tête, 28 August 1789

Gabriel stared blindly at the fire, lost in his own thoughts. He was rather well to live, as he had been almost every night for the past week. Since leaving Barton Court he'd done little but drink, gamble, and brood. And White's was a good place to do all three.

Life in town was dreadfully dull just at the moment. He could find nothing to distract him from his obsession with his garden nymph. Lady Hardy, whom he'd been half-heartedly pursuing before George's party, had made him a brash offer the night before, but he hadn't been able to convince himself to be interested in that very lovely lady's charms, or to avail himself of the similar offer put forth in a heavily scented note sent round by the opera dancer who had been his distraction of choice all summer. The one bored him, the other repulsed him.

He couldn't possibly miss Imogen so badly. He barely knew her. He kept catching himself scanning the street for her, feeling foolish moments later when he remembered that whatever woman he'd thought might be her couldn't possibly be. Imogen was miles and miles away in Suffolk. Probably up to her elbows in the garden, busy putting in a new formal herb garden, or trimming the roses.

He'd bumped into George on Bond Street. Up for a fitting with her mantua maker. It had taken all his willpower not to inquire after Imogen. George—damn her—had mentioned they would all be attending the races at Newmarket, and there had been a distinct challenge in her eyes when she said it, as well as an emphasis on the word *all.* But for the life of him he couldn't decide if she was dropping a hint, or warning him off. One simply never knew with George.

Gabriel had rarely had trouble understanding women, but he was starting to conclude, that was because the women he'd been dealing with had very clear agendas: mostly getting him into bed, and keeping him there longer than whoever his last flirt had been. They didn't take any figuring out, they were blatant and uncomplicated in their desires and methods. Women like George and his cousin were entirely different animals, and he was beginning to realize that he really had no idea what went on behind their eyes. He'd always thought he'd understood George perfectly. She was, after all, his closest friend. But lately, he wouldn't have felt comfortable betting that he knew what she was thinking.

He was deeply enmeshed in his own thoughts, chasing the idea that George might have been encouraging him to attend the races, when he was interrupted by a deep chuckle. His head snapped up. He glared when the duke raised one imperious brow.

"My dear boy," Alençon began, continuing to stare him down, his amusement clearly radiating from his eyes. "Don't waste your famous glowers upon me. I'm impervious to 'em, and far too old to even consider accepting a challenge. We'd look ridiculous." Gabriel rolled his eyes and took another gulp of his brandy. The duke had a knack for making him feel as if he were a badly behaved eight-year-old. "And stop knocking that back as if it were orjet. That's good brandy, and you're obviously well sprung as it is. Wasteful."

A waiter appeared, bearing Alençon's own brandy, and Gabriel defiantly ordered another. The duke shook his head reprovingly. "You're going to regret that tomorrow," he said, taking a sip of his own drink. "Unless it's your intention to drink yourself blind, dumb, and mute?"

Gabriel glowered at him again. He didn't want to be cross-examined by the duke. And drinking himself stupid was exactly his intention. He wanted to get blind, stinking drunk. Outrageously foxed. Thoroughly jug-bitten. He wanted to sleep the night through without dreaming of Imogen. Damn it all, he wanted to be miserable by himself.

The duke sipped his brandy, watching him with a condescending smirk that almost made Gabriel squirm. It took all his focus to keep himself slumped in his chair, his legs stuck out towards the fire, crossed at the ankle. But he was not going to snap to attention as though he'd invited Alençon to join him. The waiter arrived with Gabriel's brandy, and Gabriel quickly took a large slug of it.

The duke sighed, sounding thoroughly bored. "I can only suppose this disgustingly indulgent show is due to the inaccessibility of a certain lady," he said, his voice pitched low so it didn't carry. "Don't let George see you like this, or the cat really will be out of the bag."

Gabriel stiffened and pulled himself up into a more dignified position. "I don't know what you're talking about, Your Grace," he enunciated carefully. "I've always been partial to what you call *this disgustingly indulgent show.* It's what my life centers round; part and parcel of my existence. I would think you'd know that by now."

"Silly, silly, boy," the duke said, shaking his head and rising. "Don't think for a moment you can treat me like a flat. Tell me this is none of my business. Fine. But, please, I've known you most of your life, and blue-deviled is blue-deviled. I'll leave you to your brooding though, since you're obviously enjoying it. Carry on." The duke waived one hand encouragingly and then with one more infuriating half-smile, departed.

Gabriel glared at the duke's retreating form, tossed back the rest of his brandy, and called for another. Nosy, interfering, old busy-body. Couldn't a man drink in peace?

Chapter 9

A certain countess would appear to have deserted the field entirely. How very unsporting of her . . .

Tête-à-Tête, 9 September 1789

Imogen was seated in the garden, a book unopened in her lap, and Caesar dozing at her feet when the countess descended upon her. She'd been absent from Barton Court for over two weeks, leaving Imogen with only the earl for company. And though Lord Somercote was unfailingly kind, apart from a mutual adoration of George, they had little in common. Left to her own devices, she frequently caught herself thinking of Gabriel; a most unproductive, and lowering, occupation.

Mrs. Staunton had been safely delivered of twin boys only four days previously, but she had yet to begin receiving callers. So Imogen and the earl had had to content themselves with congratulating the colonel on his very good fortune and asking him to give his wife their best wishes for her health and that of the boys.

When George appeared, rolling down through the gardens with her long, mannish-stride, Caesar snapped out of his stupor and went scrambling up the walk to greet her. She stopped to thump the dog soundly on his side, making him roll his eyes in joy, then hurried down to join Imogen.

She threw herself into a chair, and heaving a great sigh, sunk into a most unladylike slouch. "I've been party to a positive orgy of shopping. We shall be quite the smartest women at the First October races."

"I should think," Imogen began, "that we should be likely to be the *only* women present."

George went off in a peal of laughter, startling the dog who woffled before laying back at her feet. "Not at all. There are always a goodly number of ladies present at all the races. But not so many that we shall be in danger of becoming lost in the crowd," she added wickedly. "Lord Morpeth has a horse running, as do Alençon and Carr, who dabble jointly. I just love going to the races. You'll see, it's addictive."

George sat up again and began petting her dog, who had heaved himself up and was drooling copiously all over her skirts. "Have you seen Eleanor and the twins yet?" she inquired, suddenly changing subjects.

"No. I did call with the earl when the colonel sent news of his sons' arrival but his wife was not yet receiving visitors and the twins were asleep."

"Perhaps we can invade tomorrow?" George suggested. "I'm simply dying to see our newest additions, and to see how Eleanor is getting on. Twins. Can you imagine? No wonder she was so uncomfortable when we saw her last."

Imogen blew her breath out in a sympathetic puff.

"Twins certainly would explain poor Mrs. Staunton's discomfort."

"Come inside, you'll freckle if you sit out here all day." George pushed the dog away and stood waiting with obvious impatience.

"Very well, lead me to your treasure trove."

The countess had not exaggerated when she'd referred to her shopping spree as an orgy. Her boudoir was strewn with parcels, trunks, and bandboxes, a great many of which, Imogen was embarrassed to discover, were intended for her.

While she knew George meant it kindly, to accept so many gifts all at once caused an uncomfortable pang. Especially when she could hardly appear so churlish as to refuse the things George had bought for her. But there were so many of them. George appeared to have run mad in the capital, and to have purchased nearly an entire new wardrobe for them both.

As the countess and her maid sorted through the packages, Imogen's pile grew and grew. There were hats and bonnets, new gloves in a multitude of colors and lengths, new nightgowns and a very elegant dressing gown, a long redingtote *à l'Allemande,* with large gold buttons and a high, mannish collar, a huge bearskin muff, and a swansdown tippet. There were fripperies, such as hair ribbons, and silk flowers, and a quantity of silk stockings, some of which were even fashionably striped.

"I also bought fabric for new walking and carriage dresses for us both," George said, glancing about the ruin of her boudoir, with a distracted, slightly harried look on her face. "And I think we both need new habits as well," the countess pronounced with a mischievous smile.

"George," Imogen protested, staring down at the huge pile of things the countess had brought her, all her misgivings suddenly boiling up. "It's too much. Really. I can't possibly . . ."

"Pooh," George replied, turning her head as she studied a reflection of herself in a calash bonnet of morone-colored silk. "None of that now. I told you when you came to stay that I'm extravagant by nature, and you promised to not allow yourself to be embarrassed by whatever small things I might be moved to give you. You'd best take this, too," she added, dropping the bonnet back into its box. "It doesn't suit me nearly as well as it will you. Red really doesn't flatter me at all, I don't know what I was thinking when I bought it."

"But, George . . ." This was not what she'd been picturing when the countess had mentioned *small* things.

"But nothing." George brushed her concerns away with a wave of her hand. "I'm quite determined to puff you off at the races, and no amount of protesting, or caviling is going to stop me. So just take them," she added, her tone brisk, but her eyes still smiling.

Imogen smiled back at her and shook her head. George was being ridiculous. Though she should have been expecting it. The gown that had arrived for the ball was apparently just the start of it. "I'll promise to try and not be so proud and disagreeable, and I'll even accept this appalling large collection of finery, if only you'll promise not to run mad again."

The countess grinned, all lop-sided cheer, and agreed to attempt to curb her more outrageous urges, so long as Imogen would continue to accept the things she purchased when her compunction to shop won out. Imogen cautiously agreed, fearing that what she'd just done was to hand George *carte blanche* to supply her with anything and everything that caught her fancy.

And seemingly, almost nothing escaped her notice. Imogen's shoulders sagged as she spotted an ivory spoked fan amongst the jumble of things intended for her. She was going to be almost as well supplied for the coming season as she would have been if she was still married to William. Possibly better supplied, as her former husband would never have approved of some of the more outrageous kicks of fashion that were now in vogue.

This conclusion was reinforced when George said to her as the maid directed several footmen to carry Imogen's new things down to the dowager house, "Besides, my dear, you're simply not going to be allowed to settle in here and disappear like some poor relation. Don't imagine I'd allow it for a moment." Feeling both exasperated and disgustingly happy, Imogen hugged the countess, and willed herself not to cry. She was not going to cry.

George hugged her back, and then waggled her eyebrows at her, "Shall we spend the rest of the afternoon choosing designs for our new gowns? I've brought back the latest issues of all the fashion magazines, and I'm determined that our dresses will be ready for the races, and for Lord Glendower's shooting party."

"Shooting party?" She'd heard on numerous occasions that George was the only woman who attended Lord Glendower's annual party. Even his wife excused herself to visit one of her numerous sisters for the duration.

"You didn't think I'd dream of going without you?" George replied, not looking up from the toilette she was studying intently. "What do you think of this one? For the corded silk?" Imogen took the magazine, glancing over the plate showing a woman in an elegant, *redingote du matin,* worn over a white petticoat with contrasting ruffles. Mentally stripping away the monstrous Nicolet headdress, and the heavy trimming of bugles, Imogen nodded appreciatively, and handed the magazine back to George.

"I like it. Very elegant. I especially like the waistcoat peeping out at the bottom."

George nodded and folded down the corner of the page. Imogen thought about bringing up the subject of the shooting party again, but knew that there was probably no point. The countess was hard to gainsay, and if she was determined to drag Imogen to the shooting party, then chances were high that that's exactly what would happen. By now Imogen had enough experience with George's methods to just acquiesce with good grace to the inevitable.

They spent the rest of the afternoon curled up on the sofas in George's boudoir, flipping through the pages of the *Galerie des Modes.* George had brought back several copies, and by the time the earl poked his head in to check on them, they had dog-eared numerous pages, making notes in the margins as to which fabrics to use for the design, and which of the numerous frills and furbelows shown on each dress to leave off.

"Mrs. Gable was asking if you ladies would like tea?"

he said, seating himself upon the arm of the sofa George was ensconced on. He put one hand on the back of the sofa, behind his wife, and leaned over to peek at the page she was currently studying. "I like that."

"Listen to this," George said, holding the magazine up and reading from it, "'Fitted redingote of deep lilac, shot with white; longer than they were worn last month, and trimmed with mink.' Do you hear that, Imogen? I sincerely hope you were paying attention. This month they are longer than last month," she repeated for emphasis, and laughing, tossed the volume aside. "I must be one of the most unfashionable women in all of England. I'm still wearing the same Redingote I bought last year. Thank heavens I've bought you a new one. Otherwise we'd be terribly dowdy. I can't believe that Alençon condescends to associate with us."

Imogen choked, and the earl laughed appreciatively. "Yes, my dear," he said finally, his teasing eyes glancing about the room to take in all the new purchases George had just made, "I'm embarrassed to be seen with you, myself. Been meaning to drop you a hint."

George rolled her eyes and slapped at him playfully, shooing him off to assure their housekeeper that tea would be very welcome.

Still feeling oddly out of sorts, Imogen retreated to the dowager house after dinner. She wasn't the best company at the moment, and certainly didn't want to spend the entire evening with the earl and countess, who'd clearly missed one another during their brief separation.

The sight of the two of them gave her a pang, like a

bubble bursting inside her chest. It was petty of her to be jealous. It wasn't as though she and William had ever been anything like the Somercotes after all. They had been a very proper married couple, and would never have done anything so unfashionable as to hang on one another in public.

Annoyed with herself, she sat down at the pianoforte, and began to play; pounding her way through a Bach concerto. Bach always made her feel better. The music was so strong, so emotional. You couldn't possibly concentrate on how you yourself were feeling when you played it, you had to give yourself over to what he had been feeling when he wrote it. And she particularly liked the physical sensation of playing Bach when she was upset, or angry. It simply felt good.

The dramatic notes were clearly audible, drifting out over the garden when the earl and countess walked past, taking a moonlit tour through the garden.

George paused to listen. "She's not happy." She squeezed her husband's hand.

"Brimstone?" Ivo inquired.

"I'm not sure." George stopped on the steps as they turned to go back up to the house. "She just feels restless to me."

She was almost positive that Gabriel's absence was responsible for her friend's depressed air, though she was not going to discuss it at length with her husband.

Ivo could be very dull at times such as these.

His advice would be to not interfere, not get overly involved or invested. He would tell her that it wasn't any of her business, and that Gabriel wouldn't welcome her thrusting herself into his personal affairs, but he'd be wrong.

Gabriel had certainly always taken a brotherly interest in hers, and the least she could do was do the same. Besides, she and Victoria had had plenty of time to discuss the very promising nature of Imogen and Gabriel's romance when she was in town, and to think of various schemes for promoting it. One of which was to get them both to the First October Races.

Exposure was the key. She was sure of it.

Chapter 10

Could Lord S——'s new distraction be the reason he makes no protest to his wife's flaunting herself about on the arm of the Angelstone Turk?

Tête-à-Tête, 3 October 1789

Imogen was well aware of the timing of all the races. They were, after all, popular events with the men of the ton, and as a political hostess she'd had to be aware of such things to avoid planning conflicting events.

The First October Races were exactly what the name implied. They took place on the first Monday in October, thereby preceding the Second October Races and the Houghton meeting, which brought the racing season to a close. No more formal races would be run until the following spring, when the Craven would be held on the Monday after Easter, and the entire sporting world would once again make the pilgrimage to Newmarket.

The young Prince of Wales was an a avid patron of the turf, frequently running his own horses, and could be counted upon to absent himself from London for all the major race meetings. She still recalled with particular relish when one of her rival hostesses had planned an elaborate masked ball, sent out the invitations, and was horrified to discover that she'd chosen the eve before the Oaks, and that nearly everyone who was anyone would be at Epsom Downs. Imogen's own Venetian breakfast, offered a well planned three days later, had been a smashing success.

Imogen flexed her foot in the stirrup and clucked to her mount. They were almost to Newmarket, having set out just after breakfast, and Quiz was beginning to slow down. The elderly bay gelding was her favorite amongst the many horses in the Somercote stable, and she'd been delighted with George's suggestion that they all ride to Newmarket. They'd sent their trunks along in the carriage the day before, and even now their things and the Tregaron's grooms should be awaiting them at the Slug and Lettuce, a favorite inn of George's set. Imogen reached down and patted Quiz soundly on the neck, eliciting a snort and a head shake.

"Almost there, old boy," the countess said, glancing over at her friend. "Talavera's getting tired too, but not Cobweb," she noted, as her husband's horse gave an irritated little cow hop.

"No, not Cobweb. He's rather annoyed just now at being forced to bring up the rear," the earl replied, taking a firmer grip on the reins. "Nasty brute that he is."

Imogen pressed her lips together and did her best to resist laughing. The way the earl said it, *nasty brute* was undoubtedly an endearment. Much like when George referred to Gabriel as a *dreadful provoking beast,* or her godson as a *thatch gallows.*

As they neared the town, the road became choked with men on horseback, and vehicles of every description imaginable, from the most elegant equipages to the humblest gigs, as well as mail coaches with their tops full to overflowing with passengers.

When the rooftops of Newmarket came into view a man's voice called out, "I'll be damned. It's Mrs. Exley." And they all reigned in, pulling off onto the verge, and turning in their saddles to observe a very elegant gentleman mounted on a solid chestnut hack.

"I say," the man continued, stopping beside the countess, "that's quite a horse you have there." He studied Talavera intently for a moment, entirely missing the amused glance George threw her husband. "Spanish?"

"Dutch," the countess replied, reaching out to scratch her mount's neck.

"Dutch, you say," he mused, finally looking up from the horse. "Hmm. Well, a beauty all the same. And I say," he said a second time, catching a glimpse of the earl's horse as Lord Somercote rode over towards them. "That's a splendid animal as well. You can't tell me he's not got a splash of the Spanish."

"Guilty as charged," the earl answered, raising one brow inquiringly at his wife. Imogen bit her lip to hold back a laugh. One simply never knew who might claim an acquaintanceship with George. She seemed to know and be known by everyone from Princes, to dandies, to pugilists.

"Somercote, this is Lord Fitzwilliam, who I've known for an age. Lord Fitzwilliam, this is my husband, Lord Somercote."

"Well, well," Fitzwilliam said, smiling in a very open, friendly manner, taking in the earl with a bit more enthusiasm. "Guess I'll have to get used to calling you *my lady* now."

George shook her head at him and introduced him to Imogen as well. "Here for the races?" he asked her, blithely stating the obvious. "Good, good. You keep an eye on my Pewett. Won the St. Ledger this year, and I have every hope of doing the same here."

He chatted on for a few minutes with the countess about the other contenders, and then, with a neat bow of his head he excused himself and rode off down the road, whistling through his teeth.

Imogen glanced at George.

"Obsessed with horseflesh," George explained, turning her horse back towards Newmarket. "Wait and see Ivo, he'll make you an offer on Cobweb before we head home. I recognize his acquisitive gleam."

The earl answered his teasing wife with a smile and a shake of his head. Imogen had no doubt she was right, but there was no chance at all that the earl would be induced to part with Cobweb. The big grey dapple was his longstanding favorite.

After weaving their way through the crowded streets, past braying donkeys, roving orange girls, and what seemed like hundreds of carriages, they rode into the yard of the Slug and Lettuce and handed their mounts over to their waiting groom. "Anyone else here yet, Catton?" George inquired, as her long time retainer took the reins from her.

"Yes, my lady," he replied, drawing out the *my lady*, in an affected way. "Sir Bennett, Lord Worth, Lord Alençon, Lord Carr, and Lord St. Audley are all here. I believe they're in the tap room. There's only the

Misters Angelstone, Lord Layton, and the earl, his father, still wanting."

"Excellent," the countess pronounced, linking her arm through Imogen's. "Thank you, Catton." The groom nodded, and led the horses away to be unsaddled and stabled. "And now, Ivo dearest, I think Imogen and I shall go up to our rooms and tidy up, and then we'll join you for luncheon." The earl sketched them both a quick bow, and strolled off towards the tap room.

Up in her room Imogen washed her hands and face, took off her hat and set about attempting to resurrect her hair. She was still struggling with it when the countess knocked and summarily entered her room.

"Ready?" she asked brightly. "Apparently not," she added, shutting the door behind her. "Here," she came around behind Imogen and batted her hands away, "let me do it. I love your hair," she sighed, deftly twisting up the riot of springy curls and pinning them in place.

"Somebody has to," Imogen mumbled in return, frowning at her reflection. George caught her eye in the mirror, and shook her head at her. Imogen quirked up one side of her mouth, and watched as George finished pinning up her hair, carefully drawing out a few curls at the nape, and taming them with a bit of water.

"There now," George said, stepping back and admiring her handiwork.

Downstairs the tap room was filled with gentlemen, a great many of whom were by now familiar to Imogen. The sporting set was quite large, but most of the core constituency had been present at the Somercote's house party. They were all drinking ale, making quick work of the hearty plates of food supplied by the inn keeper and his surprisingly amiable wife, and talking horses nonstop.

George and Imogen took seats at a small table partially occupied by Bennett and Morpeth and proceeded to eat, surrounded by the mad hubbub of the room. Imogen chewed her food slowly, glancing thoughtfully around the room, content to watch and listen. George was already in the thick of it, arguing the various merits of several contenders.

"Too short in the back, I tell you," she insisted, "and ever-so-slightly cow-hocked."

"Is he?" Bennett asked, his brows drawn together in a frown.

"Absolutely." George pronounced with her usual conviction. "You won't catch me putting my money on one of Brown's showy hacks. They've all got that snaky, little Arab head, too, which I can't abide."

"I'll agree with you about the snaky little heads," Bennett said, still frowning, "but I'm going to have to take a good look at his rear action before agreeing that he's cow-hocked."

"Ten pounds on it, just between friends?" George suggested, her teasing smile peeping forth.

"And who's to be the judge if I say the colt's legs are straight and true?"

"Oh, you're to be the judge. I trust you. You'd never be able to bring yourself to pronounce such an animal sound for a few guineas."

When they'd finished their meal and the countess was still avidly discussing horseflesh with Bennett, Imogen wandered about, shyly greeting her fellow guests, until she found herself being solicited to take a stroll by the Duke of Alençon.

"Come along, my dear," he urged, holding out one hand, "you shall accompany me to meet Carr at the stables to see how our little filly Aérolithe is fairing."

She glanced at George and the countess waived her off. "Make sure you take her to Gregson's for tea," George called after them as they made a push for the door.

Once outside the crush was only marginally easier to maneuver through than it had been in the tap room. The streets were choked with Corinthians, military officers, navel men, country squires, cits and tradesmen, and bloods and blades of every description.

Here and there, there was a bonnet to be spied amongst the men, and every now and again Imogen got a clearer view of one or another of the women who'd also chosen to attend the races.

The sight was not wholly reassuring.

The majority of the women she saw were clearly not ladies, or even members of the upper echelons of the demimonde. Most of them were shockingly vulgar, in both their persons and their voices, which could occasionally be heard bantering with the men thronging the streets.

Averting her gaze from a particularly bold piece, who was sashaying down the main thoroughfare her nipples clearly visible through her fichu, Imogen found herself suddenly gazing across the street and meeting Gabriel's surprised eyes. He smiled and then a coach trundled past them, blocking him from her view. Alençon craned his neck for a better view and paused on the sidewalk, clearly waiting for Gabriel to join them.

More than a little pleased to have spotted his nymph almost immediately upon his arrival, Gabriel waited impatiently for his chance to dash across the busy street. Dodging a rather rickety gig and weaving his way skillfully between a mail coach and a closed carriage, he hurried across the choked thoroughfare. The duke greeted him with a little lighthearted raillery, chuckling in his usual provoking style. Imogen bit one side of her lip and blushed slightly.

"We were just on our way to look in on my Aérolithe, my boy," the duke said, his eyes full of mischief. "Care to join us?"

"Delighted." Gabriel fell in behind them as the duke set off again.

Imogen had her hands firmly locked about the duke's velvet-clad arm. A few spiraling curls danced about the standing collar of her redingote. Dark against the milky skin of her neck. Gabriel held his breath for a moment, wanting nothing so much as to lean forward and place an openmouthed kiss to the exposed nape of her neck.

Closer to the stables the crowd thinned and he was able to come abreast with Imogen. He gazed down at her, smiling to himself. He could see the hand of George at work again.

"Is that a new hat?"

"Yes," Imogen responded, her color still unusually high. "The countess brought it back from London."

"Amazing," Alençon said, gazing at her with open admiration. "Simply amazing. George picked that out you say? She has always had the most regrettable taste in headgear. It's hard to credit it."

Imogen frowned at the duke, while Gabriel laughed. "That's not true, and you know it, Your Grace," he insisted. "You're thinking of that horrible thing Lyon bought her in Paris, which I'll admit, was a monstrosity. George rarely bothers to wear a hat, but when she does, they're always tasteful."

"Except for the monstrosity from Paris, which, must I remind you, she wore constantly, the whole summer through, not to mention her penchant for stealing her brother's hats, and now her poor husband's."

"Your Grace," Gabriel protested. "George was a new bride when Lyon bought her that hat. You can hardly blame her for wearing it."

"There is no excuse for that hat. None," the duke insisted with a shudder. "Ask any of the Macaronis, they'll second me on this."

"I'm sure they will. Just as I'm sure they'd approve Miss Mowbray's *Chapeau Jockei.*"

Before they could continue their quarrel, Carr appeared from the end of one of the long barns, and threw up an arm, calling them over to join him.

As they approached the Duke of Bedford, Alençon dropped her arm to run his hands knowingly over Bedford's filly. Gabriel promptly stepped into the breech, hands sliding knowingly along her arm, drawing her to him.

She shut her eyes for a moment, dizzy. Let the soothing scent of the barn wash over her. Hay, horse, dung, sweat, leather . . . she caught a whiff of sandalwood. Angelstone. She swallowed hard and followed him down the barn.

They finally found Aérolithe, Carr and Alençon's blood bay filly, and after billing and cooing over her, and hand feeding her slices of dried apples, the duke suggested Gabriel and Imogen take themselves off to Gregson's. "We're going to be here for hours. And I'm sure we're boring Miss Mowbray to tears. Be a good lad and take her off for some tea," he said with a sly twinkle.

Imogen blinked at them all, stunned to have been so easily pawned off, but Gabriel smiled wolfishly, and agreed that tea would be just the thing. With her hand tucked firmly between his arm and his chest he led her out of the barn and turned them both back towards the heart of Newmarket.

It seemed to Imogen that the crowd melted away as they passed through it; parting much like the red sea had for Moses. She was hardly aware of walking at all. Her stomach was in a knot, her heart was racing, and her mouth had gone suddenly dry. Her ears were ringing, and while she knew Gabriel was speaking to her, she couldn't hear a word. She was dazed. Dazed, and excited . . . and floating.

His nymph's thoughts were elsewhere.

He'd paid her several rather warm compliments, specifically designed to throw her into a flutter and put her to the blush, but she'd only nodded absently, and smiled a bit vacantly in response. He gave up teasing her, concentrating instead on steering them safely though the mob which choked the streets.

They, themselves, were creating quite a stir as they moved through the crowd. He nodded to a London acquaintance and smiled at the look of shock he saw on many of the gentlemen's faces.

The sight of a lady on his arm other than the Countess of Somercote or his cousin was one which was virtually unknown. Imogen was clearly neither of those ladies.

Gabriel saw several gentlemen stiffen as they passed. It didn't surprise him that they recognized the former

Mrs. Perrin. Though she'd been absent from polite circles these past five years, she'd been a toast, a well known hostess, and had ended her career as a famous adulteress. Nonetheless, their shocked faces told him they were surprised to see her squired about by himself.

Undoubtedly word was already flitting around Newmarket that the beautiful Portrait Divorcée had resurfaced, and she was now in the keeping of none other than the infamous Brimstone. Gabriel glared at the stiff-rumped Lord Talgert, who quickly looked away and scurried off. At least Imogen seemed blithely unaware of the whispering notice swirling around them.

Gregson's was oddly quiet, an island of calm in a town besieged. "Did you know Mrs. Staunton presented the colonel with twins?" Imogen asked, obviously searching for a safe topic.

He chuckled. "My cousin informed me of the Stauntons' new additions. Both boys if Torrie is to be believed."

"Yes." Imogen blew on her tea before taking a sip. She set the delicate cup aside to cool, hands flitting around the saucer, adjusting the cup's placement.

Nervous.

He smiled again.

Gabriel pulled Imogen in tightly against him and steered her around a group of town bucks who were swaggering down the narrow sidewalk. One of them tipped his hat and another one winked at Imogen, earning a glare from Gabriel. Insolent puppies. If he'd had George on his arm he'd have wiped that grin from the whelp's face. But he didn't; he had Imogen, and he didn't want to shock her . . . at least not publicly.

Back at the inn they found that the few stragglers had now arrived, and George was holding court over all the men in the tap room, happily chatting with her former father in law and Morpeth. Gabriel escorted his nymph over to the countess and smiled widely when George leapt up to greet him. He gave her a quick hug, wrapping one arm carelessly about her waist, and then paused. He stood staring down at her.

"George," he said, trying to keep his mouth from dropping open in disbelief. "You little devil. When were you going to tell us?"

She blushed and gave him a half-smile, half-grimace. "Not till the shooting party. Damn you, Gabriel."

The tap room had grown suddenly quiet, everyone's attention drawn to the tableau taking place near the windows. "What's that then, George?" Bennett inquired, raising his brows.

George glared at him one last time, then glanced across the room to her husband. The earl smiled and shrugged.

"Victoria's going to kill me when she finds out she's the last to know," George said with a nervous little laugh.

"Not if my wife or mother get to you first, baggage," Lord Glendower shouted. The whole room burst into laughter.

"And poor St. Audley is going to be green that we all knew first," Viscount Layton said, crossing the room.

Gabriel gave way as her former brother-in-law pulled her in for a quick hug. "Not everyday I find out I'm to be an uncle," Layton added, with a grin.

The countess endured a good ribald ribbing from her friends, while the earl looked on smugly, accepting the congratulations of his circle with a satisfied smile.

Imogen watched them all tease and scold George, shaking her head. It was no wonder the countess had stayed silent. It was like a seven-day-wonder had suddenly appeared in the room, with all of the men simply fascinated by the simple fact of George's pregnancy.

After the first swell of commotion died down, Imogen glanced up to find Gabriel approaching her with a glass of wine in either hand. He handed her one and claimed a seat at her table. "You'd think it was a miracle," she said, listening to the room hum with chatter and excitement.

"And you think it isn't?" he asked, looking incredulous. "Think about it. George, pregnant. *George.*"

Imogen raised her brows and shook her head slightly. She still didn't understand their response to something as natural and commonplace as a married woman falling pregnant.

"Well, I mean . . . it's George," he said again, lamely, seemingly unable to come up with any other reason for their surprise. "Julian," he called, waving his cousin over, "back me up on this. George?" he asked with an exaggerated blinking of his eyes and raising of his brows.

"I know," the other Mr. Angelstone replied, with a low whistle. "George."

"I think you're all mad," Imogen announced, rolling her eyes.

"No, really, it's George for Christsake, she's—she's . . ." Julian struggled to find the right words.

"She's one of us." Gabriel gave voice to what they all seemed unable to quite explain. "George is one of us, and the idea of one us pregnant is bizarre, to say the least."

Imogen laughed. She couldn't help it. The idea that

most of these men had never fully accepted or understood that the countess was, in fact, a woman was simply too funny. She laughed until she cried, and then when she realized the whole room was staring at her, she gasped out, "George . . . too funny . . . think you're a man." And burst right back into a fit of the giggles.

The countess's smile quirked up on one side, and she too began to laugh. The men simply stood about staring at the mad women in their midst. When the ladies finally got themselves under control, George called for a glass of water to try and alleviate the hiccups she'd suddenly caught, wiping her streaming eyes with the back of her hand. They really did think of her as one of them. Accepted her as such. Imogen found the idea was both comforting and immensely amusing.

Imogen yawned, and poured herself another cup of tea. Everyone had been up late, playing cards, studying the racing forms, and continuing to amuse themselves with the idea of the countess's pregnancy. Even after she'd excused herself and gone up to bed sleep had been impossible. Gabriel had caught her eye as she was leaving, and her stomach had turned over. She'd lain awake half the night, wondering if he would come knocking, but he hadn't.

Stifling a sigh, she ate a piece of toast, and stared out the window. Half the men had already breakfasted and left, and the other half had not yet left their rooms. Only the earl and Lord Morpeth were in the tap room with her, and they were both silently reading the paper the landlord had thoughtfully provided.

George swept in, smartly attired in a double-breasted

caraco with revers and a small shoulder cape. She paused to kiss her husband good morning, then took a seat next to Imogen. She poured herself some tea and spooned a large amount of marmalade onto a triangle of toast.

Morpeth eyed her toast thoughtfully. "I take it you're not suffering the usual bane of women who find themselves in an interesting condition?"

"Not at all." George took a large bite of her toast and chewed it contentedly. "Though the smell of ale makes me queasy, and the thought of brandy makes my head swim."

Morpeth chuckled and assured her that Victoria had been much the same. "Torrie couldn't drink at all when she was pregnant with the boys. She swears that's how she always knew: when the smell of champagne made her sick."

George laughed, and between bites, gave Imogen a good idea of what to expect for the rest of the day. After breakfast they'd head down to the stables, then out to where the races would be held, then to The Blue Garter for luncheon, and then back out for the afternoon race.

"Tonight we'll host a party here to toast the winners, and then in the morning we'll head back to the Park," she said, finishing up her toast and her plans at the same time. "Come." George dusted the toast crumbs from her hands. "Let's be off."

Gabriel and his cousin Julian appeared as they were putting on their hats. Julian suggested they wander down to secure themselves a good view of the race.

The crowd would gather on foot, on horseback, and in their carriages all along the raceway. Alençon had driven up in his own magnificent closed coach, and had offered the use of its roof to the ladies. The gentlemen escorted

George and Imogen down to the track, doing their best to keep them clear of the surging crowd.

The crowd of spectators was already quite large, and was growing by the minute. Even with an Angelstone cousin on either arm Imogen was considerably jostled by the time they reached the duke's coach. Gabriel was actively thrusting men out of their way, much as Lord Somercote was attempting to do for his wife.

Unfortunately for the earl, half the men present knew George, and they were overjoyed to see her. They were all stopped every few feet by some well-wisher, or old acquaintance. And George, as usual, was happy to see them all.

When they finally reached the coach, Gabriel boosted Imogen up to the driver's box. George scrambled up behind her, and promptly sat down, queen of all she surveyed. Imogen dropped down beside her, starting to catch a bit of the countess's excitement.

From the top of the coach they had a commanding view of the field. The duke's coachman had positioned the coach so that the box faced the track, but had left room for the standing crowd in front of it. He'd unhitched the team and returned them to the stable, leaving one of the grooms to guard the coach. Their arrival had relieved the groom of his duty until after the race. With a vale from Gabriel clutched in his hand, the groom disappeared into the crowd.

Imogen amused herself watching the crowd as it ebbed and swirled around the coach. Beside her, George was busy chatting with Lord Morpeth, while the others wandered away for a closer look at the field of contenders for the day's first race. The crowd was made up of men from every walk of life. Cits and farmhands rubbed shoulders with liveried servants, country gentlemen, Corinthians and members of the militia. Here and there she spotted a well dressed lady of the ton, or an even better dressed member of the demimonde.

Gentlemen flocked to their coach, and soon Imogen had been introduced to the few remaining members of the Corinthian set who had yet to come her way. She'd met Lord Craven, and Tom Johnson, the rough and tumble champion pugilist. She'd even re-encountered Lord Fitzwilliam, and shared an amused glance with George when he'd expressed his dismay at missing the earl.

"Wanted to make him an offer on that magnificent horse of his."

"George," Imogen said as soon as he'd gone, "he's going to drive Lord Somercote mad."

"Nonsense," the countess responded with a wicked twinkle. "It will do Ivo good to learn to say no. Besides, an offer of purchase from a man such as Fitzwilliam is a compliment of the highest order. Ivo should be flattered."

Imogen laughed and shook her head at her friend. George delighted in twitting her husband, and luckily the earl seemed to thrive on her teasing. When she looked back out towards the track, it was to see a dark, very handsome man threading his way through the crowd, watching them intently. From the cut and style of his clothing, it was obvious he belonged to the sporting set, from his bearing, that he'd at some point and time been a military man, and from the smile on his face, that he was extremely happy to have spotted George.

"George," Imogen prompted. "Another friend of yours?"

The countess looked out into the crowd and suddenly squealed. She was yelling, "Darling! Darling!" as she leapt down from the coach and flung herself into the man's arms. Startled, Imogen stared down at them.

The man hugged her close and swung her around, to the imminent danger of the surrounding spectators. He whispered something that made them both laugh, and then set George aside to shake hands with Lord Morpeth.

"Imogen," George called, motioning her to climb down. "I'm simply ecstatic to introduce you to a very old friend of mine, whom I thought to be still in the thick of things in India. Imogen, this is Major Lindsey Darling. Darling, this is Miss Imogen Mowbray."

"Actually," the gentleman said with an apologetic smile, "it's Lord Drake now. I sold out, when m'father died, nearly eight months ago now."

"Oh, Lindsey . . ." George extended a hand to clutch his sleeve.

"It's perfectly alright." He patted her hand. "The old reprobate went out in style, half a bottle of good burgundy in him, and a mistress barely a third his age under him. Nothing the undertaker could do to get the smile off his face."

Imogen goggled at him, unsure how to respond, but the countess burst into laughter. "You are impossible."

"All true," Lord Drake protested. "Ask Alençon or Carr if you doubt me."

"I don't doubt you for a minute. Remember, I too knew your father. And you're still damn lucky that I'm not your step-mother. Lord knows he asked me often enough."

"The old boy always did have a soft spot for you," Drake replied with a laugh. "I'd have paid a monkey to see his face if you'd accepted. I hear you've news as well though. Re-married, and not to me. Though you promised so faithfully that I was next. I always knew you were a heartless tease."

"A fickle jade. That's me," the countess agreed with a cheeky smile. "You can meet him tonight, my new lord and master. We're hosting a small party at the Slug and Lettuce."

"I look forward to it," he said with the slightest of bows. "Now I'd best be off if I want to get my wager in. George. Miss Mowbray. Morpeth."

George sighed as they settled back onto the box and Lord Drake disappeared into the milling crowd. "Very satisfactory," she said, taking her seat. "Another of my boys clearly in need of a little meddling. You wouldn't care to be a viscountess, would you, Imogen?"

Chapter 11

Has a certain fiery-haired opera dancer grown tired of Lord T——? It would seem so, judging by the performance she gave last night in the green room . . .

Tête-à-Tête, 5 October 1789

The race was over all too quickly, in Imogen's opinion.

There was a shot, then the thunder of hooves as more than twenty horses flew past, their jockey's distinctive silks nearly impossible to distinguish in the tumult. The crowd yelled and cheered. Imogen felt the rush of excitement down to her toes.

The countess was watching the race through a pair of mother-of-pearl opera glasses, bouncing up and down on her seat. She gave a triumphant yell as the race finished and lowered the glasses.

"Well?" Imogen asked eagerly.

"Aérolithe, by at least a furlong. There was nothing even close to her."

Imogen gave an excited whoop and George glanced

over at her. "I told you it was thrilling," the countess said with a touch of smug hauteur.

"Going to turn our newest member into a turf addict, are you, George?"

Imogen jumped at the sound of Gabriel's voice. He was standing beside the coach, one hand resting on the iron coachman's step. She'd been so absorbed in the race she'd not even noticed his arrival.

"Too late," Imogen announced with a slightly guilty grin. "It's done. I only wish I'd had my own horse out there vying with the others."

"Would you like to see if we can find Alençon and Carr?" Gabriel asked.

"Could we?"

"Certainly," Gabriel replied, amused by her awed tone. "That would be the perfect ending to your first race."

Imogen jumped down from the box into Gabriel's waiting arms. The tingle of awareness that passed between them only added to her excitement. She was having a splendid day. Gabriel set her down and took possession of her arm.

"We'll be back for the next race," Gabriel called over his shoulder.

He gave his nymph's hand a squeeze and smiled down at her. He wished he could divert her to some secluded spot for an hour or so, but she was so eager to find the duke she was practically dragging him through the crowd, and he strongly doubted there was a quiet spot anywhere in the vicinity on a day like today.

Imogen was blind to the amused glances their

progress was eliciting. Throughout the crowd they encountered a wide assortment of Gabriel's friends, acquaintances, and enemies.

By the time they'd pushed their way through the crowd surrounding Alençon and Carr the festivities were over. Imogen looked absurdly crestfallen to have missed the awarding of the prize.

"Perhaps we will be lucky again when she runs later in the month," Carr said, smiling indulgently. "If you care to, you shall spend the day with me, and if Aérolithe wins, you may collect the prize with your own hands." Imogen smiled, and eagerly accepted the earl's invitation.

"Carr, my dear, dear friend," the duke drawled. "You're going to spoil the girl. And don't think for a minute you're going to cut the rest of us out with such an obvious ploy."

"Such things have been known to work," the earl replied.

The duke glowered theatrically at his friend and Gabriel broke in. "Before either of you makes Miss Mowbray another offer that she can not refuse, I think I shall take her out of your reach." He nodded to the elderly roues, and deftly turned Imogen around and led her away.

"Somewhere towards the rear of this throng there should be mongers sent out by the various inns. Would you like a pasty, or something of that kind? Or would you like to join the others at the Blue Garter?"

"Anything we can find will be fine. I'm famished, but not picky."

"Beautiful *and* gracious."

Imogen glanced up at him, her brows drawing together. "A lady can but try."

Gabriel gave a bark of laughter. He thought he'd lost her there for a minute. She'd looked so serious and concerned. Whenever he crossed the line into flirtation she stiffened up on him. He spied a boy with a cart and waved him over. The push cart was piled high with pasties, apples, cold capons, coarse farmer's bread and a large wheel of cheese from which he was cutting slabs. Imogen took a pasty and an apple, while Gabriel selected two pasties, and a thick slice of bread and cheese.

They ate quickly, standing right where they were. Imogen was smiling and laughing, as happy as he'd ever seen her. He was desperately restraining the urge to kiss her. He'd been busily scouting out any quiet corner, hidden nook, or private spot, to no avail. The field was teeming with people. There were no such desirable spots available. When they'd finished their lunch, Imogen delicately wiping her hands on her handkerchief, he resignedly suggested they return to the coach.

"The afternoon race will begin soon, we'll want to be in place before the start."

When they reached the coach, it was deserted save for Alençon's groom. Gabriel, recognizing the opportunity for what it was, flipped the man a crown and sent him off.

With a suggestive smile he opened the door to the coach, and glanced from Imogen to the coach's interior, and back again.

Imogen bit her lip and allowed Gabriel to hand her into the coach. He hopped in after her, shutting the door behind him with a decisive click. The curtains were already drawn, and the dim interior just allowed Imogen to make out his smile as he pulled her into his lap.

Imogen squeaked, and then shivered from head to toe as Gabriel's mouth covered hers, every bit as hot and urgent as it had been in her dreams these weeks past. She could feel his straining erection pressed against her hip, and feel his hands roaming over her. He'd been dreaming of her, too, she was sure of it. With a triumphant moan she wrapped her arms around him, and returned his kiss, her tongue dancing with his.

All too soon he locked his hands onto her shoulders and pushed her gently, but firmly, away from him. One of them had to maintain some vague shred of common sense. And apparently it was going to be him.

"The others will be back soon," he said. "Shall we play cards while we wait?"

Imogen shrugged. If he wasn't going to continuc to kiss her, she supposed cards would suffice to pass the time. He pulled a folding table out from the door panel, and fished a deck of cards out from the cubby below the seat. "It's a poor substitute for what we could be doing," he said with a regretful smile, "were we not surrounded by several thousand men."

Imogen swallowed hard and smiled back at him. It was suddenly very warm inside the coach. She shook a few stray curls back from her face and took a deep breath.

Gabriel set the cards down, twitched back the curtains, and dropped the windows, allowing the light breeze in. "What shall we play?"

Imogen watched him shuffle the cards; his long fingers seeming to caress the cards, putting her forcibly in mind of those same hands on her. In a tight voice she suggested Piquet.

"Stakes?" he asked, his smile growing even more intimate as he dealt the cards.

"Well . . ." Imogen drawled, trying to sound flirtatious,

and unflustered, "this morning I believe I had a whopping two pounds and six shillings in my reticule, and I'm willing to risk it all."

"Penny a point and a shilling per trick? I had something a little more valuable in mind." His smile was positively indecent. Imogen knew exactly why George had once told her he was dangerous. That smile was incendiary. Her blush began at her toes and ended at her hairline. She could feel it.

"Penny a point, and a kiss per trick," he continued softly, glancing at his cards. "And a night in your bed if I win the hand."

Not surprised by his choice of wager, and not opposed either, Imogen quirked a brow and felt her blush recede. There was no reason for her to be embarrassed. He wanted exactly what she did, he was just better at expressing that fact. She always seemed to get flustered.

Practice certainly did seem to make perfect. Determined not to be cowed, Imogen slipped her foot out of her slipper, and slid it carefully into his lap until she encountered his still half-engorged cock.

"And if I win?" she asked archly, attempting to get a little practice in herself.

"I suggest you lose."

"But that wouldn't be sporting," she reminded him, her toes now lightly caressing him through his breeches.

"Imogen," he growled. "I'd like to not present myself at full mast when George returns."

Imogen removed her foot, with a slight moue of dissatisfaction. "Spoil sport." She slipped her shoe back on, and looked at him attentively. "We still haven't agreed what I get if I win?"

"A night in my bed?" he suggested helpfully.

"Now that would be something worth winning."

Gabriel grinned, an entirely feral expression that made her feel molten to the core.

By the time George appeared Imogen knew she was in over her head. Gabriel had won four hands to her two, and he was looking forward to redeeming his vowels. Electricity pulsed from her nipples to her groin. Her knees shook.

She was looking forward to it too, no point in denying it.

Chapter 12

Rumor has it that Lord A—— and Lord C—— have come to blows. Was the dispute over horses, or a certain dowager? We wait with bated breath for details . . .

Tête-à-Tête, 5 October 1789

The afternoon race, the race they'd all come to see, was even more thrilling for Imogen than the first. She was riding high upon a wave of flirtation and anticipation, her body still humming from Gabriel's touch. The countess had lent her the opera glasses, and Imogen was glued to the race. The gritty looks of determination on the jockey's faces, the flying manes and tails, the flared nostrils of the horses.

She loved it all.

It gave her a thrill she could feel just behind her sternum, of a kind that she'd never felt before, except, perhaps when Gabriel looked at her, dark eyes full of innuendo and desire.

When the race was over, and the Duke of Grafton had

collected his prize, George suggested they return to the inn. "I for one am terribly thirsty," she announced, taking her husband's arm and smiling up at him beguilingly.

Ever his wife's slave, the earl acquiesced to her wish, and they wandered off through the already dissipating crowd. Everyone else followed along behind them, the countess's suggestion of a drink holding universal appeal.

Imogen had Gabriel on one arm, and Viscount Layton on the other. The viscount was regaling them both with his afternoon's adventures. He'd won a little more on the first race than he'd lost on the second, so he was in a particularly good mood.

The tap room was filled with gentlemen who'd already grown loud and rowdy. They were busy settling up, buying each other drinks, and toasting Carr and Alençon's filly. Squire Watt was alternately trying to purchase Aérolithe or Cobweb, or perhaps both, while Alençon and Carr were basking in the reflected glow of their win.

As they joined the fray, Layton dropped Imogen's arm and went off to work his way up to the bar to get them all a drink. He returned some while later with ales for himself and Gabriel, and a cider for Imogen.

Drinks in hand, they moved further into the tap room, Imogen satisfied to sip her cider and listen to the gentlemen talk about the races, recount famous events from the past, and speculate on the last two meets of the season. As the evening wore on, and the drinks continued to flow, Imogen found herself growing sleepy. She'd never been much of a drinker; she simply had no head for it. She had had an exciting day in more ways than one, and she could feel a small flicker of anticipation burning within her whenever her path crossed Gabriel's, or she looked up and her gaze met his. His eyes were always quizzing her, even as he spoke of horses, boxing matches, or the many other sporting concerns his circle frittered away their time pursuing.

The inn had provided what they referred to as a plain ordinary upon request; shepherd's pie, parsnip soup, soda bread, and pear tarts. When she and George had eaten, the countess stretched and announced that she was off to bed. Imogen excused herself as well, and without so much as a tale-tell glance in Gabriel's direction, accompanied George from the room.

"They're all going to drink themselves stupid," George said as they went up the stairs. "And I find that's not nearly as entertaining when I'm dead sober."

Gabriel watched his nymph disappear, and felt a surge of desire so keen he had to swallow hard to keep from charging after her. He knew she'd be expecting him, and that knowledge was a delightful secret burning in his chest.

His mouth was dry, and his hands were tingling. He was only vaguely listening to the story Alençon was telling. His attention was focused on what would even now be transpiring upstairs.

His nymph would take down her hair, strip off her jacket and petticoats, her corset, and shift. She'd remove her shoes and stockings. Perhaps she would pull on her nightrail and dressing gown, perhaps not . . . He slugged back the last of his drink and excused himself for a smoke and a piss.

He wandered out the back door and across the now quiet yard to the inn's water closet. He unbuttoned his breeches and relieved himself, hurrying in the hope that no one would join him for a smoke.

Imogen had been gone almost an hour now, surely she

had had plenty of time to get ready for bed by now? Still buttoning up the fall of his breeches he returned to the inn and ducked into the hall.

All clear.

With one last glance about he darted up the back stairs, if anyone caught him he could always say his cigarillos were in his room, which was conveniently across the hall and down one door from Imogen's. He'd managed that much last night.

Once he gained the upstairs hall he walked as quietly as his boots would allow to Imogen's door and scratched softly, afraid to knock lest he wake George. An eternity later the door eased open and he saw his nymph peak out. She smiled enormously, and stepped back to allow him to slip in.

He shut the door behind him and leaned back against it, reaching behind his back to turn the key in the lock. It gave a soft snick and Imogen began to giggle.

She clapped her hands over her mouth and looked up, eyes brimming over with laughter. Gabriel stared down at his nymph, slightly horrified.

"Shhhhhhhhhhh." He smiled at her. "You'll wake George," he whispered, repressing his own rising laughter. "Imogen . . ." He bit his lip hard as a chuckle escaped. What the hell was going on? He was a dangerous rake, a master of seduction, a veteran of the *ton,* and she was laughing at him. There was nothing funny happening here, and yet, he couldn't resist the urge to giggle like a naughty four-year-old. Imogen had collapsed upon the bed, fully supine, her whole body convulsing with silent laughter. Gabriel tiptoed across the room and threw himself down beside her.

"Damn you, woman," he ground out between fits.

"It's just . . . I mean, I'm—and you're . . ." She went off again, unable to sustain her explanation.

"I'm what?" Gabriel demanded, suddenly perfectly serious. He propped himself up on one elbow and stared down at the mirth filled face of his nymph. Something was not adding up here. This afternoon she'd been a minx, and a bold one at that, and now she was anything but. Her giggles were the furthest thing possible from the husky, seductive laughter he would have been expecting.

"You're a rake," she managed to say, the fact seeming to send her over the edge again. "I, Miss Imogen Mowbray, Divorcée, am alone in my room with a rake." She stifled another fit of the giggles with the heel of her hand.

"Why yes, you are," Gabriel almost purred, now fully in command of himself. They were veering from their course, but it wouldn't be all that hard to steer them back. "You, Miss Imogen Mowbray, are alone with a man who's been banned from Almack's, escorted out of Bath, and who has every intention of collecting on the wager you so skillfully lost this afternoon."

Imogen went suddenly still, her hand dropping away from her mouth as he leaned over her, rolling more fully onto his side, and sliding one leg over her hips, trapping her on the bed.

Gabriel leaned down farther, capturing her mouth with his, and when he felt her quiver, and not—he was positive—with desire, he pulled back and looked her right in the eye. "Don't you dare," he warned sternly, before returning to the eminently enjoyable task of kissing her.

Responding, if not to the command in his voice, then to the reality of the situation, Imogen wrapped her arms around his neck and kissed him back, tongue fencing with his, exploring his mouth as her hands explored his body.

Satisfied that she'd gotten over the bizarre humor which had possessed her, Gabriel rolled back just a bit; just enough so he could look down at her. She was wearing a simple calico dressing gown, all flowers and butterflies, over a perfectly modest white cotton nightrail. No lover of his previous acquaintance had ever appeared before him in what she actually wore to bed. The ladies of the demimonde were professionals, and they had all the trappings there of: silk nightrails and bed jackets, along with dressing gowns designed to titillate and taunt. And none of the young matrons of the *ton* he'd carried on with over the years would ever have admitted to owning something so serviceable and dowdy. But it suited his nymph. It was sweet, and pretty, and oddly attractive in its own way.

It was real.

He reached out and deftly untied the ribbons holding her dressing gown closed. Her nightrail had a narrow drawn-thread edging. It was so damned wholesome. This was what women wore to bed all over England. Safe, happy, comfortable women. Wives. The kind of women who didn't have affairs with men like him. Even her hair was primly pulled back and braided.

She'd gotten ready for bed, not for him.

Oh, she'd known he was coming, but she hadn't varied at all from her normal pre-bed routine. That sudden realization gave him a pang of uncertainty. He shouldn't be here. Imogen might have been more than seven, but she really didn't know what she was doing. He sat up and stared doggedly down at his boots for a moment, unsure what to do. He wanted her—God knew he wanted her, his erection was ready to burst the buttons right off his breeches—but he shouldn't be here.

Imogen pushed herself up onto her elbows, suddenly confused. He'd been kissing her, he'd started to disrobe her, and then he'd just stopped.

"Gabriel?"

"I, ah . . ."

He was going to leave. He'd spent all this time convincing her, seducing her, flirting with her, and now he was going to leave. She'd done something wrong. Or at least, she hadn't done something right. Imogen pursed her lips and thought quickly. She could just let him go, but if she did, he was unlikely to ever come back. Once he'd decided she was off-limits, she didn't think he'd change his mind.

She pushed herself up and got off the bed, moving around to stand in front of him. Her breasts were just about eye level when he was seated, and she stood in such a way that he couldn't miss them.

"Gabriel," she said again, in a more serious tone. When he failed to look up, she reached out with one hand and forced his chin up. She caught his eyes with hers and smiled down at him, mischievously. "What are you thinking?"

"I'm thinking I shouldn't be here."

"Stuff. The whole world thinks I've been doing this for years. For Christ's sake, Gabriel, I was divorced for being an adulteress. I've not a shred of reputation left. And besides, I lost a wager."

He smiled a bit sadly at that. Shaking her head at the general perversity of men, Imogen put her hand on his chest and pushed him slowly back on to the bed. She'd be damned if he left now. "Don't be stupid, if I didn't want you here, you wouldn't be here, I'm not a child you know, and my door does have a lock."

"But—"

"No buts." She shrugged out of her dressing gown and let it fall to the floor.

"Imogen," he growled reprovingly.

"Gabriel," she mocked him in exactly the same tone, unbraiding her hair and giving her head a shake. Her curls sprang loose, cascading in spirals over her shoulders.

If he backed out now, he'd never come back. She was sure of it. And if she lost her nerve and let him leave, she'd never find it again. Not just with him, but with anyone. If he left now, she'd be alone forever.

Gabriel sucked in an agonized breath. He hadn't realized she had so much hair, or that she was aware of his fascination with it. But she obviously was, for that was not the maneuver of a woman who was unaware of her power, or unwilling to employ it to her ends. That was not the maneuver of a woman who didn't know exactly what she was doing.

She climbed into the bed and curled up against him, leaning over him almost exactly the way he'd just done to her, then she kissed him, sure as any courtesan. That magnificent hair fell over them in a curtain, and he reached up to run his hand over it, careful not to catch his fingers in the curls.

There was certainly nothing seductive about accidentally yanking a lady's hair; pulling it on purpose was an entirely different thing, however. He locked his hand in the hair at the base of her skull, and slowly tightened his grip, exactly like she'd done to him during their encounter in the garden.

His nymph gasped, excitedly, and let her neck go limp

so that her head fell back, exposing the extremely elegant curve of her neck. He put his lips to the tender pulse point, opened his mouth more fully, biting her very, very softly.

She ran her hand down over his chest, fingers pulling at the layers of coat, waistcoat and shirt. She reached his breeches, and the completely evident proof of his desire. She flattened her hand over his shaft so that it was cupped between her thumb and the side of her palm, and then slid slowly down the length of him, and back up again.

Gabriel pushed himself up against her hand. He couldn't help it. He really should get up and leave, but she wasn't going to let him. Lucky him. He'd tried to do the right thing—something he'd certainly never even thought to attempt before—and cotton nightrail or not, she wasn't behaving like a wholesome little wife. Thank God. Knowing he could only allow her to push him so far before he lost all semblance of control, he grabbed her wrist and pulled her roaming hand up to his chest.

"You can do that some more later, minx."

Imogen giggled again, but this time it was a wholly different giggle. This giggle he knew how to interpret. With an amused but reproachful smile he thrust her off of him and sat up again. He tugged off his boots, and unbuttoned the knees of his breeches, then stood to disrobe.

Imogen just laid on the bed watching him. He peeled away his coat and waistcoat, untied his cravat, and then unbuttoned his shirt and pulled it off.

"Don't stop now." Her voice was pitched low, but the excitement, desire, were unmistakable.

Gabriel raised his brows haughtily, and never taking his eyes from her, flipped open the buttons to his breeches, enjoying having her watch him. When he had the satisfaction of seeing the beginnings of her blush, he looked away long enough to strip off his breeches, along with his drawers and stockings.

She smiled tentatively and scooted up onto the bed, making room for him. Gabriel pulled the small box he'd been carrying all day in anticipation of tonight from his coat pocket and climbed into the rather small bed. He thrust the box under the pillows.

He reached down and began to slowly draw up her nightrail, continuing until he had her bare to the waist, then he sat up, straddling her thighs, and pulled it right over her head. In the dim light provided by the few candles in the room he could almost, but not quite, make out the color of her nipples.

He'd been so looking forward to that . . . he sighed, and smiled wickedly down at her. Things to look forward to. He could see that they were small, dark against her pale skin, and tightly budded.

He pressed her down into the bed; kissing her hard and fast. Her tongue darted out, bold, sure. It twinned with his and then retreated. It was exciting to know that he was kissing her, he was making love to her. It was different than having a woman make love to him, though he was certain, judging by her earlier fit of aggression, that they'd get around to that . . . perhaps when she called in one of her vouchers.

Imogen reached up and slid her hands into his hair. He had wonderful hair; thick and dark with a slight curl to it. He was lying fully atop her, weight crushing her into the mattress, kissing her hungrily. His teeth clashed with hers in his urgency, and then he suddenly abandoned her mouth and began to work his way down her neck to her breasts, where his hands were already busy, stroking and rolling her nipples between his thumb and forefinger. He replaced his hand with his mouth. She gasped and arched.

Gabriel smiled, his teeth still lightly gripping her nipple. She could feel the smile against her skin more than she could see it. His hand slid down her stomach, and curved it along her inner thigh. Imogen moved her thighs apart, too eager to be missish, and he slid his long clever fingers into her cleft, lightly stroking her until he found the exact spot he was looking for, just as he had in the garden. He slid further down the bed, so that he was resting on his stomach between her thighs, watching his hand upon her.

Imogen studied him in the dim light. The lean torso, the sculpted perfection of his back. He really was beautiful.

You weren't supposed to say that about a man, but he was. He was more than handsome; or something other than merely handsome. Naked, he was glorious; smooth, and golden, in a thoroughly un-English way.

When her breathing hitched he stopped sliding his thumb up and down over her clitoris, and instead slid one long finger into her, and then another. Her whole body went rigid and she stared down at him.

Gabriel chuckled and pushed her thighs further apart, leaning in to lick her. Imogen clapped both hands over her mouth, barely cutting off the shriek she couldn't prevent.

William had never done anything her mother had not prepared her for in the rather startling speech she'd given Imogen the night before her wedding. This had certainly not been part of that lecture.

When she'd heard her friends mention this as one of their favorite types of bed sport, she'd always been vaguely repulsed. It just didn't *sound* like the sort of thing one would enjoy. Now she understood their glowing reports. What Gabriel was doing was simply amazing.

He had an indecently talented tongue.

He slid one arm under her thigh and brought it up and around her hip, his hand splayed out on her belly, lightly holding her down. She couldn't take much more, he was simply going to have to stop.

She tried to say his name, but couldn't catch her breath enough to do so. She tugged at his hair, she pulled one leg up and put her foot on his shoulder and shoved, all to no avail; he had her fast. She bit the heel of her hand, forcibly cutting off a shriek she simply couldn't stifle. She'd never been loud in bed, but somehow knowing she had to be quiet made everything feel more intense . . . or maybe that was just Gabriel.

Gabriel was more than a little amused by her reaction to having his mouth and hands on her in such a delightfully intimate way. She could pull his hair all she wanted, he wasn't about to stop until he'd driven her right over the cliff.

He'd been imagining and dreaming about doing this with his nymph for at least a month now, and he wasn't going to be denied. She was holding her breath now, only occasionally taking loud, gasping breaths. Luckily the rooms on either side of hers were occupied by men who'd likely be downstairs for hours yet. When she began to whimper and thrash he knew she was close. The leg which she had been using to try and dislodge him had stopped pushing against his shoulder, and was now trembling against him, her thigh pressed hard against his shoulder.

Gabriel tore himself away, laughing as she whimpered

in protest, and dug the box out from under the pillow. He flipped it open, the scent of brandy filling his nostrils.

Imogen stared at him, confusion writ plainly on her face. He pulled the brandy-soaked sponge from the box and held it up. "Simple whore's trick." She frowned, then jumped as he circled her clitoris with the cold sponge. "And damned effective in my experience."

He licked the brandy from her, moving the sponge down her cleft, guiding it up inside her as he sucked. She began to tremble again, hands clutching at him, legs moving restlessly. She gave one last muffled shriek, her whole body bucking and then going rigid.

Satisfied, he stopped, raising his head to watch her face. She looked dazed. Shocked. She looked thoroughly replete.

He wiped his chin with one hand. Imogen drew several gasping breaths, letting them shudder back out. Gabriel smiled, working his way up her torso, returning to her breasts to suckle and tease her out of her lethargy.

Imogen wriggled and gasped when he bit down on her breast with a little more force than he'd used before, arching her back and pressing her breast up towards him. He slid up a few more inches and returned to kissing her, fastening his mouth to hers hungrily.

She'd just had at least a small release, but he was still in a state of almost painful anticipation. With an easy twist of his hips he positioned himself, maneuvering so that he was lodged just inside her, poised for entry.

Imogen pressed herself towards him, as wanton as he could have ever dreamed. Acquiescing to her evident desire for him to hurry, Gabriel drove himself deep inside her in one fluid motion. She made an odd, almost purring sound—half gasp, half sigh; her breath shuddering in and out of her nose—and broke off their kiss, throwing her head back and angling her hips to increase the depth of his penetration.

Gabriel withdrew slightly, then slid his forearms up under her shoulders, so that his weight was on his elbows, and his hands on the bed, resting beside her head. In a much better position now, he began to move atop her, grinding himself into her with every long, hard stroke.

Her legs came up, knees pressing against his ribs, feet on his buttocks, urging him deeper. Gabriel locked his hands in her hair and pulled her head back, licking and biting her neck, trying to remember not to leave any marks. Though if he did, at least for once her damn fichus would be useful.

She began to thrash beneath him, and then with a convulsion that involved her entire body, she simply shattered; her legs locked about him, holding him fast. Her release washing over him was all he needed to find his own; he'd been resisting for several minutes now, desperate to make sure she found hers first. Pressing his face into the hollow of her neck and clenching his teeth to prevent himself from shouting he came, spilling himself into her.

When he thought he could move again, he raised his head and grinned at her. She was still drifting, eyes soft and unfocused. He nipped her earlobe, worked his way down across her jaw and returned to kissing her. She was infinitely kissable, her mouth proving to be every bit as promising as he'd first supposed back in George's garden.

Roused from the sleepy and rather contented state he'd put her in, Imogen was startled to feel him growing hard inside her. He hadn't really lost his erection to start with, but the size of it had tapered off; now he was clearly fully engorged again. It had only taken minutes. She hadn't known a man could do that. William had always simply rolled over and gone to sleep.

He began to move slowly, not withdrawing and plunging in as he had earlier, more of a gentle nudging in and out, his pelvis rocking against hers. She clenched and unclenched around him, then did it again; the wave of small orgasms almost too much to bear.

Her vision flickered, everything going black for a moment as she came. Gabriel sighed, and raising himself off her slightly, increased his pace until a moment later he too shuddered and gasped, thrusting himself into her one last time; sinking into her as deeply as possible.

With one last kiss Gabriel withdrew and slid over to lie beside her on the bed.

Imogen rolled over onto her side and he gathered her up against him. She dropped her head down onto his shoulder and slid one knee up to rest on his thigh. Gabriel dropped a kiss on the top of her head, content with the world and his current place in it.

She was his, plain and simple. And whether that meant for a month, or year, or however long it took for them to grow tired of one another, it was enough for now to simply be sure in his own head; she was his.

Imogen kissed his chest, and mumbled sleepily. Gabriel roused her enough to get her under the covers and slid in next to her, pulling her back into his arms once they were both under the blankets.

"You're not leaving?" she asked, glancing up at him.

"Not just yet. I'll wait a couple of hours, until everyone has gone to bed."

"Good." She snuggled into his side and promptly closed her eyes, content to trust him to escape her room on his own.

Lying there he found himself very much looking forward to the next several months of shooting parties and race meetings, not to mention the upcoming Little Season.

She hadn't had anyone in her bed in years, he was certain of it. Gabriel let his thoughts roam over the various things he'd like to do to and with his nymph. The options were almost endless. She's obviously had a very limited introduction to bed sport. Once again cementing the fact that Perrin was an idiot. An undeserving, incompetent, idiot.

Gabriel glanced down at her; she was already soundly asleep, her face pillowed on her hand, resting on his chest. Worn out.

The infamous portrait of her had been a seven-day-wonder; everyone had gone to see it. At the time he'd thought that it was much ado about nothing. Now he was sure of it.

He had the most infamous portrait in England in his collection, and he was now the lover of the lady depicted in it. He kissed his sleeping nymph again and settled in; he was undoubtedly going to remain right where he was for a good long while, as he had not the slightest desire to move. Life was a beautiful thing.

Chapter 13

If the gossips are to be believed—and in this case we think that they certainly are—the Portrait Divorcée has already transferred her affections from Lord S—— to the Angelstone Turk. Alas, no duel appears to have been required . . .

Tête-à-Tête, 6 October 1789

Imogen couldn't help smiling the whole ride back to Barton Court.

She'd had a very fine morning. Gabriel had flirted with her all through breakfast, but it aroused no suspicions. Almost all the gentlemen flirted with her; just as they did with George, though perhaps, in not quite so warm a vein. She had smiled, and teased him back, all the while wishing they could run back upstairs. It didn't seem fair that after one night they had to part.

Even the knowledge that she wouldn't possibly see him for more than a fortnight couldn't dampen her spirits. Not today. Today she felt invincible. He'd kissed her hand, in a mockingly grand manner that had sent George into whoops, and had asked almost off-handedly as he'd tossed her up into the saddle, if she'd be attending the Earl of Glendower's shooting party.

Before she could answer, the countess had said, "Of course she will," as though the question were absurd. So now she had something specific to look forward to . . . she'd see him again in a fortnight.

When she'd woken up alone, she'd been vaguely uneasy about what would come next. How did these things work? She didn't know, and she didn't have anyone to ask. It didn't feel right to talk to George, since she was Gabriel's friend, and she couldn't write it in a letter—she just couldn't—so Helen was out as well.

She was stuck muddling through on her own.

She wished now she'd paid more attention to the intrigues of the affairs her friends had conducted, but at the time she simply hadn't wanted to know what Helen and the rest were up to.

There'd been no sign of his presence in the room this morning; no forgotten stocking, or misplaced glove; not even a dropped cufflink. Her nightrail and wrapper were draped neatly across the foot of the bed, and her slippers positioned beside it, just as though she hadn't kicked them off haphazardly while making her way to the bed, nearly hysterical with laughter.

He was nothing if not thorough, in every way, she thought with another irrepressible smile. She'd been smiling so much she felt as though her face might crack.

Luckily the countess put her smiles and good humor down to her newfound love of the turf, and spent much of the ride filling Imogen in on all the major figures in the racing set, who was a member of the Jockey's Club, which racing stables were the most famous and successful, which of the founding famous horses each line held to, or blended in their stock. All of it interesting information, and all of it lost on Imogen. She simply couldn't think of anything but Gabriel. She was half afraid she was in love with him; she was certainly infatuated.

Back at the park they found Caesar very happy to see them, and a letter from Colonel Staunton inviting them to dinner, any night they should please. There was a pile of invitations and general correspondence for the earl and countess, and even a letter for Imogen from Helen.

She wrote that town just now was very slow; so many of the gentlemen being absent due to the manifold opportunities for sport being offered in the country at this time of year. Not only was the race season wrapping up, but fox hunting was in full swing, and all manner of game was in season: pheasant, grouse, woodcock. Left to her own devices, Helen was finding things in town quite flat. The only real entertainment was being provided by Lord Dalton, who had left his wife, and was openly living with his mistress, and that the whole city was riveted by reports of a man strangling shop girls in Whitechapel. Bow Street was said to be looking into it, which at least made the public at large feel safer, if not the poor girls standing behind innumerable counters all over the city.

Imogen read her letter and immediately wrote back. Her quill spilled details of the races, who she'd met, and mentioning her upcoming trip to Winsham Court for Lord Glendower's annual shooting party. It skittered and spat a line of ink across the page when she thought of Gabriel. She couldn't put that in a letter.

On Thursday they went to dine with the Stauntons,

and spent a very pleasant evening there, fussing over the twins. There really wasn't all that much to say about them just yet, but they were, nonetheless, adorable. The two small boys seemed entirely identical to Imogen, though their mother insisted she could tell them apart without the aid of the brightly colored floss tied around their wrists.

"Eleanor claims it's quite easy to distinguish them," the colonel said, staring down perplexedly at the boy he held, "but I must confess that I can't do it."

"You can't tell them apart, Papa, because you think of them as a set." Simone leaned over her new half brother, and twitched the blanket back from his face. "Toby here is the watchful one, while Bryan over there, is the demanding one. They're entirely different," she said, seemingly disgusted by her father's inability to tell his own children apart.

"Perhaps to you and your mother, poppet," George said. "But I'm forced to concede that, like your father . . . they seem just alike to me. I'm sure it will become easier for the rest of us as they get older," she added, by way of a peace offering.

Simone made a slightly rude noise in the back of her throat and stared at her former guardian reproachfully. "You can't tell them apart either?" she asked in an appalled voice. "And I was sure Papa couldn't do it because he's a man."

"Well," Imogen jumped in, her eyes dancing, but her tone perfectly serious, "I'm sure your mother can tell them apart because she's their mother, and mothers have a special sense about these sorts of things. And I'm sure you can tell them apart because you've trained your eye so carefully with all your art lessons, but you'll have to let the rest of us get to know the boys better. In time we too will be able to tell which is which. Even your poor father," she suggested wickedly, causing everyone, the colonel included, to laugh.

Not at all mollified, Simone harrumphed, and sat back down next to George. The countess caught Imogen's eye, and wiggled her brows up and down comically. Imogen stifled a laugh. George was simply too wicked sometimes, now was not the time to make her laugh.

"Imogen!"

The angry shout carried all the way across the garden. Imogen skidded to a stop, afraid she was going to vomit. Her hands began to shake. She could have sworn the flowers trembled, buds furling in fright.

Her brother couldn't be here.

There was no reason for Richard to be here. The garden spun, a sickening sea of green. The scent of freshly mown lawn washed over her and she swallowed down her gorge.

She glanced towards the top of the garden. Richard was practically running, his face bright red, the skirts of his coat flying out behind him.

How had he even known where to find her? Why would he care to? He'd sent her one letter since her divorce. Refusing the use of a long vacant cottage on the estate he'd been given when he'd reached his majority. Why would he be here now?

"Does Lord Somercote know you're here?"

His face went from red to mottled puce. Sweat ran down his temple, oozing out from under his wig. "I don't need that damn lap dog's permission to speak to my own sister."

"I never said you did. I merely asked if his lordship was aware that you'd invaded his gardens."

Please let someone know he was here. Please.

"Besides, Richard. You've made it quite clear you have no interest in my well-being, so why would I think you were here to see me?"

"Why would—of all the—you damn—" he sputtered to a stop.

Imogen stared him down. Richard had always been a bully. He was like a savage dog. If she showed any fear at all he'd tear her to pieces.

He took a deep breath, his color still high. He reached in to the pocket of his coat and pulled a newspaper out. He shook it at her, crumpling it in his fist.

"I warned you. Gave you every chance."

Imogen took a step back. He was clearly out of his mind. She'd be lucky if he didn't beat her to death here and now. Lord knew he'd tried once before . . .

"Brimstone? Of all the men in England you make a public show of yourself with the Angelstone family mongrel?"

Imogen took another step back and Richard surged forward, grabbing a hold of her arm. "There's been a general call for women to be transported to New South Wales. You're going to be on that ship."

Imogen jerked, trying to pull her arm free. "You can't have me transported on a whim." She pulled again, pushing with her free hand, her heart beating frantically.

"On a whim? Perhaps not. But for theft? We've been wondering what happened to mother's pearls ever since you left. Now we know."

Fingers digging into her he dragged her towards the stables. "I've come to fetch you to Bow Street. If you come quietly maybe we'll simply pack you off to Madras to become some fat major's mistress."

Imogen swung, her fist connecting with his ear. Richard let out a bellow that was quickly cut off by the explosion of a gun being fired. He dropped her arm as he turned towards the noise, sending her flying into the flower bed.

She pushed her hair out her eyes in time to see the countess cock a second pistol as an army of footmen and grooms came running from all directions.

"Would it be simpler if I shot him?" George called, taking aim.

"Much." Imogen yelled back. "Except that he's my brother."

"A family reunion. How charming. It's too bad we have guests coming and Mr. Mowbray's presence would unbalance my table. I'll make sure and mention your visit to the earl, though."

Richard sputtered and reached up to adjust his wig, fat fingers fumbling with it. "You can't—"

"Goodbye, Mr. Mowbray." The countess nodded and the wall of footmen behind her spilled over.

Her brother stood his ground until one of the beefier grooms grabbed hold of his shoulder and propelled him towards the stables.

One of the footmen helped her to her feet and Imogen brushed at her skirts. Rage filling her.

"Up to the house," George said in a tone that brooked no opposition, placing her hand on Imogen's elbow and steering her back towards the steps.

"I'm not safe," Imogen replied, restraining herself from throwing off George's hand.

"What you need is a drink. Everything looks better from the bottom of an empty glass."

Practically twitching the whole time, Imogen allowed her friend to drag her up to the house. Once inside, George pulled her into the library.

Imogen dropped in the reassuring embrace of one of the large chairs near the fireplace, while George set her pistols down on the desk and poured her a very full glass of brandy. She handed it over, and sank into the chair beside Imogen's.

"Drink up."

Imogen took a gulp and gasped as it hit the back of her throat. It burned all the way down and made her eyes water. She blinked and took a smaller sip.

"That's a girl. Finish up, and I'll pour you another."

Imogen drained the glass and held it out. George filled it again bringing the decanter back with her.

"To what do we owe the pleasure of your brother's visit?"

Imogen opened her mouth to reply, but nothing came out. She was simply too angry to speak yet. She took another sip of brandy, letting its warm glow spread through her body.

George settled back into her chair with the causal nonchalance for which she was famous. "I'm going to guess one of the London gossip rags has made you their latest victims?"

Imogen nodded, still not trusting herself to speak.

"Don't pay it any mind," the countess advised. "It doesn't mean a thing. They've been saying worse about me for years. You should have seen the things that were being written when Ivo and I were courting. Let alone the things they wrote about me before that. I don't know when I would have found time to sleep."

"But no one in your family was threatening to have you transported." And she was a wealthy woman with a powerful family. Always had been.

"Transported?" George's eyes flashed. "You should have let me shoot him."

Gabriel stared down at the most recent edition of Lady Banbury's scandal sheet and cursed. His cousin Victoria had sent it round, folded up inside a sheet of foolscap upon which she had written, *Damn you.—V.*

He hadn't been thinking. He'd made sure to keep George and the rest of them in the dark, but it hadn't even occurred to him that the gossips would take such vicious notice of a single outing. She'd been seen on his arm for less than an hour, in a very public place. But the column spoke for itself:

As mentioned here before, this author has heard over and over from the gentlemen of her acquaintance, of the beauty of the mystery lady seen on the dangerous Brimstone's arm at the First October Races. This same lady is reported to have been seen in the company of the even more deadly Lord Drake, and the equally reprehensible Lord Alençon. Such a wild group of cicisbei has not been seen in recent years. I am happy to announce that it required little effort to discover the lady's identity. It seems that the infamous Portrait Divorcée has reappeared, and is keeping company with one of, or pos-

sibly many of, society's most scandalous bachelors. This comes as no surprise after the episode which ended her marriage, but one would have thought the lady would have learned her lesson. This author is forced to wonder, has the devilish Brimstone found a new way to keep himself entertained when the lure of his usual pursuits wanes? And is poor Mr. Perrin aware of his former wife's current tastes in entertainment?

As he read the column over, phrases jumped out at him: *Mystery Lady . . . one of, possibly some of.* Gabriel cursed again and clenched his teeth. He'd dearly like to throttle Lady Banbury, whoever supplied her with information, and her damned publisher. Imogen had been skittish enough as it was.

This couldn't possibly be good.

If Torrie was angry, George was likely to be in a rage, and Lord only knew what his nymph's response would be. He'd be lucky to get within ten feet of her at the shooting party, if she even showed up.

Horrible thought, that. She might not even attend. And even if she did, he might not want to; George was sure to be out for blood. She'd specifically warned him off, and he'd ignored her. Gabriel crumpled his cousin's note and the column and tossed it into the fire. Taking a savage satisfaction as they blossomed atop the coals.

Chapter 14

Not even the considerable charms of London's most beautiful widow have proven enough to lure Lord St. A——from his monastic ways. What a pity . . .

Tête-à-Tête, 16 October 1789

Imogen sat beside George in the countess's phaeton. Driving had been a compromise with the earl, who had wanted his now noticeably pregnant wife to take the coach, while she had wanted to ride. They were bowling along at a spanking pace, behind the countess's greys, on their way to Winsham Court.

No argument Imogen had put forth had swayed her friend in the least. George insisted Imogen attend. If for no other reason then that to not do so would reinforce the damage the gossips had done, and possibly make her brother think she'd been deserted. It would make it appear as if Imogen was being shunned, and nothing, as Imogen knew, drew the attention of the scandal mongers like the scent of wounded prey.

Though she knew George was right, Imogen was still not feeling at all confident. Before her mother and Helen's letters she'd been happily dreaming about two weeks with Gabriel. Now she was almost dreading them.

A private affair was one thing; a public intrigue was something else. People were already watching, and any signs of an illicit relationship would spread like wildfire. None of their close friends would gossip, but Lord Glendower's party would not be limited to their small, select group.

She couldn't endure being raked over the coals again.

She gripped the side of the seat as George swung through the gates of Winsham Court, and the phaeton sluiced slightly from side to side as the wheels rolled onto the gravel of the drive. The earl, riding behind them, gave a yelp, and George slowed her team. They traveled up the shady drive, until finally the house came into view. Imogen gave an appreciative gasp and simply stared. The seat of the Earls of Glendower was every bit as amazing as the guide books made it out to be. The house was massive; four stories of soft yellow Bath stone that reflected the light back with a soft glow. The drive circled up to a semi-circular dais of steps that led to a massive door.

Imogen smiled, and looked about, trying to take it all in.

"Wait until you see the courtyard," George advised her. "What's in the courtyard?"

"It's not what's in it. Lyon's grandfather had the entire thing glassed in, and then fought with the tax assessor tooth and nail. The earl insisted it was all one window, but the tax assessor wanted to charge for every pane. I think the earl died still fighting, and the current earl finally paid the bill simply to have it over and done with; much to the dowager's annoyance. It's amazing. Multi-story stone staircases up to the first and second floors, massive fireplaces on two sides, and a fountain in the middle. You're going to love it. When we were young, and it was snowing, we used to practice batting there, and my changeling led a charge through the great hall, and once round the courtyard a few years ago. I thought the poor dowager countess was going to faint when the children erupted through the front door on their ponies."

George steered the carriage around the side of the house and drove it back to the stables. Still happily chatting about past events which had defined life at the Glendower seat. The earl dismounted and tossed his reins to a groom, then stepped over to the phaeton. George held the horses steady while her husband helped Imogen down, and then handed the reins over to one of the waiting grooms and allowed Ivo to help her down as well.

Once on her feet, George led them in through the side door, and straight to the billiard room, where they could hear the sounds of a game in progress. Inside, they found the earl playing billiards with Carr, while the rest of the guests either looked on, or clustered about the two tables playing cards. George swooped in, greeting everyone brightly, leaving her husband and Imogen to trail in behind her. After making the rounds, she dragged one of the men over to Imogen, and introduced him.

"Dorry, this is my friend Miss Mowbray, she's rather new to us, so do your best to put her at ease. Imogen, this is my very old friend Lord Dorrington. He's mostly home in Ireland, so I'm very excited to find him here today."

Imogen smiled and gave her hand to the man. He was shorter than most of his friends, barely taller than she was, handsome in a comfortable way. His coat was loose, his neckcloth loosely knotted, but his boots fit him perfectly, and were shined to a mirrored perfection.

The Irish earl bowed over Imogen's hand in a friendly, but thoroughly perfunctory manner, and asked if she and George would like a drink. He was obviously not much of a ladies man. Imogen smiled at him with a friendly twinkle. Good thing too, as she had more than she could handle at the moment.

"Traveling is thirsty work, or so I always find," he said, smiling back at her.

While he was gone Imogen had a chance to glance about the room. Gabriel definitely wasn't there, but his wasn't the only face that was missing, so some of the guests must either be arriving late, or already taking advantage of one of the many activities the estate could offer just now.

Imogen accepted a glass of madeira from Lord Dorrington, and crossed the room to greet their host's son. She rather liked the bluff Lord Layton, he was friendly and entertaining, without ever being flirtatious, or making her the least bit uncomfortable. Cut from the same stamp as his father, clearly. Imogen had the distinct impression that the countess's first husband had been the wild one.

Layton was playing hazard with Sir Robert Bennett and Lord Morpeth. Bennett currently held the dice, but he paused to welcome her, and invited her to join them.

"I'm afraid you all play too deep for me," Imogen responded with a grin. "I'm more in the habit of playing for lottery fish with the children, but I'm more than happy to sit and watch." She took the proffered seat beside Lord Morpeth and sat chatting with them and watching them play until the butler appeared and informed them that their trunks had arrived, and were being unpacked.

"Thank you, Griggs," George said, rising and smiling at him. "Are the earl and I in our usual room?"

"Of course, my lady," he responded, with just a hint of a smile. "And Miss Mowbray is in the Three Graces Room, as you requested."

"Excellent. Imogen, are you coming?" She turned and looked at Imogen inquiringly.

Imogen excused herself from the table and followed George out of the room and up the stairs. George, chatting all the way, pointed out various *objet d'art* and familial portraits, including one of her former husband and his brother. Imogen stopped and gazed up at them.

"He was very handsome," she said, stating the plain truth of the matter. The painter had even captured the devilish twinkle in his eye.

"Yes, he was," George agreed a bit wistfully. "Very handsome, and full of life. Lyon was always something of a rogue, and everybody adored him. It was impossible not to."

The countess gave herself a shake and Imogen realized she'd made something of a *faux pas*. No matter how much in love with her current husband George might be, it was clear that she'd always have a spot in her heart for her first.

Turning away from the portraits, they went down a long hall and George let Imogen into a large corner room where they found a maid already busily unpacking Imogen's trunk.

"I'll come back to collect you for dinner in an hour or so," George said. "Just listen for the bell. The house can be confusing, and Ivo and I are in another wing entirely."

Imogen glanced around the room. It was huge, with pale blue walls, and a raised bed with curtains of a slightly darker brocade that matched the drapes, the upholstery of the chairs arranged before the fireplace, and the cushions in the window seats. There were large windows on two sides of the room, and several Persian carpets on the floor. It was a beautiful room. There was a landscape painting on one wall, and on the mantel the set of three rather ugly Sevres figurines, depicting cavorting naked goddesses and plump cherubs.

Imogen requested a pitcher of hot water so she could wash her face and hands, and while the maid was gone, stripped out of her habit. Once she was clean, she selected a gown, and then allowed the girl to help her dress.

She dampened her hair to bring the curls back under control, and managed to pin it back up in a becoming manner. When she was done dressing, she unpacked her personal things, then curled up before the fireplace to read *The Spectre.*

An hour later she hadn't made any headway; she kept reading the same paragraph over and over again, her eyes reading each word, but her brain not stringing them together into comprehensible sentences. Finally she closed the book and simply sat staring into the fire.

Was Gabriel coming? Was he already here? If so, what should she do? How should she act? She wanted to tumble into bed with him, gossips be damned, and indulge herself for the next two weeks in a passionate affair. Something to store up for all the cold winter nights to come.

This might be her only opportunity for such a thing, and she wanted it, badly. But her practical, logical self knew that to do so wasn't the wisest thing she could do.

The hazards and pitfalls were many, and all too easy to stumble upon.

If she wanted to reenter society, even on a small level, she should endeavor to keep Gabriel, and anyone like him, at arms length. Any further public association could only cause her trouble, and ultimately lead to her being shunned in the few places she was still welcome.

It was simple for the countess to snap her fingers at society's dictates, she had money, family and rank backing her up. And should her brother choose to put his threat into action, there would be little she could do to defend herself.

She shook her head and sank further down into the chair. It was easy to think clearly here, now, while she was alone; another thing entirely to do so with Gabriel's sleepy eyes upon her, or worse, his hands.

When he looked at her, she couldn't think straight, and when he touched her, all ability for thought simply left her. And when he smiled, she simply couldn't resist. He had the most tempting smile she'd ever encountered.

She gave a gusty, disgusted sigh, and opened her book again. George would be here any minute, and the last thing she wanted was to be caught moping. A few minutes later, while she was still struggling to enter the world of the novel, the dinner bell sounded, and almost simultaneously there was a loud rap upon her door and George sailed in.

"We've got a few minutes yet, the gong only means we should assemble in the drawing room. We won't go in to dinner for another half hour or so."

At George's urging, Imogen set her book aside, and accompanied her back downstairs. They were joined by several other guests on the stairs, and they found the rest of them assembled in the drawing room.

The earl crossed the room as they entered and slipped his arm around his wife's waist, bending to drop a casual kiss on her temple. George smiled up at him and stepping back, slipped her arm through his.

"Good God," Lord Drake said, his mouth curling up into a teasing smile. "Is it possible for the two of you to become any more unfashionable?"

"I hope so," the earl responded with perfect good humor.

The viscount shook his head reproachfully, his eyes merry. As the earl and countess crossed the room, he turned his attention to Imogen. "Miss Mowbray, I'm happy to find you as beautiful as ever."

Imogen blushed hotly. The viscount spent several minutes gossiping with her about the current events taking place in London, never once coming anywhere near the rumors currently being bandied about concerning her, before Mr. Bennett arrived and displaced him at her side.

"Miss Mowbray," he said, faintly smiling, "How lovely to see that you've joined us. Usually there is only George here to flirt with, and I find that rather trying. Rather like attempting to turn one's great-aunt up sweet."

Imogen laughed, clearly able to picture exactly what he was complaining about. While he rattled on about the Quorn and the local cheeses, she studied the other guests.

Where was Gabriel? Was he staying away because of the gossip? Did she want him to?

Chapter 15

We sincerely apologize for our earlier reports of fisticuffs between two of our more distinguished peers. It seems the truth of matter was that the tails of Lord C——'s coat had caught fire . . .

Tête-à-Tête, 16 October 1789

Gabriel felt his stomach clench as he entered the dining room; dinner was in full swing, the soup course had already been cleared, and the next was now being placed upon the table. He was sure he should be smelling the savory roast and buttered parsnips, but the only scent he was aware of was that of Imogen's perfume: a faint hint of roses.

He glanced around the table, smiling with relief when George greeted him with her usual wicked smile. Either she hadn't seen the papers, or for some inexplicable reason of her own she was not reacting as he'd expected.

Please let it be the latter. Please.

He simply wasn't prepared to deal with George in the first flush of anger.

Imogen was seated halfway down the table, between Sydney and Drake. She looked sufficiently amused by her dinner companions, and amazingly delectable. Her hair was slightly disheveled in a way that made him long to shake it loose from its pins. Curls twisted about her head, fell into her eyes, twined about her ears . . .

Gabriel filled his plate and ate slowly, easing himself into the conversation around him, doing his best to avoid staring at Imogen. He knew he'd missed her these past weeks, but his wishful thinking of the days past had coalesced into simple lust the second he'd entered the room.

Happy to be back in familiar territory, he stole a glance down the table, and was pleased to catch her watching him, soulful eyes wide, pupils large and dark. He smiled, trying to keep his thoughts and intentions cloaked.

It wouldn't do to be caught with too predatory an expression on his face. Any interest at all would rouse George's attention, but simple politeness wouldn't catch the male guests' attention. Or not more than usual. Half the men here were trying to figure out how to get her into their beds, he'd bet his favorite team on it.

Sydney and Bennett were both overly solicitous, and Drake, well, Drake was an even worse roué than he was. He might be considered bad ton, but Drake had such a wild reputation he was excluded from even the larger venues that Gabriel still graced by invitation.

Imogen met his gaze, but glanced away immediately, turning her attention to her plate, until Sydney said something that elicited a smile. Gabriel gave himself a mental shake and turned his attention to Morpeth, who was discussing their all joining the hunt at Quorn the next day. No reason to drive himself crazy over Sydney

Exley. Syd was simply not in the petticoat line; she couldn't be with anyone safer, especially in this crowd. Drake, on the other hand, he'd be keeping an eye on.

After dinner they all retired to the drawing room, settling in around the scattered tables to play whist and piquet, while a footman wandered about, filling their glasses.

His nymph was demurely ensconced with George and Lord Exley before the fire. She looked tired, skin stretched a little too tightly over her cheekbones. Her glance slid over him, skittered away like a bat.

"Listening to my father and George hash over all the last few months has got to be dreadfully dull for you," Syd said, extending one hand to Imogen and helping her up from her seat.

"You'll be much better off with us out on the terrace," Lord Dorrington added, seconding his friend.

His nymph glanced to George, who waved her off. "You go, too," she said to her husband. "You don't want to listen to this."

The earl smiled, but shook his head. "Not a chance. I'm simply agog to hear how the Cooper children have been fairing, and to find out about Mrs. Swift's new son."

George raised one brow, but she seemed content for him to stay. Amazing. George was displaying alarming signs of domesticity.

A faint shudder worked its way down his spine. It was all so terribly wrong.

Layton and Dorrington had already escorted Imogen out to the terrace, his cousin and Morpeth drifted out, followed by Bennett and Drake. Gabriel fell in behind them, hands already searching his pockets for a cigarillo.

He pulled a cigarillo and a spill from his pocket,

twirling the small twist of paper as he walked towards one of the lamps that illuminated the terrace. He lit the spill and used it to light the cigarillo, all the while keeping an eye on Imogen.

He bit the side of his cheek and studied the tableau before him. His nymph was sitting perched upon the wide stone balustrade, in animated discussion with all three gentlemen. He puffed on his cigarillo and repressed the urge to wade in and send them about their business.

Drake glanced over at him, a mere flick of his eyes, but the smirk on his face said it all. Gabriel wasn't surprised that Lindsey Darling would catch on so quickly, he'd always had a sixth sense for ferreting out what you least wished him to know.

Refusing to be drawn, Gabriel leaned against the balustrade and bided his time. He crumpled what was left of the spill to ash and let the wind carry it away. He wasn't about to pursue her in as blatant a way as he would have to in order to break into their ranks.

For the moment he was content to simply watch her, to indulge himself with a few entertaining fantasies, and to wonder and worry if she had been made aware of the gossip circulating London. She hadn't come near him all evening, and that led him to believe she had been. Rotten luck.

He grimaced, and took a long drag on his cigarillo, savoring the spicy flavor of the tobbaco. She couldn't avoid him all night . . .

Lying in bed later that night he began to regret his strategy. Watching Drake flirt with her, and Bennett teach her to play hazard had been more than annoying; it had been torture. He supposed he was lucky that St. Audley had thus failed to put in an appearance and further cut him out. At it was, she'd eluded him all evening, and now he was alone in his cold room, filled with unanswered questions, and almost overwhelmed with lust.

This was not the reunion he'd been hoping for. He kept forgetting she wasn't one of the ton's practiced flirts. That even if she wanted him—and he wasn't entirely sure that she did—she wouldn't think to casually tell him which room was hers.

Just being in the same room with Imogen made his blood heat, and when she looked at him, her lower lip caught between his teeth, and a worried expression clouding her eyes, it was all he could do not to simply pull her into his arms and kiss such doubts away.

He rolled over and punched the pillow into a more comfortable shape and flung himself down again.

When he'd joined the crowd teaching her to play hazard, she'd waited a few minutes, and then excused herself. When he'd found her seated with George and Carr, she'd glanced around the room searchingly, eliciting invitation from Drake to join him for a game of chess. Damn him.

Thoroughly put out, Gabriel rolled over again and buried his face in his pillow, too wound up, and too irritated to sleep.

Chapter 16

Reports that a certain viscount has abandoned the court of the Lady Corinthian appear to be premature.

Tête-à-Tête, 17 October 1789

Seated atop one of the countess's hunters, Imogen clenched her knees together around the horn for balance, and clucked her tongue at the animal as she pulled his head down and sought to calm him.

"Hazard is a lively mount," the Earl of Glendower said, smiling over at her in a paternalistic fashion. "But there's not a bit of vice in him, he just needs a good run."

Imogen smiled back at her host, then turned her attention to the footman offering her a stirrup cup. Settling the reins in one hand she took the cup and tossed its contents back. She held the whiskey in her mouth for a moment before letting it burn a track down her throat. She returned the cup to the waiting footman and reached down to pat Hazard on the shoulder, hand sliding smoothly over his shining coat.

It had been years and years since she'd been on a hunt, and she could feel the excitement thrumming from the large animal and up through her. She was every bit as impatient as he.

The great south lawn of Quorn Hall was filled with riders and their fidgeting mounts. Footmen were wandering about, handing out glasses of whiskey, while off to one side the Hunt Master was conferring with the Master of Hounds. The dogs were busy frolicking about the huntsmen in a seething pack.

Imogen shivered and pulled her hat down more securely. The morning fog had yet to burn off, and was beginning to resemble clouds rather than mist. The air smelled wet, and the ground was damp; the grass still rather slick with dew.

Dangerous conditions for a hunt, but no one seemed deterred. Looking at the clouds again Imogen gave a quick prayer for the rain to hold off. She wouldn't mind so terribly much riding back to Winsham Court in the rain, but she really wasn't prepared for a neck-or-nothing dash through it.

Glancing around she noted with misgiving that there were no other ladies present today. The fact was hardly surprising, as very few women hunted, and there was no ball being offered in the neighborhood in association with the day's sport. Such an event might have added one or two more ladies to their ranks.

Imogen was certain that the countess would hardly have noticed her solitary state, but she felt amazingly conspicuous. Several gentlemen, upon recognizing her mount had stopped to inquire after George, and been disappointed when Imogen informed them that the countess would not be joining them this year, but most had simply eyed her askance, or ignored her completely.

George might be accepted, but no other lady was likely to be likewise welcomed. Luckily her own party was quite large, and they'd been unfailingly considerate all morning. It was hard to feel snubbed while surrounded by a veritable wall of cheerful masculine bodies.

Last night George had insisted Imogen go, even though she herself was declining to hunt this year, due to her husband's concerns. The earl was adamant about George's staying out of the saddle for the duration of her pregnancy, as her reckless riding could endanger both her and their child.

"He's being ridiculous really," the countess had said with an indulgent smile, "but I can't make him see reason. So I'll acquiesce, and sit home alone all day while you all enjoy yourselves."

Imogen had quickly volunteered to forgo the hunt and bear her friend company, but George had laughed the idea off and told her to go. She had plenty to catch up on with the local villagers, and she planned on spending the day visiting at the cottages. So here she was, mounted on George's favorite hunter, her stomach tied up in knots, and Gabriel watching her like a hawk who's spied a rabbit, which certainly didn't help matters.

She bent to adjust her stirrup leather, which had twisted, but couldn't get her skirts out of the way. She was still fiddling with it when Gabriel suddenly materialized beside her.

He simply shook his head at her, and gently pushed her leg up and out of the way, hands sliding under the skirts of her habit.

"Are you going to be jumping?" he asked, his tone

only implying mild interest. He adjusted her stirrup, and then double checked her girth, taking advantage of the opportunity to lean in close to her, fingers brushing over her knee.

"No," Imogen responded a bit breathlessly, feeling ridiculously flustered. "I'm neither that talented a rider, nor stupid enough to think I am."

Gabriel gave her mount a slap on the neck, and looked up at her. "Very few women are," he replied. "George, well . . . she's a madcap, and always game, but I can't tell you the number of times I've had my heart in my throat watching her fly over a fence the rest of us have gone round."

"You won't be watching me take anything higher than a small style or ditch," Imogen responded, clamping down on the fluttering feeling in her stomach and returning his smile. "I'd be off in a trice, and I really don't think I could take the indignity of falling off in front of all these people."

"Better not to take the risk?" he asked, his hand lightly circling her ankle as he assisted her foot back into the stirrup. And while she knew he was literally speaking of the risk of jumping, she couldn't help but think there was an implied reprimand for her avoiding him since his arrival.

"Yes," she replied, struggling to keep her face blank, "decidedly so."

The Hunt Master gave a loud "Halloo!" and Gabriel broke away from her with a start. He dropped her ankle, and glanced around. With an almost angry twitch he turned and swung up into the saddle. With another "Halloo!" and a loud blowing of the horns the dogs were cast and everyone sped off after them, grass and mud flying, coating those caught in the rear.

Imogen moved off to one side, trying to avoid the worst of it, leaning low over Hazard's neck and urging him on. The horse was clearly confused when she steered wide, taking him through the gaps in the fences, rather than over as George would have done. But he didn't protest in the slightest; he was, as George had promised, a magnificently responsive animal.

Up ahead she could see Lord Glendower, closely followed by his son, and a large pack of the other guests from the shooting party. Beside her were Gabriel, Lord Dorrington, and Drake. After the first field she gave up trying to keep track of her own party, and simply concentrated on keeping up with the hunt. When the first drops of rain began to fall, she glanced about, and didn't see a soul she knew.

The hunt didn't appear to be slowing down any, and even a quarter of an hour later when the rain increased beyond a sprinkle most of the men thundered on, though a few began to break off and turn about.

Imogen reigned in and searched the remaining riders. None of them were from the Glendower party. She'd completely lost them all, and she wasn't exactly sure where she was. They'd been racing about hither and yon for well over an hour by now.

She bit her lip and squinted up at the leaden sky. It wasn't going to let up anytime soon. She was already soaked through at the shoulder, damp linen and wool clinging to her skin. Clucking to Hazard she put him into a gallop and set off after the disappearing hunt. If she lost them now she could spend the rest of the day riding about in the rain, completely lost.

Chapter 17

Can it be that the Portrait Divorcée is about to take center stage in yet another scandal? One can always hope.

Tête-à-Tête, 17 October 1789

Teeth chattering, Imogen clung to her saddle as she followed the tracks of the few dedicated riders who were left. A horse and rider slid in beside her, pushing Hazard to one side.

The gelding tossed his head, warning off the intruder and skidded to a stop. Gabriel put a steadying hand on her hip.

"They've all scurried off to a dry barn or farmer's cottage. We should do the same," he yelled over the sound of distant thunder.

"Where?"

"My cousin, bless him, has a hunting lodge not far from here, maybe another mile or so back down the last road we crossed. I imagine most of the others are already there."

Too cold and wet to worry about who might or might not be at the hunting lodge, or the fact that she was alone with Gabriel—exactly where she'd promised herself not to be—Imogen wheeled her horse about and fell in beside him.

All she cared about was the promise of being warm and dry. They found the road, and the horses slogged through the deepening mud, their pace slow and dogged. By the time they reached the lodge it was raining harder than ever. Imogen's feet and hands were numb.

The small dark lodge was the most welcoming thing she'd ever seen.

She followed Gabriel around to the back of the house, where he hurriedly dismounted and wrenched opened the barn door. "Come on, love," he said, reaching up and plucking her from her saddle. "It doesn't look like any of them are here yet. Let me get the horses settled and we'll get ourselves inside the house."

Imogen stood dumbly watching as he removed the horses' tack, rubbed them down with hay, and put them each in a loose box with a bucket of grain.

She should help, but she could barely move. Her sodden skirts were getting heavier by the minute, the weight of them, coupled with her own fatigue threatening to pull her down at any moment. So she simply stood, leaning against the stall for support, thankful Gabriel was there to take care of things.

When he was done he ushered her back out into the rain, shut the barn door snugly behind them. With a grin he practically dragged her up to the house.

"Wait here," he said, placing her under the slight eve near the back door. "The doors are usually locked, but the window into the pantry has a broken lock; or it did the last time I was here," he added with another wicked grin, before disappearing around the corner.

Imogen huddled against the door, trying to keep out of the rain as much as possible. The feathers on her hat, once so jaunty, were sopping wet and dripping cold water down her neck. She glanced about, desperately hoping one of the others would come riding in.

Gabriel's cousin had taken part in the hunt. Surely he at least would be arriving shortly? She hugged herself and shivered again as the wind whipped up and the rain blew at her sideways. After a few interminable minutes, she heard the sound of the latch being thrown, and the door swung inward. She stumbled in, and Gabriel shut the door behind them.

"The caretaker appears to be missing," he said. "Perhaps he was assisting with the meeting today. I'm going to go and get a fire going in the front parlor. Why don't you run upstairs and see if there's anything in any of the bedrooms you can change into. I'm sure Julian at least has a nightshirt and a banyan stashed up there."

More than ready to be warm and dry Imogen hurried up the stairs, nearly tripping over her skirts several times, trying not to think about the prospect of spending the entire day, and possibly the night too, trapped here alone with Gabriel. She was half hoping no one else showed up . . . and half dreading that whoever did show up might not be one of their own small party, and then the fat really would be in the fire.

If the Earl of Morpeth, or Viscount Layton found them alone together, it wouldn't matter at all. But if some stranger found them . . . she couldn't bear to think about it. The gossip would be deadly, defense impossible.

The first chamber yielded nothing more than two

cravats forgotten in the back of a drawer, and a single cufflink lying forlornly on the dresser top. The second room proved far more rewarding. It was obviously Gabriel's cousin's room. The wardrobe contained several nightshirts, a mishmash of abandoned shirts and forgotten breeches, a magnificent brocade banyan, and a much plainer flannel one which Imogen unhesitatingly claimed for her own use.

She pulled off her boots, peeled off her habit, and her underthings, and quickly pulled on one of Julian's nightshirts. It was freezing in the house. She could only hope that Gabriel had had no problem lighting the fire down in the parlor.

Still shivering she shrugged herself into the robe. She poked about a bit more, looking for a pair of slippers. She was still hunting through the drawers when Gabriel knocked on the door.

"The fire's lit downstairs," he said through the door.

Imogen padded across the cold floor and opened the door. Her feet burning with the cold, her toes were on fire. He was standing in the hall, dripping onto the floor, a large towel in one hand.

"Here, love," he said, with a warm, slightly teasing smile that made Imogen's stomach turn over. "Go down and get warmed up."

Imogen took the towel and with a silent nod of thanks fled downstairs. Even dripping wet and spattered with mud he was handsome enough to make her rethink her decision to avoid him. Doing her best to regain control of herself, she sat down on the hearth rug, as close to the fire as she could get without scorching herself, and toweled off her hair.

* * *

Once his nymph had disappeared Gabriel allowed himself a smile of pure satisfaction. He really had expected Julian and several of the others to have preceded them, but this was far preferable. He'd never have imagined that he'd be able to spend an entire night alone with Imogen, and be blameless in its instigation, but he was certainly not the kind of man to look a gift horse in the mouth.

Divesting himself of his dripping garments, Gabriel couldn't stop himself from picturing the various ways the two of the them could while away the hours while the storm raged. He'd never so enjoyed the prospect of a day trapped inside.

Following Imogen's lead he donned one of his cousin's nightshirts and his brocade banyan. In the back of the wardrobe he unearthed an embroidered pair of slippers identical to the ones their Great Aunt Effie had given him four or five Christmases back.

When further searching failed to turn up another pair, he tucked a pair of woolen stockings into his pocket for Imogen. Pretty as her bare feet might be, he didn't want to ruin the next two weeks by allowing her to get sick.

Before returning downstairs he lit the fire in the bedroom, and spread their clothes out to dry as best they might. Then he went on the real treasure hunt. What were the odds his cousin had brought a ladybird here?

He dug through the nightstand, pulled out a book, a fascicle of letters, an empty leather jewelry box that at one time had certainly held a matching pair of armlets, but no condoms.

Damn.

He plunged into the dresser. He couldn't be this unlucky. He couldn't be . . . but he was. Nothing in any of the drawers that would be of any use. Nothing in the traveling desk either. Not even in the secret compartment underneath.

Damn. Damn. Damn. What kind of monk had Julian become? Thoroughly irritated he descended the stairs, Julian's gaudy slippers slapping with every step.

Imogen was huddled before the fire, braiding her still damp hair, practically lost amongst the voluminous folds of her borrowed nightthings. She'd rolled the sleeves up to free her hands, but she couldn't help but resemble a child. With her hair strangling about her face and her hands fumbling with the poker she looked all of twelve.

Thank god she wasn't.

As he entered the room her head snapped around. An odd assortment of emotions flitted across her face: wariness, embarrassment, desire. The last flared in her eyes even as her cheeks bloomed faintly red and she ducked her head to avoid meeting his eyes.

Gabriel crossed the room and held out the stockings. "They're not as beautiful as my cousin's slippers," he said, unable to keep the seductive purr out of his voice, "but they'll keep your feet warm."

And he'd keep the rest of her warm. There were plenty of things they could do that wouldn't result in a pregnancy. The kind of lovely things one could do at the Opera, or in a secluded nook at a ball . . .

Imogen took them from him, her blush growing hotter. She made no move to put them on, just staring at them as they lay in her lap, as though they were the carcass of a bird, gifted by a cat.

"I'm going to explore the kitchen. Stay here and get warm." He glanced back to catch her hurriedly pulling on the stockings, shapely calves glowing in the firelight as the wool slid over them.

His stomach clenched in a rush of pure desire, and his cock throbbed impatiently. Gritting his teeth and blowing his breath out between them he forced himself to leave the parlor. If they didn't eat now, they weren't likely to, and he was starving. A man could not live by sex alone . . . though he might be willing to give it a try.

At least they'd both die happy.

The larder was well stocked. His cousin's crusty old groom had indeed stepped out on some business or other, and would no doubt reappear when the rains abated. He'd been half-afraid he'd find nothing but stale tea and the skeleton of a mouse.

He gave the handpump several quick strokes and filled the kettle. He could heat the water on the hob in the parlor. The tea things were easy to find, the small tea chest was even unlocked.

Inside the cold larder lay an already roasted and partially carved joint of beef, which he promptly made further incursions upon. He added a small wheel of wax-encased cheese to his booty, as well as several apples, and a loaf of seemingly day old bread, which he carved up into slices for toasting.

He commandeered the toasting fork, which dangled from a nail by the kitchen hearth, and assembled it all on a large platter.

He carried the whole thing into the parlor, set the tray down on the floor before Imogen, and dropped down to sit across it from her; Imogen simply gawked.

"Old Piers does rather well here." He placed the kettle on the hob and pushed it closer to the fire. "Give that here." He commandeered the poker and pulled some of the burning embers out under the hob. "There's no milk for the tea, but a bit of whiskey will do us both better anyway."

He groaned as the warmth from the fire began to suffuse his garments, pushing the cold aside. He poured a dram into the two cups and pushed one towards his nymph. She reached for it with an unsteady hand.

Was it him or merely the cold? He rolled his head, feeling the bones of his neck and shoulders pop.

They drank in silence, both staring into the fire, letting the warmth sink into them. Gabriel distracted himself with the toasting fork, making a small toasted cheese sandwich which he offered to Imogen, still bubbling on the end of the fork.

She took it with the first genuine smile he'd seen since Newmarket. He watched with a singular fascination as Imogen blew to cool it, and then pulled it apart with her fingers and ate it bit by bit. She consumed the next one he offered her too, then she sat back and rubbed her neck with one hand.

"Better?"

"Yes," she admitted with the lazy smile of a contented cat. "Do you think any of the others are likely to join us?" she asked with a look he couldn't quite interpret, almost as though she were unsure which answer she wanted.

Gabriel knew exactly which option he preferred, and lucky him, he appeared to be getting his way. "I think it highly unlikely that anyone is still out in that." He nodded his head towards the window, through which the raging storm was clearly visible. "I imagine they're all snug in Barrow at the Mad Boar, drinking themselves silly and pinching the bar maids."

"Oh," Imogen gulped, her slightly worried expression

making Gabriel feel like a beast. It wasn't his fault they were trapped here alone together; though he supposed it was going to be entirely his fault that he had no intentions of being a gentleman about it and spending the night cold and alone.

She stretched and adjusted her legs, shifting so that she was slightly further away from the fire. "Perhaps the rain will let up soon," she said with false hope.

"Perhaps," Gabriel replied, removing the kettle from the hob and filling the tea pot. The scent of bergamot rose with the steam. Even if the storm did let up, the roads would be quagmire, and near impassable in the dark.

Imogen picked up an apple and bit into it, more to give herself something to do than because she was still hungry. Her mind was running in twelve directions at once, her attraction at war with common sense.

She couldn't lie to herself, she wanted him. Even the shame of finding her name in the scandal sheets couldn't dull the attraction he held for her. Nor could her brother's threats. She was damned already, what difference could tonight make?

At Winsham Court she could have rebuffed him, or at least she could have kept herself surrounded by de facto chaperones. But there was no avoiding him at the moment, and likely no rebuffing him either. She was well aware of her own limitations.

Even if she went upstairs and locked herself in one of the bedrooms like some hysterical schoolgirl, she'd only end up opening the door when he knocked.

And he would knock.

She was sure of it. He'd been watching her with a particularly hungry expression since they'd arrived at the

Court, and he wasn't the kind of man who abounded with self-control.

When she finished the apple, Gabriel took the tray back to the kitchen, and returned with a bottle of brandy and two glasses. He pulled two of the room's chairs over to the fireplace, and arranged them on either side of the small table that had been under the window.

"Do you fancy backgammon or cards?" he inquired convivially, almost as though seduction was the furthest thing from his mind. His eyes gave him away. They bubbled like a hot spring.

"Backgammon," Imogen replied, the knowledge of the vouchers they'd exchanged the last time they'd played cards flashing to the fore of her mind as the words left his mouth.

"Backgammon it is." He pulled a box from one of the shelves and opened it to reveal the ivory and ebony pieces, which he laid out on the marquetry game board which made up the center of the table top. He reached down and helped her to her feet, the almost electric leap of awareness between them making her drop his hand as soon as she was standing.

She wiped her hand nervously on her robe and hastily took her seat, feeling oddly better with the solid table squarely between them.

Chapter 18

Tongues are wagging all over Town about a certain countess being in a most interesting condition . . . speculation is rife as to just who the father will prove to be.

Tête-à-Tête, 17 October 1789

Gabriel smiled knowingly and settled into the vacant seat across from his nymph. He poured them both a large brandy and sat back, waiting for her to make her first move.

It was growing steadily darker outside. The rain showed no sign of letting up. The clock on the mantle chimed the hour, and he realized with amazement that they'd been in the lodge for more than four hours already, and he'd done no more than touch her hand.

Quite a lowering thought really.

By now he would have had any other lady of his acquaintance naked and tumbled into one of the comfortable beds upstairs. Instead he was sitting here with slightly cold shins playing backgammon, struggling to find just the right way to approach her. One false move could very well result in her angry retreat, cursing them both to a lonely, unfulfilling night.

That was the last thing he wanted.

The first game ended quickly, Imogen's thoughts were clearly elsewhere. Gabriel only wished he knew where. She was a mass of conflicting signals, and he was reluctant to bring up the issue of their names being openly linked, for fear that instead of clearing the air, it would shatter the tenuous understanding they seemed to have come to. His nymph was no fool. She was well aware of where this day was leading, prevaricate as she might.

He was used to being the victim of the scandal sheets. He even enjoyed seeing his face at the top of the Tête-à-Tête on occasion. Such events were usually good for a laugh. But there was nothing to laugh over this time.

The last time the tabbies had gotten their claws into his poor nymph they'd torn her apart. He was sure she'd meant to cut him, or at least to hold him at arms length. He was equally certain she'd not have succeeded.

Whatever her plans may have been, they were useless now. At least she would have that to salve her conscience with; circumstances clearly beyond her control.

Over their second match Imogen strove to collect her thoughts and to concentrate on the game. But she had very little luck. He wasn't going to have to bother seducing her, she was quite successfully doing it for him. She couldn't stop thinking about their night together in Newmarket; picturing it, reliving it. She felt like a cat in heat, and she almost couldn't believe that he wasn't aware of her state. She was practically panting. So much so that she couldn't follow the game.

Luckily, he wasn't in a much better state. A rather

quiet hour later Imogen claimed victory in their third match. She plucked her last piece from the board and grinned. Their hands brushed as they collected the pieces and Imogen's breath hitched. Her eyes flew to his, and she simply stared, trapped. It was the most damnable thing.

Gabriel returned her gaze steadily, merely raising one brow in response. If he gave the slightest push she'd fall readily into his arms, but clearly he was going to make it her choice. Her decision. Damn him.

He was not going to play the seducer. He was going to force her to be a willing participant in whatever might come.

Imogen smiled tremulously and held out her empty glass. Another brandy could only help.

Gabriel smiled back at her, his expression turning wolfish, as though he knew exactly what she was thinking. And he probably did . . . she pressed her thighs together to alleviate the ache building in her groin.

Why didn't he just carry her upstairs?

He filled both their glasses, raised his in a silent toast and drank.

Imogen swallowed hers in a single gulp, cursing the fact that her play for time had only resulted in further confusing things. His eyes seduced her, but he made no other move . . . he didn't even touch her.

Frustrated, not at all sure what to do next, she rose and excused herself, assuring Gabriel that she would be right back. Nerves and too much tea had taken their toll, she simply had to find a chamber pot, and she desperately needed a few minutes to gather her wits.

When she returned the room had been set to rights, the backgammon set put away, the furniture back to its original positions. Gabriel was kneeling, stoking the fire, light playing over his hands, burnishing his hair. It glowed faintly red where it spilled over his shoulder.

She watched him work. It was amazingly attractive to see a man do something so basic for himself. She wandered quietly back towards the fireplace. How on earth could she have thought she'd be able to endure his presence for a full fortnight without succumbing?

Not a soul alive would believe that the Portrait Divorcée had spent an innocent night alone with the ton's infamous Brimstone, so why should she bother denying them what they both wanted? She poured herself more brandy and sank down beside him, welcoming the heat of the fire as it chased off the chill.

Gabriel glanced over at her, a seductive smile tilting up one side of his mouth. He poked the fire a few more times, rearranging the newest log so that it would burn better, then hung the poker on its brace and gingerly took a seat beside her.

"Warm enough, love?"

"Yes." Her decision made, she wanted to get on with it, before she changed her mind, or her common sense got the best of her. She wasn't quite sure what to do next. She was alone, scandalously undressed, with one of society's more notorious rakes. Who'd have thought she'd have to do anything?

She risked a glance at him. He was staring at her, quietly absorbed. Their gazes still locked, she caught one side of her lower lip between her teeth; pondering her options.

She could feel the strength of his desire like a physical tug; it washed over her, warming her in ways the fire never could. He reached out and plucked her glass from her hand, setting it behind him, along with his own.

She leaned towards him slightly, and he pulled her against him, sliding her across the polished floor and into his arms. His mouth came down on hers, and she twined her arms around his neck.

This was what she wanted; what she'd been waiting for all night.

Gabriel slanted his mouth over Imogen's, invading her mouth with his tongue, taking acute pleasure in the give and take as their kiss deepened and she returned his every caress with an urgency that left him shaking.

There was simply something amazing about a woman who responded so fervently, who called forth an equally strong response in him.

Overwhelmed with lust, he'd do anything in his power to please her, to make her want him with the same bone deep intensity that he felt whenever he saw her. He didn't want her to be able to avoid him, to put him off, to ever deny him as she had the night before. He didn't want her to be able to even contemplate such resistance.

She was practically purring, twisting about, adjusting the way her hips fit into his lap. She ground herself lightly into him, making him moan and grip her hip tightly with one hand.

"Enough, vixen," he growled, taking her earlobe between his teeth.

"Really?" she asked coquettishly, gasping when he reached up to tug her braid, pulling her head back and exposing her neck. He took his time exploring her ear, and then her jaw and eventually her neck; his lips, tongue and teeth slowly moving over her already flushed skin.

She gave a soft moan when he bit down ever so slightly on the tender muscle where her neck connected to her shoulder. Her hand fluttered along his back, as though she didn't quite know where to put it. He blew softly on her wet skin, and returned to kissing her.

He could spend hours kissing her; if only the now painful throbbing of his cock would let up. She wasn't helping either, naughty girl that she was. If she didn't watch out she was going to end up pinned beneath him right here on the hard parlor floor; which would be a shame, considering there were no less than six, soft, empty beds only a short flight of stairs away.

With super human effort Gabriel broke off their kiss, and took a few deep, calming breaths. He met Imogen's desire glazed eyes and dropped his head to rest his forehead against hers, his eyes closed but his entire body painfully aware of hers. Her scent, her shallow breaths, her impatient hands.

"Shall we adjourn upstairs, nymph?"

Imogen moved her head slightly away from his, rubbed her cheek against his, cat-like.

"Nymph?" she asked, brushing her lips across his, and rubbing her other cheek on his.

Gabriel choked. "Did I say that out loud, love?" When she sat back slightly and nodded he gave her a chagrinned smile. "My Garden Nymph. Just as I first saw you. 'Haste thee Nymph, and bring with thee, jest and youthful jollity; quips and cranks, and wanton wiles, nods and becks, and wreathed smiles.'"

Imogen felt her face and neck flush, the skin warming perceptibly even though it was already stinging from the fire's heat. She slid out of Gabriel's lap, rising as gracefully as her bulky night things would allow. She glanced down at him, and couldn't help but laugh at the ludicrous expression on his face.

He thought she was offended. She smiled and held out her hand.

"Are you coming?"

With a boyish grin he was up beside her. He screened the fire, and then in one quick motion she was swept off her feet, and gathered up against his chest.

"Gabriel," she protested.

"Yes, love?"

"Put me down. I'm perfectly capable of walking up the stairs myself."

"No you're not," he replied, carrying her out of the parlor and up the stairs with no visible effort. "You're far too overwhelmed by my attentions to do any such thing."

"I am?" She slanted a glance up at him.

"You are," he assured her as they reached the top of the stairs.

"Very well," Imogen said with a theatrical, languishing sigh.

Gabriel chuckled, and juggled her a bit as he opened the door to his cousin's room. He kicked the door shut behind them. Imogen felt herself go airborne, and her eyes went wide as they met Gabriel's just before she hit the bed, and she heard herself squeal in the most childish fashion.

She landed in a tangle of bed clothes and collapsed back on the bed, laughing. After a few moments when she realized Gabriel had made no more to join her, she pushed herself up and glanced about the room in confusion. She found him busy stirring the fire. He added another log, and put the screen back in place.

Turning back towards the bed his gaze met Imogen's, and she saw heat flare in his eyes. He smiled deviously, his face half lit by the flames. A seductive devil. This was how Lucifer should be depicted. Not as a demon, with horns and cloven hooves. God's chosen one. The most beautiful angel in creation.

"Do you have a vinaigrette?"

She cocked her head, staring at him dumbly. "Yes. It's in my pocket."

He turned and rifled through her clothing, coming up with the single embroidered pocket she'd worn beneath her habit. He fished inside, his hand so large it barely fit though the slit.

"Ah." He pulled the silver container out and held it up like a prize. "Perfect."

"Perfect? It's a vinaigrette. Do you feel faint?"

He flipped open the lid and folded the grill back, exposing the vinegar soaked sponge inside. Understanding exploded inside her. She bit her lip and shifted back further onto the bed.

He truly was the most wicked man she'd ever met. Who else would think to turn something so innocuous, so feminine, to such device use?

He tossed his cousin's brocade dressing gown onto the floor. Pulled his nightshirt off over his head in one fluid motion that seemed all too practiced. No doubt it came to him as naturally as breathing.

He was meant to be naked. His lithe, athletic body begging to be captured in marble. Though there was something decidedly non-classical about the erection he was sporting. None of the statues she'd ever seen had been anywhere near that well-endowed.

Imogen smiled hugely as he climbed onto the bed, crawling over her and pushing her gently onto her back. He slid his hands under the hem of her night shirt, and pushed it up and over her head. He gave it another tug, and flung it off to one side, leaving her naked beneath him.

He took one nipple between his teeth and bit down lightly, making her gasp. He laved the ridged peak, his tongue circling and teasing, while his fingers delved in-between her thighs, taking up where he had left off earlier.

Imogen had nothing to do but lay back and take it all in; sensation overwhelming her, pushing her inevitably closer and closer to what she recognized was going to be shattering release. She was shaking with need, her head thrashing back and forth and her hands clenched in the bed sheets when he succeeded in driving her over the edge. Imogen shrieked, then clapped her hand over her mouth, mortified.

Gabriel chuckled wickedly, sure his nymph had never before so lost control of herself. She'd been genuinely surprised by her own noisy release. Dying to see if he could drive her to it again, he reached for the vinaigrette and plucked the sponge out of it. He slid it into place then positioned himself between her thighs and entered her with one hard thrust. Beneath him she gasped and he felt her clench as she enveloped him completely.

Balanced above her, he teased her slowly, nudging into her with sure steady strokes. When she began to sob, her breath catching in her throat and her chest heaving, he changed the rhythm of their joining, rocking his hips against hers, bumping her sensitive clitoris with his pubic bone with every stroke.

With another strangled scream Imogen exploded into climax again, her legs gripping him with all the strength of an avid horsewoman, her spine arching, and her fingers digging almost painfully into the muscles of his back.

He paused to kiss her deeply, basking in the deep throbbing contractions of her release, then rededicated himself to finding his own completion, driving himself into her with hard, fast thrusts that quickly brought about his climax.

Imogen was breathing in shaky gasps, crushed beneath him when Gabriel came back to himself. She was gazing vacantly at the ceiling, trying to get herself back under control. Something he clearly couldn't allow.

"Well, love," he said, shifting slightly off her and kissing her again. "Shall we see if you can be louder yet?"

In response Imogen smiled and kissed him back, sliding her free leg up to cling to his side, her foot riding his hip bone. "Louder?"

"Louder," he reiterated. "Much, much louder."

Chapter 19

What can one make of the news that Lord St. A—— is hopelessly enamored with the former Mrs. P——? Can it be true?

Tête-à-Tête, 18 October 1789

Imogen woke early, to find Gabriel studying her in the half light of dawn. When questioned as to exactly what he was doing, he smiled.

"I'm trying to come up with the proper name for the exact shade of your nipples. They're not Aurora, nor Morone, and they're definitely not Terre d'Egypte." He peeled back the covers, exposing her breasts more completely to the light. "And they're not Incarnate, or Bristol Red. I think the closest I can get is Lustre-gallant." He bent forward and took one of the objects of his musings between his teeth, flicking its responsive peak with his tongue.

Imogen hissed, her body convulsing. Let him muse colors like a draper all he wanted. Let him compare her to silk, or paint, or food. Let him quote Shakespare, Donne, or Milton. She didn't care, so long as he continued to touch her exactly as he was doing right now. He'd slid one devilish hand down her stomach to deftly stroke her already slick hidden folds.

When she began to squirm, he redoubled his assault, until she climaxed with a series of shrieking gasps. When she quieted, he stopped, rolling off her, and propping his head up on his hand, stared down at her, his eyes locked with hers. "Well, nymph?"

"Very well," she replied with a hint of a purr, stretching until her elbows popped and her feet quivered, "but we can't possibly be finished."

She glanced at his engorged cock, and he laughed. "No, we're certainly not finished," he agreed, reaching out and yanking her to him.

Riding back to Winsham Court was as unpleasant as she'd expected it to be. The day was overcast and there was a decided breeze, and to make matters worse, both their clothes were still extremely damp, and it was Sunday, so all the world turned out to stare.

It had been nigh impossible to muster any enthusiasm to leave the bed, let alone the hunting box. Eventually they had to though. The caretaker would undoubtedly return at some point during the day, and she didn't relish being found there by him. It was going to be hard enough to brush through this without that.

Glancing over at Gabriel she caught him smiling. They must present quite a sight. They were both thoroughly disheveled, and more than a little crumpled. Gabriel's usual suave air was hampered by a hat with a slightly floppy brim, and the sad mud-spattered state of his boots, while she looked for all the world like a drowned rat. Her hair was in a fuzzy braid down her back, and curling up like mad, while her habit was simply a soggy mess; muddy and rumpled.

They hadn't discussed what had occurred, or where this might all be leading. In the heat of the moment it seemed unimportant, and in the cold light of dawn, impossible to broach.

Imogen was sure she didn't want to know. It was easier to simply let things happen, and deal with the aftermath. Her brain turned over the various problems that presented themselves.

What if they were found out? What if, all precautions aside, she fell pregnant? What if her brother made good on this threat? Even now a warrant for her arrest might already be in the hands of the runners.

When they arrived at the Court, George took one horrified glance at them and burst out laughing. "Hot baths," she announced. "And tea with brandy. Up you go, both of you. Drake came in much in the same state an hour ago, and poor Dorry arrived with the sniffles and his hair full of hay. We'll be lucky if the cold doesn't settle in anyone's lungs. Go on. Up."

Imogen hurried up the stairs, eager to escape before George's imagination and curiosity got the better of her. Having seen them come in together, she was certainly going to put two and two together, and start asking some very pointed questions, and before that could happen, she wanted to be warm and dry, and possibly drunk.

Imogen stripped out of her wet things, grateful for her maid's assistance. The tub had already been hauled to the middle of the room and filled. Steam drifted upwards from it. She tossed her robe over the rack before the fire and slipped into the tub, wincing as the heat made her frozen toes and fingers sting. She laid in the tub, half dozing until her maid startled her awake.

"Do you need anything, ma'am? Tea's here."

"No," Imogen replied, slightly chagrinned. "I'll be out in a moment."

The girl poured water over her head, rincing the soap from it. Imogen squeezed it out as best she could and climbed out of the bath.

In no time she was ensconced in front of a cheerful little fire, with a pot of hot tea, a plate of warm scones, and a cream pot filled with brandy to add into the tea. She wiggled her feet in her slippers and poured the brandy into her tea, amazed at how wonderful it felt to be warm. Eventually she found herself yawning, and without a second thought, she crawled into bed for a long nap.

When she finally came downstairs again, it was nearly time for dinner, and those who weren't suffering from their tempestuous adventure the day before, were gathered in the billiard room, watching their host and the Duke of Alençon play. Neither of the older men had so much as a sniffle to testify to their previous day's adventure.

Imogen leaned against the side of the table, balanced on her hip, and watched until dinner was announced. They ate amidst several loud conversations concerning their various plights during the hunt. Most of the men had ended up at the inn, just as Gabriel had suggested. Lord Layton had ended up in a crofter's cottage, but everyone else had made directly for the Mad Boar.

"Whatever became of you Gabriel?" his cousin asked, wolfing his food down ravenously.

Imogen held her breath, unable to swallow, wine burning her tongue.

"I found Miss Mowbray soaked to the bone, and abandoned by all of you. We found safe harbor at the Rose and Anchor. It's not what any of us are used to, but it was dry and the beds seemed free of vermin."

"You must have gone on much longer than the rest of us. We turned off as soon as the rain started."

Imogen repressed the urge to squirm and took another healthy draught of wine. It wasn't her fault she'd been trapped alone with Gabriel, and even if they'd behaved with perfect, staid propriety, the table would still be rife with speculation and curiosity.

Not that they had behaved with anything close to propriety. Grateful that she wasn't blushing, she leaned back as the footman removed her plate to make way for the final course. The countess was watching her rather closely, and Viscount Drake had already made several comments. Nothing mean spirited, merely teasing in a manner she was sure he often employed with George.

An affair with Gabriel was going to be complicated, and nerve racking, but she wasn't going to delude herself into thinking that she wasn't going to continue sleeping with him.

He wanted her, and she found it nearly impossible to deny him. She'd never encountered a man before who made her feel that way. She'd rarely crossed her husband, but not for the same reason. William had simply been unpleasant when contradicted, but something about Gabriel made it hard for her to think straight. She wanted to do whatever lay within her power to please him.

Call it infatuation. Lust. Love. It didn't matter.

After dinner she began sneezing, and George bustled her out and sent her off to bed. "Have another brandy, and get into bed with a hot water bottle," the countess advised her. "We can't have you getting sick; the boys would never forgive you."

Exhausted, as much from straining beneath the party's rampant speculation, as from her cold ride and lack of sleep, Imogen dragged herself up the stairs and rang for her maid. Alone in her bed, the sheets warmed with a brass warming pan, and her feet tucked up with a hot brick, she snuggled into the down pillows and pulled the blankets closely about her neck . . . but sleep wouldn't come.

Her mind was still whizzing about, not settling on any one topic for long, just skimming them and flitting on, afraid to examine the last few days too closely, but unable to stop thinking about what had happened. About what might happen next . . .

She sighed and plumped her pillow. Truth be told, she simply didn't want to be alone. Exasperated, she climbed out of her warm bed and poured herself another brandy from the decanter the maid had delivered earlier. Sipping it before the dying fire she set herself to examining her options, only to give up in disgust.

There was no good option.

They all ended with her in a worse position than she was now, because eventually they'd be found out, and then what little respectability she'd managed to cling to would be gone.

Wealthy widows took lovers.

Poor Divorcées became mistresses.

The distinction was rather clear, and not really open to

interpretation. If she wanted him—and she did—she was going to have to be clear on what the cost might be.

With her brother's threats ringing in her ears she crawled back into bed and pulled the blankets all the way over her head.

Chapter 20

Just how many men can one woman hold in thrall? And is our most delightfully infamous Divorcée endeavoring to find out?

Tête-à-Tête, 19 October 1789

Gabriel could not throw off the sense that something was wrong. He was warm and dry, his valet had arrived bearing a steaming pot of coffee, and a freshly ironed issue of the Morning Post which was only two days old, but still . . .

Possibly it was simply that he'd spent the previous night alone, prone to his own raging desire, fighting with himself over whether or not he should go in search of his nymph.

Lord knew he wanted to, but she had gone to bed sick, so perhaps a little forbearance was in order. Besides, stumbling about the Court searching for her was a recipe for disaster. He'd end up in someone else's room, with no way of explaining himself except the all too obvious.

He drank his coffee and read the paper while his valet laid out his clothes and moaned softly over the condition of the boots he'd worn on the hunt.

"What's to do today?" Gabriel inquired, folding the paper and setting it aside.

"Grouse hunting, sir," his valet responded, shaking out a coat of oatmeal twill. "The day being fine, his lordship has ordered the guns made ready, and the gentlemen are to assemble in the gun room at eleven."

"Wonderful, Rogers. Wonderful," Gabriel said, perking up considerably as he envisioned an entire afternoon tramping around with Imogen on his arm; so many opportunities to disappear, or fall behind . . .

The weather was beautiful; crisp and sunny, and after her previous lessons at Barton Court Imogen found she was able to handle the gun with a bit more confidence. She still handed it over to one of the gentleman for reloading, but she was comfortable carrying it, and quite proud of the fact that she almost hit something.

Besides, how could she not have enjoyed the day, when Gabriel was there to flirt with her, entertain her, to offer her assistance over fallen trees, stone fences, and any other obstacle they encountered. And he did it all without ever seeming to hover over her, or to be too obviously keeping track of her. He just always seemed to be in the right place at the right time.

No one gave them a second glance.

When they had filled the game bags, they turned as one back towards the Court, the earl suggesting they all stop in the village for a drink. After finding the road, it was easy enough for them all to make their way, so long as they stuck to the verge and avoided the still muddy track where the carriages ran.

Imogen stopped when her boot lace came undone. She handed her gun to Gabriel and bent to tie her shoe. That done, she stood up and noticed with a resurgence of the slightly embarrassed awareness she'd been feeling all day that she and Gabriel were now alone. The country lane they were on wound its way through the woods, and just ahead it curved around and disappeared into the trees.

"Come on, love," he said, helping her up, and glancing up the road. "George is bound to send one of the boys back for us in a moment or two." She stood up, and he bent his head and kissed her briefly, just a quick caress of his lips.

Imogen stared up at him, witless. How could he possibly think that was a good idea? For one, they could get caught, and that would never do, and secondly, a brief kiss only served to make her all the more unsatisfied with their present situation. The last thing she needed was to be even more aware of him.

Gabriel held himself in check as his lips left Imogen's. If he kept her balanced as precariously as possible, she'd fall right into his arms when he chose to finally give her a little push.

With both their guns securely slung over one arm, he offered her the other and escorted her on down the road. Long before they reached the inn they came back into view of the rest of the party.

Gabriel made no move to hurry his nymph along. He was more than content to bring up the rear. At the inn they found the rest of the party noisily filling the tap room, and were handed mugs of hot rum punch as soon as their guns were set aside. Imogen quickly found a seat. She smiled faintly when Gabriel slipped in beside her, his thigh riding hard against hers, pushing in under the table.

She drank her punch with gluttonous hurry and Gabriel got her another. She had a third before they all set out for the short walk back to the Court, all of them—save George—mildly unsteady.

At the Court, his nymph turned her gun over to the earl's gamekeeper for cleaning, but sat alongside him and watched as he absently cleaned and oiled his gun, while they all debated the merits of a fishing contest, versus another day's hunting. The fishing won out, mostly because George couldn't join them on the hunt field.

The guns clean and tucked away in the cases that lined the walls, they all went off to their rooms to change for dinner. Following the group up the stairs, Gabriel noticed with a delighted shock that Imogen went directly to the door at the end of the hall.

That meant the only thing between their rooms was their dressing rooms, which he knew for a fact shared a door; all of the rooms in the Court did. It had been designed in a pattern of room, dressing room next to bathing chamber, then the same mirrored on the other side. All the way down. So that some rooms adjoined directly, and others via the dressing rooms. But they did all adjoin.

Curious.

Was George up to something? Something other than facilitating his amorous adventures? It was unlike her to provide him with such easy access to his quarry, and he knew for a fact all their room assignments had been planned out by her.

Once in his own room he quickly checked the door between his dressing room and what he now knew to be Imogen's. Locked. And no key in sight. Which meant Imogen had it on her side. Pondering exactly what his mischievous friend could have meant by their room assignments, he rang for his valet and prepared to change for dinner.

Chapter 21

Is the new head of the Darling family the latest man to be scalded by scandal broth of the Portrait Divorcée's brewing? Numerous people seem to think so . . .

Tête-à-Tête, 26 October 1789

Quivering with a combination of nerves and the chill of a crisp fall night, Imogen sat by her fire, waiting for Gabriel. After dinner, while they'd all played cards and smoked on the terrace, he'd bent his head and whispered "Unlock your dressing room door before you go to bed." Then he'd wandered off again to play billiards with Lord Drake.

The decision in her own hands, she'd dithered over it all evening; locking and unlocking the door in question no less than four times before leaving it unlocked and forcing herself to retreat to the fire.

Her stomach twisted into knots. Her head swam. Succumbing was easy, making a choice much, much harder.

Hearing the sound of male laughter from down below,

she stood up in a panic and moved to lock the door again. Locked was much wiser.

She had barely stood up when she heard the dressing room door creak open, and Gabriel, already attired in his banyan and slippers walked into the room.

"Change your mind, love?" he inquired, stopping in the doorway and leaning up against the door jam.

Imogen smiled a bit wildly, and bit her lip in consternation. He'd known exactly what she was doing. She blew her breath out and laughed softly. "Over and over."

Over and over . . . but she'd already inserted one of the sponges he'd given her.

"Last chance," he said, not moving from the doorway. "Shall I turn around and go back to my own bed?"

Imogen shook her head no and Gabriel smiled back at her, relief flooding through him. For a minute there he'd been convinced she was going to take him up on his offer. The thought was intolerable.

He was going to have to do something about her reticence. He just couldn't figure out exactly what. He'd never had a lover before who was unsure about her choice. Hell, he'd never even had one he'd had to really pursue.

But for the moment he was content to simply pull her into his arms and offer the most obvious kind of reassurance. What his nymph needed was further proof that she belonged to him, and that he belonged here with her.

Moving carefully, but with decision, he untied her wrapper and slid it off her shoulders, amused to find she hadn't bothered to don a nightgown. He could feel her blush as her skin heated beneath his hands more than he could see it in the fire lit room.

Imogen followed his lead and loosed the frogs of his banyan. Her fingers fumbled. She made a disgusted little sound and broke off their kiss momentarily as she tugged the final one free. Gabriel chuckled and let the garment fall to the floor, he wouldn't be needing it for hours yet.

She tugged him to the bed and fell back, taking him down with her onto the coverlet. Overly eager in a purely selfish way Gabriel rolled her to the center of the bed and slid one hand between her thighs. She was already slick and swollen. Her excited gasp when he slipped two fingers into her sheath was all the encouragement he needed to nudge her thighs further apart and ease himself into her.

He moved slowly, teasing her, rolling his hips with each thrust. He wasn't sure how long he could hold out, he was too pent up from hours spent picturing being with her, planning exactly what he wanted to do to her. Remembering the sound of her crying out in his cousin's cabin, and wishing to hear it again.

Genuine abandon was a rare and precious thing.

He paused when he felt the first rush of his climax, he could fell the ache of his building orgasm all the way to his toes. He couldn't put it off, though he was loathe to bring their play to an end.

Beneath him Imogen strained, urging him to go faster, to go deeper. Her knees drawn up to tightly grip his ribs, her feet braced against his buttocks. He kissed her again, exploring her mouth, nipping at her lips, and then when she shivered, and made a soft whimpering sound that she quickly muffled by biting down on the heel of her hand, he gave in, and propping himself more securely on his forearms and knees he turned his attention to bringing them both to fulfillment, surging in and out of her with long hard thrusts that shook the entire bed.

Imogen threw back her head, clutched one of the

displaced pillows in one hand, while she continued to hold the other one over her mouth, afraid she was going to scream and bring the entire household down upon them. It felt as if she were actually coming apart. Her vision flickered, and she felt her climax explode, making her whole body clench and throb.

Gabriel filled her, driving himself into her as deeply as possible before collapsing on top of her. Having him atop of her was heavenly. Imogen let out a long breath she hadn't been aware she was holding, practically sobbing with the aftermath of her orgasm. It didn't even seem possible that something could feel so good; that someone could make her feel so good.

She took a deep breath, ran her foot down the back of his leg, cupping his heel with her toes. Her legs shook. She almost felt sick.

Gabriel chuckled softly and lifted his head to kiss her again. He rolled off her and flung himself onto his back.

Too sated to move far Imogen curled up against him. Let herself enjoy the feeling of lying there, comfortably intertwined, until the room's chill seeped back in and she started to shiver.

Gabriel pushed her off him and twitched the covers back, holding them up while they slid beneath them and settled back into their previous positions. His arm tightened around her and he dropped an absent kiss on top of her head. Imogen gave a sleepy murmur and snuggled into his side, her face half-buried into his chest.

Half-awake Gabriel nuzzled the back of Imogen's head, burying his face in her hair. God how he loved her hair.

He'd woken already hard and impatient, but it was rare that he woke with a woman at hand, and he had every intention of taking full advantage of the circumstance. Such luxury. He almost never slept the entire night through at any of the houses he rented over the years for a flurry of different mistresses, and he'd never taken any of them home to his own bed.

Imogen was still asleep, but she made a little contented noise and wiggled back against him when he ran his hand possessively over her hip. Even unconscious she was remarkably attuned to him.

Her change in position caused his shaft to slip between her thighs. It was cradled against her slick folds rather than being pressed against her.

He clenched his jaw as his breath hissed out of him. He desperately wanted to simply roll her over, and thrust himself in, but more than that he desired to put a further seal on her seduction. To brand her as completely and utterly his. The more he saw of her, the more he wanted to see of her . . . it just never seemed to be enough.

He kissed her shoulder, nipped softly at her neck, bit the lobe of her ear, all the while moving gently against her, rousing her with a multitude of soft caresses. He knew he'd succeeded when she sighed and moved her leg up and along his, opening herself to him. She hooked her foot behind his calf and pressed herself back against him.

"Morning," Gabriel whispered, sliding his hand down from where it had been teasing one nipple to hold her hips steady.

Imogen murmured something, that might have been a rejoinder, and then gasped when the head of his shaft brushed the already tight peak just inside the valley of her thighs.

"Ummm is right," Gabriel answered her, moving against her with a little more force. He returned his attention to the back of her neck and shoulders, and gave a stuttering gasp of surprise when she reached down and cupped his shaft, pressing him securely against her, so that each shallow thrust of his cock brushed over her clitoris.

He pulled back, ready to swivel his hips against her and urge her on to the next level when she suddenly arched her back and repositioned her hand so that his next thrust buried him inside her, his shaft entering her as deeply as the position allowed. She put her hands out, splayed against the bed for balance, and Gabriel dropped his head to rest in the hollow of her neck and shoulder.

She moved against him, thrusting herself back, and he gave up any plan he might have had, and simply moved. The position only allowed for small, shallow thrusts, but she was so hot, so tight, and so damned willing that the slight movement was more than enough. He slid his hand down over her so that his fingers were pressed against her clitoris. She climaxed almost instantly. She made a strange little sound in her throat and went momentarily rigid.

Gabriel stilled, thoroughly enjoying the sensation of being caressed by her release. When she sighed and went limp he slid her leg down off of him, and without withdrawing from her, slid his own leg up and over hers, and rolled her over onto her stomach.

He ran his tongue up along her spine, nuzzling her neck with his lips and teeth. She wiggled, and moved her arms up over her head, while he pulled back from her until just the tip of his shaft was still inside her, marking his place. She mumbled a protest and he smiled into her shoulder and slid home, filling her completely.

Imogen moaned and arched her back, throwing herself into the rhythm he established. Everything he did was perfect. He knew just how to touch her, just where to touch her, and just when to touch her.

She gasped for air, half-trapped beneath him, and threw her arms out higher so that she could brace herself against the headboard. Her new purchase allowed her to push back with more vigor, and Gabriel responded by raising himself slightly onto his knees and changing the angle at which he entered her, his every thrust raising her up off the bed. He bit her hard on the back of her neck, just above the hairline, where any marks wouldn't show, and she gasped, amazed at how good such a thing could actually feel.

After a few more wild thrusts he buried his face in her hair and collapsed, his breathing ragged and uneven. Imogen bit her lip and moved against him experimentally. Was he actually finished? Or was this merely a break?

Spending hours making love with abandon had never been William's style, and Imogen suddenly found herself rather sorry for her staid ex-husband. He had no idea what he was missing, and if he hadn't thrown her off, she would never have known either.

Smiling, she wriggled against Gabriel again, then she peeked up at him over her shoulder. He was laughing silently and shaking his head.

"Wanton," he teased, raising himself off her, and withdrawing from her in the same motion. He reached down and flipped her over, simply using one hand on her hip to roll her over onto her back.

"Cad," she replied, pulling him back down to her.

"Jade," he growled back at her, sealing his mouth over hers for a searing kiss, while sliding back into her. He whispered "Now, love. Now." and she let herself go, just as he gasped and buried his head in the pillow beside her head, his release leaving him incoherent.

He rolled off her, breathing hard, and Imogen rolled onto her side, turning to face him, sliding one hand across his stomach. She folded up her arm, and pillowed her head upon it, gazing up at him sleepily, enjoying this unguarded chance to look at him. When his breathing steadied, but he still didn't open his eyes, she ran her tongue up along his hip bone. He jumped as though scalded, reached down and hauled her up so that she was lying prone beside him.

"You're going to be the death of me, woman," he said, wrapping one arm around her, effectively trapping her where he'd put her.

"That's certainly not part of the plan," Imogen replied, settling her head into the hollow of his shoulder, and snuggling up to him. "It would be most inconvenient."

"Inconvenient," he retorted. "I'll show you inconvenient." And he did so, rolling her beneath him again, and pressing his already tumescent shaft into her yet again. "It's inconvenient, my beautiful nymph, to not be able to be in your company outside of this room, for fear of being seen sporting this. It's inconvenient to want you so badly I can't sleep. It's inconvenient that you're mired in the country at George's beck and call."

Chapter 22

It seems not even her delicate condition can prevent Lady S—— from enjoying her mannish entertainments. Or so reports say . . .

Tête-à-Tête, 2 November 1789

Curled up before the fire a week later, Imogen smiled to herself and glanced up at the clock. Four o'clock. The group which had left early to go and witness a prize fight would be back in another hour or so.

The last few days had been filled with entertaining activities and amusing banter during the day, and even more amusing activities at night. Life at Barton Court had been the most pleasant she'd ever experienced, her short marriage included, but this was almost sublime.

Gabriel appeared each night, though the hour differed, depending on when the party below broke up. She no longer bothered to wait up for him, he had proven himself more than capable of waking her. She smiled again and stretched her feet out towards the fire.

In another few days the party would break up. Imogen shook her head and laid her book aside. She didn't want to think about it, but it was encroaching upon her thoughts more and more. Another three days, and then who knew when they'd see each other again?

She didn't, like her friend Helen, have a house in town to go to. A residence from which she could discretely carry on with their relationship, and no matter how she struggled with it, she simply couldn't picture herself as a kept woman. It would be too dangerous. Her family would never stand for it.

Not that Gabriel had made her any such offer, or ever indicated in any way that such an arrangement was in the offing. In public he teased her in the same vein as the countess's other friends, and in private they rarely spoke of anything concerning the next day, let alone the next month, or year.

Irritated with her line of thought, she went upstairs and grabbed her redingote, muff, and hat. A walk was what she needed, she'd been cooped up too long. Outside the gardeners were busy preparing the garden for winter. Studying what they were doing here would be just the thing to distract her.

Riding back from the prize fight, Gabriel watched a bit enviously as the Earl of Somercote lounged at his ease in his wife's phaeton, George laughing beside him at whatever he'd just said. In that instant, he found himself overwhelmingly jealous.

Jealous of the fact that the two of them needed only each other. You could have dropped them on a desert island and they'd have been perfectly sanguine about their isolation. To put it bluntly, they were happy. Disgustingly so.

He knew other happy couples, but none of those couples was quite the same as the Somercotes. George and Ivo did everything together, from planning their estate's improvements, to parties such as this. And that was what he suddenly found himself wishing for, a companion who suited him the way George suited her earl.

He'd always been so certain that love ruined everything—look what it had done to his father's life; to his own—but George had swept that certainty away. Damn her.

It had occurred to him last night, as he lay snugly in Imogen's bed with her curled up asleep against him, that he'd never been so content in his life. It had been a perfect moment. And it had started him thinking.

Why couldn't this continue? Why couldn't they make it permanent? It wasn't as if her divorce was the bar to him that it would be to many men; he wasn't a pillar of the ton, and he didn't have any parents to please. He was a wealthy man, with a large house in town, and a small country estate not far from his cousin's.

There was no reason he couldn't just marry his nymph.

None at all.

She wouldn't even object to his friends, or his way of life, since she was already a part of it, and to all appearances, enjoyed it immensely. And they certainly wouldn't object to her.

Perhaps they would even begin breeding race horses together, or if her inclination turned to travel, they could sail to Italy, visit his grandfather in Constantinople even. Their options were endless.

Chapter 23

Whatever is keeping Lord St. A—— in Town? This must be quite the first hunt season he's missed since he was breeched.

Tête-à-Tête, 3 November 1789

Imogen burrowed into Gabriel's side, burying her face between his chest and the blankets. It was freezing in the room, and in a few minutes the clock would strike five and he would crawl out of her bed and return to his own room as he did every morning.

She had no idea how he did it; years and years of playing the rake most likely. If it had been up to her to leave, they'd have been caught immediately.

Not able to sleep any longer, she cracked an eye and peeked up at him. He was wide awake and staring out at the dark room with a thoughtful expression on his face. She nipped his chest and slid up against him slightly so that her head fell naturally into the hollow of his shoulder.

"Morning," she said, yawning and turning her head up so she could look at him.

"Morning, love," he replied almost absently. "I was just thinking . . ."

"About what?" she asked, not really paying too much attention. His hand had slipped down to cup her breast and his thumb was slowly circling her nipple.

"About where we go from here." Imogen stiffened and he looked down at her sharply, his expression serious. "We all leave here in two days. You to return to Barton Court, and me to town."

"That's not worth thinking about," Imogen said, trying to keep her tone light, dismissive even. Pretending a nonchalance she was far from feeling. "That's what happens at the end of a house party; everyone goes home."

He frowned and shook his head slightly. "That's not what I mean." He narrowed his eyes at her. "And what's more, you know it."

Imogen rolled over and sat up, keeping her back to him. This discussion was going in directions she wasn't prepared to go. "Don't, Gabriel."

"Don't what, my silly nymph? Don't think about tomorrow, or the next day—"

"Or the day after that," she interrupted. "Yes. Exactly. Don't."

Gabriel gave an exasperated little snort. "I'm terribly sorry to disappoint you, love, but I've been thinking a lot further ahead than that."

Imogen twisted around and looked at him, his amused expression only heightening her disquiet. "I can't, Gabriel. I wish I could, but I can't."

"Can't what?" His eyes crinkled at the edges as he smiled. "I haven't asked you anything yet."

"This is one thing," she replied doggedly, suddenly numb to the core. "An affair is one thing," she qualified. "But I can't be anyone's mistress. Not now, not ever. I can't. You have to see that. George, your other friends . . ."

"You certainly can't be. George would skin me alive, and the rest of the boys would hunt me down and force me to put a bullet in them one by one." He gave a strange little laugh, and looked at her very intently. "But you could be my wife."

"Your wife?" The pit in her stomach turned icy. Her brother's angry florid face swam before her eyes. Robert would ruin them both if pushed. If he felt he had to. She couldn't risk that. Couldn't risk pushing him so far.

"My wife," he reiterated. "People do get married all the time you know. Even people like me."

"Not to people like me, they don't."

"What are you—"

"Absolutely not," she insisted, crawling out of bed and struggling impatiently into her wrapper.

She'd never expected him to ask her to be his wife. She could already hear the gossip such a union would incite, and she simply wasn't prepared for the ruckus her family would kick up. And neither was Gabriel.

Standing before the cold fireplace, she shivered and suppressed a half hysterical sob. This was not supposed to be happening. Why couldn't he have just let things be?

She'd been prepared since they'd met for him to offer her carte blanche, and she'd known her answer would be no. It had to be no. But marriage? She wanted to say yes. Her heart had leapt, and her pulse had quickened, but just as quickly all the reasons such an answer was impossible rushed to the fore.

It simply wasn't fair for him to put her in such an untenable situation.

Confused and caught out, Gabriel climbed out after her and came up behind her. His skin prickled with the cold, but he ignored it. He put his hands on her shoulders and squeezed.

"Why, 'Absolutely not'?"

Imogen hiccupped and tried to step away from him. He tightened his grip. "You must—I can't—Don't be . . ." She broke into outright sobs and he turned her around to face him.

He cupped her face, wiping the tears from her cheeks with his thumbs. "I'll ask again, love. Why absolutely not?" She wasn't making any damn sense.

Imogen stared up at him, her eyes continuing to well up, until he gave her a little shake.

"I can't," she finally choked out. "It's crazy to think it would work between us. That our families would allow it to work, even if we did. It would be an exercise in misery."

"Misery? That's all you see when I ask you to be my wife? Damn it, Imogen. I'm offering you something I've never offered any woman; something I thought never *to* offer."

"Don't." She dropped her head, obviously unwilling to even look him in the eye.

"You repeat yourself." He dropped his hands from her. "And I've no wish to listen to the same nonsense a second time."

He turned on his heel and stomped out, pausing only to grab his dressing gown, and to snag the key from her side of the door. He slammed the door shut hard enough to rattle the mirror on the wall of his dressing room and locked the door behind him.

He took several deep breaths, his back resting against the cold wood of the door. He had to get out of here.

There was simply no way humanly possible that he was going to be able to sit down to breakfast with her. He'd end up shaking her until her teeth rattled in her head; stupid, stubborn woman.

He was yanking on his boots when his valet appeared, armed with a pot of coffee and a freshly ironed shirt.

"Sir—?" Rodgers was clearly thrown to find him already up and nearly dressed.

"I'll be leaving immediately." Gabriel stood and glanced about the room, looking to see if he'd forgotten anything. "I've left a note on the dresser for Lady Somercote. See that she gets it."

"Of course, sir."

With a nod, Gabriel snatched up his heavy riding coat, his hat and gloves, and was out the door before his man could ask any questions. He had to get out now. Before he went crawling back into Imogen's room, begging her to reconsider. Before he strangled her. Before he started such a fight with his nymph that he raised the whole house.

His nymph.

He snorted and shook his head as he crossed the cobbled yard and made for the stable block. He supposed he'd have to stop thinking of her as such, impossible as that might be.

When Imogen did not appear at breakfast George went upstairs in search of her. As she walked down the hall she encountered a footman bearing a small trunk, followed by Gabriel's valet. He had a glossy dressing case in his hand.

He stopped when he saw her, and then bowed and extended a folded pieced of foolscap. "Mr. Angelstone asked me to give you this before he left, my lady."

"Left?" George's eyes widened with surprise. This could not be good. She'd known when Imogen had absented herself from breakfast that something was afoot, but she'd been hoping it was something good.

"Yes, my lady. Mr. Angelstone left for town before seven."

"Well . . . thank you, Rodgers." He bowed again and George opened the note and read it while he disappeared down the hall. It didn't tell her anything more than his man had; just that he'd left for town that morning, and he begged her to make his excuses to Lord Glendower.

Suddenly deeply concerned, George hurried down the hall and knocked on Imogen's door. There was no doubt possible that whatever was going on concerned them both, and George was only too well able to imagine what Gabriel could have done to precipitate things.

There was no answer from Imogen's room, so she tried the handle, only to find it locked. "Imogen?" she called, knocking again. "It's George. Open up."

After a moment she heard the lock snick, and when she tried the door again it swung open. Imogen, still in her wrapper, was shuffling back towards the bed. George watched as her friend climbed into bed and pulled the covers up over her ears.

"Imogen?"

"Go away," Imogen said, her voice muffled by the blankets.

"You and Gabriel have a fight?" George sat down on the bed.

"Not a fight," Imogen mumbled, pulling the blankets over her head.

"You're lying in bed like you're dying of consumption, and he left in a pelter at an ungodly hour, and you expect me to believe you didn't have a fight?"

Imogen peeked out and George could see that her friend's eyes were swollen and bloodshot. "Not a fight. He—He . . ." She sniffed and wiped at her eyes with thc back of her hand. "He asked me to marry him."

"Marry him?"

She'd thought he'd come around to it eventually, but not this soon. In any case, it certainly did not seem like something to cause such havoc and consternation. George patted Imogen on the back like she were a child, her brain whirling.

Gabriel had proposed, and Imogen had obviously turned him down. Interesting. Very, very interesting. This would take some sorting.

Chapter 24

St. A—— missing entirely and the Angelstone Turk departing early . . . Lady S—— must be losing her allure.

Tête-à-Tête, 17 November 1789

"Going to purchase a new set of dueling pistols?"

"I'm not sure yet." Gabriel ignored the sudden arrival of St. Audley and Layton. He'd been testing pistols for the better part of three hours, and he had no intention of stopping just because George's hounds had tracked him down.

He fired again, breathing in the acrid smoke, enjoying the foul smell of sulfur and salt-peter. The way it blocked everything out, if only for a moment.

"Well, why don't you think about it over breakfast?" St. Audley picked up one of the pistols he'd been trying and examined it more closely. "I'm famished, and the air in here smells like hell itself."

"I rather like it," Gabriel replied, firing again. "Besides, I'm not hungry."

"Well I am," Layton said. "And I could use a drink."

"I do need a drink," Gabriel agreed, laying the pistol he'd just fired aside.

He needed a lot of drinks. He'd done his best not to be sober since he'd left Winsham Court, and he'd been fairly successful. In his more lucid moments he recognized he was making a cake of himself, so he tried to make sure such episodes of clarity occurred as infrequently as possible.

When he was drunk, he was blissfully numb. When he was sober, he was painfully aware of his nymph's absence, stung by her rejection; unable to stop turning it over and over in his head.

No woman had ever had the power to hurt him, and he was finding that escape was the only answer. He couldn't sleep because she haunted his dreams. He couldn't eat because food turned to ash in his mouth and was impossible to swallow. Couldn't whore, because they were a pale shadow of the woman he wanted. All he could do was drink. Drink and gamble. God only knew how much money he'd lost in the last month. He certainly didn't; nor did he care.

Gabriel allowed his friends to steer him out of the gallery. They hit the sidewalk outside and Gabriel flinched and squinted as his eyes adjusted to the bright light. "So, George set you two on me?"

"Don't be an ass, Brimstone." Layton gave him a shove and started walking.

"My cousin then?"

"I believe Lady Morpeth did give me a message for you." St. Audley fell into step beside him. "She told me to tell you to quit making such a spectacle of yourself."

Gabriel glared, and stumbled over a loose cobble in

the street as they crossed Piccadilly. The dandy-trap spurted muck and water up onto his hose. He cursed and shook his foot. "You can tell my lovely cousin to mind her own bloody business."

"I shall tell her no such thing," St. Audley protested. "Come on, let's get that drink, you could obviously use a bit of the hair of the dog, not to mention a shave and a clean shirt."

Gabriel went along tame enough. A drink was exactly what he wanted, and while he'd rather have it on his own, at one of the numerous gaming hells that enjoyed his patronage, he'd settle for White's. It was easier than fighting. Layton and St. Audley might be two of the more easygoing members of their circle, but they were as tenacious as terriers with a rat cornered in a wall.

George watched her friend as she intently applied herself to her needlework. Imogen was working on a christening gown. She'd begun the day they'd returned from Winsham Court, and she was nearly done now. The fine white cambric was almost completely covered in complicated white on white tambor work, based on the jacket one of Ivo's great-grandfathers wore in a portrait. Imogen didn't seem to do anything but sew, play the pianoforte, and go for fast rides across the countryside.

She had refused to discuss what had transpired between her and Gabriel, telling George nothing further than she had the morning Gabriel had fled the Court. George hated it that her friends were making each other miserable, and her mind had been busy trying to find a way to bring about a reconciliation. But if she couldn't get Imogen to confide in her, her only option was to corner Gabriel, and that was a slightly more complicated undertaking. Especially if what Victoria had written was true, and Gabriel was busy drinking himself to death and gambling away his fortune as quickly as he could roll a die or turn a card.

He was going to respond like a wounded bear.

Perhaps a trip to town was in order? But first she should write Helen Perripoint. A soiree at Helen's would be the perfect excuse for them all to take a trip to town, and unlike a larger function, Imogen could hardly decline to attend an event being held by one of her oldest friends.

Leaving Imogen to enjoy the company of her tambor frame, George took herself off to the library and penned a quick note to Helen and another to Victoria. She was going to need all the help she could get if she was going to bring this matter to a satisfactory conclusion.

Chapter 25

Whatever has put the Angelstone Turk's nose out of joint? Pry as we may, no answer has been forthcoming . . .

Tête-à-Tête, 18 November 1789

Mrs. Perripoint's soiree was in full swing when Gabriel made his belated appearance. It had taken him half the night and several glasses of brandy to decide that he *was* attending.

Helen had not mentioned that his nymph would be there, but it was obvious that she was likely to be present. And he wanted to see her, desperately; almost as much as he dreaded seeing her.

He'd convinced himself that he wouldn't go; wouldn't give himself the chance to make a fool of himself again. But as the night had worn on, he had found himself wandering aimlessly towards Mrs. Perripoint's on more than one occasion. And when the brightly lit house had appeared in front of him, he'd gone up the stairs and entered the house, unable not to.

Gabriel snatched a glass of champagne from a passing footman and ran an eye over the crowd, searching for Imogen. When he spotted George off to one side, chatting with Helen and Lord Carr, he was sure his nymph was hidden somewhere in the merry horde that had invaded Helen's house.

He worked his way carefully around the room, eyes busily searching out a particular head of curly dark hair. When he finally located her, he almost wished that he hadn't. She was moving through a set, partnered by Drake.

His hand clenched involuntarily, breaking the stem of his glass. He batted at his sleeve, brushing off the droplets of champagne. A footman appeared and took away the broken glass, while a maid wiped the floor with a towel. Several of the guests were staring, but Gabriel didn't give a damn. Let them stare.

Thankful only that Imogen had not seen him, Gabriel cursed under his breath and worked his way through the milling guests, steering wide of the dancers. He found an unoccupied spot along the wall, and leaned his shoulders back against the papered surface. He really should leave, but he wasn't going to. Not until he'd seen Imogen. Privately.

Drake spun her through the steps of the dance, touching her far more than was necessary. Gabriel forced himself to watch. To stand calmly on the sidelines instead of wading out into the dancers and dragging her away from Drake.

The music finally came to a halt and Imogen escaped from the viscount. With a determined stride Gabriel crossed the room, trailing her from a distance, waiting for a chance to pounce.

* * *

Exhausted from forcing herself to participate and be merry, Imogen slipped away in search of a drink. She could feel a headache coming on, the tightness starting around her temple; throbbing behind her left eye. Ignoring the circling footmen with their glasses of champagne, she went directly to the buffet in the drawing room and poured herself a brandy.

Life with George and her circle was ruining her for polite company. Brandy, in mixed company no less. She'd discovered she liked brandy, far more than she did champagne, which would only worsen her aching head.

Drink in hand she wandered through the party. Almost everyone present was well-known to her, either from her earlier days, her infrequent visits to Helen's, or her recent absorption into the countess's set. She skirted her way around the room, looking for George.

As she passed through the hall on her way to the supper room she found herself being suddenly manhandled from behind, and hauled into Helen's small study. She tripped on her skirts and sloshed her drink all over her assailant.

"Damn it, Imogen!" Gabriel closed the door behind him and shook out his sleeve, sending a spray of liquid onto the floor. "I've already spilt champagne on this coat tonight. I'm going to smell like a tap room."

"A very expensive tap room," she protested, her head spinning. She'd been petrified he was going to be here tonight, but the night had grown late without his putting in an appearance. Just when she'd relaxed he'd not only shown up, but had whisked her away from the party and the rest of the guests, trapping her in a private tete-a-tete, which she by no means had the energy for.

He was appropriately dressed, but rumpled around the edges, his cravat knot crooked, his hair slipping from his queue, long tendrels handing about the sides of his face. He looked angry, dark eyes hooded, lips grimly pressed together. Angry, unhappy, and frustrated. All of which were feelings she was more than familiar with herself.

He stared at her for a moment, clearly unsure what he intended now that he had her cornered, then he removed her glass from her hand and tossed back the dregs of the brandy.

"A very expensive tap room," he agreed, setting the glass aside.

"We should go back." Imogen twisted her fan in her hands until several of the spokes broke with an audible snap.

"Agreed," Gabriel replied, continuing to block the door. "We should."

She looked up at him expectantly, but instead of moving aside he pulled her close and lowered his head to kiss her, his lips molding to hers in a now familiar caress. Imogen put her hands out, shoving against his chest. If she let herself kiss him back, she wouldn't stop.

He broke off the kiss and stepped back from her, leaning back against the door with a thunk. He looked broken. She was on the verge of relenting when he stepped aside and held the door open for her.

Sick to her stomach Imogen hurried past him and out into the melee. She found George as quickly as possible, and pleaded her now very real headache. She wanted to be gone before Gabriel could corner her a second time, before she could regret her refusal and go in search of him herself.

George was well pleased with the evening. She'd

thrown Brimstone and Imogen together, and the results had been exactly what she'd hoped for: Gabriel had been possessive and disturbed, and Imogen was obviously far from indifferent. All in all, a good night's work. Now all she and Victoria had to do was figure out exactly what made Imogen reluctant to accept Gabriel's proposal, and then convince Imogen that she was wrong. A task which would have cowed her, had she not been so amply provided with evidence of both her friends' desire for such assistance. Gabriel may not have known he needed a woman's meddling in his life, but he was going to be grateful that she knew it.

The first thing her plan required was a trip to see Brimstone himself. And since he'd ignored her summons the day before, she'd have to beard the lion in its den.

Chapter 26

Society's most scandalous Divorcée has returned to Town, causing a near riot at a certain widow's soirée. What a wonderful time it is to be alive and in London . . .

Tête-à-Tête, 19 November 1789

Decidedly grumpy, head pounding from the previous night's drink, Gabriel made his way downstairs. He'd been awoken without ceremony, the covers stripped from him by his valet. The man had then forced him to rise with threats of a pending invasion of females, and not of the Cyprian variety he assured him.

Rodgers had hurriedly shaved him and sent him down to his doom without so much as a cup of coffee or an apologetic word—though the man's eyes had been full of compassionate understanding. That look might or might not be enough to keep him in Gabriel's service. He had yet to decide if a look was apology enough for such rough and ready tactics.

He found George and his cousin cozily ensconced—

just as threatened—in the main saloon, a pot of tea on the table and a plate of biscuits between them. He barked for coffee and stomped into the room, glaring at them both.

"Well, Brimstone?" His cousin looked at him reprovingly. "You could at least say good morning."

"Is it a good morning?" He sank into a chair across from them, his banyan and slippers loudly proclaiming his irritation with their invasion. He'd be damned if he dressed for them to rake him over the coals.

"A very good morning," George assured him, a mischievous smile, which he instantly mistrusted, on her lips.

"And why is that?" he asked, his voice dripping with irritation. "Because I've been rousted from bed when I had just managed to fall asleep? Or because I'm now confronted by two hoydens with unknown—but certainly dangerous—intentions? Wild women, who have further encroached by undermining my staff I might add."

"It's a good morning because we're here to help you, you dolt," Victoria said with asperity. She clinked her spoon in her cup as she stirred her tea.

"That is, if you deserve it," George qualified, refilling her own tea cup.

Gabriel eyed them both with misgivings, but refused to be drawn. They'd tell him exactly what was afoot when they had finished roasting him to their satisfaction, and not a minute sooner. If only Torrie would stop making that infernal racket with her spoon. She knew how it irritated him, and she was far too well bred to be making such a rude noise by accident.

His coffee arrived and he sat back to wait for their pronouncement. Whatever it was, their presence couldn't bode well for him. They were darlings, both of them, but interfering, social queens at the same time. Always so sure they knew what was best for everyone else.

After a few minutes of silence, he glared at them and set his cup down with a thump. If it was about his nymph, George was far more likely to play the avenging angel than the Good Samaritan. Something was certainly in the works, and he couldn't imagine any other topic that would bring them down upon him at such an hour, but he also couldn't imagine why George was looking so pleased with herself.

"So are you going to tell me why you're here, or do I have to guess?"

Bad enough that Imogen had rejected him yet again, now he had these two meddling. He was a fool for wanting her, and a fool for having proposed, and thrice times a fool for continuing his pursuit in the face of her rejection. But there was no way he was going to give up. He'd get her by hook or by crook, fairly or unfairly. He'd get her any way he could, and the sooner she realized it, and gave in, the better off they would both be.

George eyed him coolly while his cousin glared right back at him, as though he were one of her recalcitrant offspring.

"Don't come the matriarch with me, Torrie. I'm not one of your sons, and I'm not your husband. Save that look for someone it works on."

"It doesn't work on Rupert," she replied haughtily.

"Or Hay," George put in, still wearing her mischievous smile, an odd contrast to his cousin's serious expression.

"Or Hay," the countess agreed, clinking her spoon again. "And I'll look at you anyway I please, idiot."

Gabriel narrowed his eyes but held his peace. If he got her wound up, he'd never find out what was afoot.

"Help me with what?" he drawled, trying to sound as bored as possible.

"Help you with Imogen," George replied in her straightforward manner, taking the wind out of his sails.

"If we think you deserve help that is," Victoria added waspishly, echoing George's earlier pronouncement.

Gabriel shot her a scathing glance and turned his attention back to George. "And what makes you think I want your help? Or need help for that matter?" he asked, doing his best imitation of his cousin when she was trying to be condescending.

Both women stared at him, eyes slightly enlarged with surprise, and then burst into raucous, unladylike laughter. George laughed until she cried, tears streaming down her face, which did nothing to improve his mood.

"Don't be stupid, Gabriel. I've never seen a man in need of help so badly," she asserted wiping her cheeks with the back of her hand.

"Except perhaps your poor husband when he was courting you," he snapped, his color mounting as he got angrier and angrier.

"Exactly," George responded with enthusiasm, her eyes sparking.

Trapped by her sudden twisting of his taunt, Gabriel shifted uncomfortably in his chair, glowering at them both. He didn't want or need their help. Imogen would come around on her own, he was sure of it. He just had to keep working on her. He'd be damned if he won her consent because of any strong arming from these two.

That would be unbearable.

"Poor Ivo didn't have the slightest idea how to handle me. Any more than you have about my poor Imogen."

"If you're implying that I'm as clueless as your befuddled earl, I'll—I'll—I'll—" He gritted his teeth, unable to think of anything awful enough to threaten her with.

"Ivo is not befuddled." George glared at him, eyes snapping with a very familiar anger.

If he could push her further she'd lose her temper entirely. "Confounded? Clueless?" Gabriel offered, his tone taunting. "What about lackwit?"

"We're not here to talk about George and her husband," Victoria interrupted them. "We're here out of concern for you." She held up a hand when he started to protest. "You can't go on the way you are now. And you can't continue to carry-on with Miss Mowbray in such a brash, obvious fashion. Her reputation won't stand it. And quite frankly, neither will yours."

"Why *are* you pursuing her?" George blinked at him innocently, as though he couldn't smell a trap.

"Yes, why can't you simply leave her alone?" his cousin asked, looking at him almost mockingly. "She doesn't seem to want you." She jabbed the final prompt in, her expectant gaze flicking momentarily to George.

Exasperated, Gabriel hooked one hand under the low table between them, sending it flying. The tea things scattered and smashed against the fireplace, the table crashing with a loud thump against the marble façade.

"Because I want her." He leaned forward in his chair, staring both women down. "It's that simple, I want her."

Gabriel's butler burst into the room, followed by his housekeeper, the first footman, and two of the maids. Gabriel glared at them. "You can clean it up when I'm done here," he shouted at their retreating backs.

George's smile grew, cocking up on one side, while

his cousin settled back into her chair as though nothing at all had just occurred.

"Then you'd better figure out how to get her, hadn't you?" George said, her expression suddenly benevolent. "And I'd advise to start with the brother."

Chapter 27

The sight of Lord St. A—— ape drunk in the street has become an all too common one. One would think the cause would have been driven to take pity by now. . .

Tête-à-Tête, 19 November 1789

Imogen ruthlessly jammed the gown she was holding into the trunk, hopelessly crushing it. She didn't pause when George entered, but continued to shove it down.

George eyed her thoughtfully and dropped into a chair a few feet away. "Going somewhere?" the countess inquired, as if what was going on wasn't perfectly obvious.

Imogen stiffened. She stopped what she was doing momentarily, leaving the train of the gown dangling out of the trunk like a waterfall of calico. She was behaving badly, and she knew it, but she had to escape. To get away from Gabriel, from town, from everything; to return to someplace quieter, somewhere she could think logically again. Someplace her brother wouldn't find her . . .

"You and the earl have always made it clear that I am

welcome to the use of your carriage whenever I might want it. To date I never have." She paused to pull the crumpled gown from the trunk and fold it neatly before putting it back in, rearranging the crushed dress in her trunk. "I'd like to return to Barton Court to get my things, and then I have to leave. Edinburh, maybe even Dublin. I don't know . . ."

"Of course," George replied, her tone as conciliatory. "I sincerely hope you're not taking such a step because of Gabriel. I assure you, there's no need for such drastic action."

Imogen goggled at her, her brows drawn together in a frown. "There's *every* need," she insisted passionately, aghast that the countess truly didn't understand the position she was in.

She was on the brink of causing yet another scandal. A scandal which would forever cement the image of her as little better than a Cyprian in the eyes of the world. And she was going to drag the countess's friend down with her.

If he continued to badger her—to propose to her, to kiss her—she was going to falter, and then their marriage would be the talk of the town. The infamous Brimstone and the Portrait Divorcée. She'd make a laughing stock of him, and he'd ruin her.

Her brother would cause all the trouble he could, too. And knowing Robert, the trouble would be considerable. He hated her, and he loathed Gabriel. He'd delight in torturing them.

All she'd wanted was a quiet place to live, a few friends, and perhaps to make herself useful. Why did he have to go and complicate things? Rakes were not supposed to propose marriage. They were supposed to avoid it like the plague. But Gabriel—damn him—wasn't playing by the established rules.

He'd been the very pattern card of the charming, dissolute man-about-town. The perfect choice for a simple, quiet affair. The kind of thing Helen had been recommending to her for ages. Why did he have to break character and ruin everything?

The countess's brow puckered, and she held out her hand. "Come and explain it to me then. I didn't press you the last time this came up, but I do know Gabriel rather well. Perhaps I could help?"

He was going to kill Robert Mowbray.

Wrap his hands around the little toad's neck and squeeze until it popped right off. Gabriel raised his walking stick and knocked on the door to number twenty-six Queen Street with enough force that the silver head dented the wood.

She'd said no because some underhanded threat Mowbray had cooked up. Water spilled off his greatcoat, pooling on the small porch. He raised his cane and knocked again.

The door cracked open and he brushed past the startled footman hard enough that his wig was knocked askew. She'd said no, and she hadn't told him the reason. Damn her. Why hadn't she told him?

"Mr. Mowbray's not at home, sir." The footman adjusted his wig, attempting to reassert his dignity and his authority.

"Of course he is. Saw him come in myself. He's just damn lucky I value my membership at White's too highly to have cornered him there. Mowbray!" His shout echoed off the wainscoting.

Several doors opened all at once. A wisp of a maid ducked back into whatever room she was cleaning, like a mouse scurrying to hide. A second footman appeared from below stairs, clambering down the hall with a loud, graceless tread.

"Mowbray, in private, or in public. It's your choice."

His quarry appeared at the top of the stairs, red-faced and quivering with the impotent anger of a King Charles Spaniel cornered by the butcher's dog. "I have nothing to say to you Angelstone. Get out of my house."

"But I have several things to say to you, Mowbray." Gabriel stalked up the stairs, taking each step with deliberation, his eyes never leaving Imogen's brother.

Mowbray held his position until Gabriel reached out and grabbed him by the lapel. "Come along, then." He dragged him down the hall.

Gabriel propelled his prisoner through the first door, sending him sprawling onto the floor. "Clumsy oaf, aren't you?"

He turned his back and crossed the room. Above the mantle a barefoot goatherd wooed a blushing shepherdess under a canopy of linden trees. "A Boucher? Really?" He turned around in time to see Mowbray heave himself to his feet. "I wouldn't have thought it of you. I'd have put you down as more of a Cozen's man. Maybe a Jones?"

"I'll kill you. I'll—I'll have you arrested for housebreaking. I'll—"

"You'll shut up, and perhaps by doing so you'll live long enough to sire a dynasty of little Mowbrays on that cow of a coal heiress you've married."

"My wife sir is none of your business."

"A fact for which I am eternally grateful. My hat's off to you on that account. I don't know how you can bring yourself to the point." Gabriel allowed himself a faint shudder.

Mowbray's mouth opened and closed like that of a clockwork toy. The vein in his forehead stood out, throbbing.

"Having an apoplexy?" When he didn't fall to the floor in a twitching heap Gabriel smiled. "I suppose that was too much to hope for." He sighed and removed his gloves slowly. "I understand your mother's pearls have gone missing?"

Mowbray eyed him warily.

"I would suggest you check with her dresser. Perhaps they were sent out for repair? Or maybe they were simply left behind when you came to Town? At any rate, there'll be no more mentioning them—or anything else but your deepest felicitations—to your sister. Do I make myself clear?"

"Or what?" Mowbray attempted to brazen it out, raising his chin so that he only had one, rather than his normal two.

Gabriel spun his walking stick in a lazy circle. "You seem to forget that while I may be, how did you put it—'the Angelstone mongrel' was it?—that I'm still an Angelstone. I'm the great-grandson of a duke. The brother-in-law of an earl."

Gabriel allowed that to sink in. "And I'm one of three men in England who can touch Angelo. I'm more than happy to give you a personal demonstration if you'd like?"

Mowbray's face twitched as though he were having a fit.

"I thought not." He pulled his gloves back on. "It's

been a pleasure, sir. I'll make sure and send you an invitation to the wedding."

Gabriel slouched down in his chair and blew out an irritated breath. He'd endured another helpful visit from George this afternoon, in which he'd been told in no uncertain terms to leave Imogen alone. To allow her to come around to the idea slowly before he pressed his case.

Damn all helpful, interfering women. Damn them especially for being right. At least he'd been able to relate his interview with Mowbray. That had pleased her to no end.

He got up and poured himself a drink and stood staring at the portrait of Imogen that hung over the mantle. He set his glass down hard enough to break it, amber liquid streaming down the marble.

There she was, the teasing smile he'd come to know so well just peeping out, the shoulder which had been her downfall revealed in all its glory. He retreated to the center of the room from which he could better study the larger than life rendition of his nymph. She hadn't changed much since it had been painted. Perhaps she was a little thinner, a little more serious, but not one jot less beautiful.

It really was an amazing portrait. It captured Imogen perfectly, from her wildly spiraling curls, to her elegantly shod feet. Firth had even managed to show the subtle sparkle of her eyes, and the enigmatic smile that lurked in the corner of her mouth.

There didn't seem to be anything so terribly provocative about it. But people saw what they wanted to see, and it only took one society tabby with a wagging tongue to have started the rumor, and then people would have wanted to believe it; to watch the downfall of such a beautiful young political hostess.

That prospect would have been titillating and extremely satisfying to those members of the ton who reveled in the downfall of others. Irresistible, in fact. Lord knew they'd dug their claws into him often enough for him to sympathize.

And it was clear from the painting that whether she'd been guilty or not, the artist had been in love with his subject. She'd have been better off going to Gainsborough or Reynolds rather than to the young rising star.

With a groan Gabriel threw himself back into his chair. This was not how he'd planned things. Not how things should be. He should not be trapped here alone with nothing but a facsimile of his nymph. Even one as enchanting as this one.

By all rights he should be sitting across from the flesh and blood woman—or better yet—making love to her in the bed behind him.

Chapter 28

We can only speculate as to what the Angelstone Turk could possibly have to discuss with the Portrait Divorcée's brother . . . and speculate we shall.

Tête-à-Tête, 3 December 1789

The night of the Morpeth's ball Imogen realized she hadn't seen Gabriel in weeks. A long collection of days in which she'd been hauled around the city, to musicals, dinner parties, boating parties, the theatre, the opera, even to a cricket match; if it was a social event of any significance, she'd attended.

She had been, if not deluged, then at least slightly flooded with invitations. Everyone wanted her at their parties; if for no other reason, than that they were hoping the hinted at liaison with Gabriel would come to a head there, burning their event permanently into the memories of all the attendees.

To date she had been happy to disappoint them.

Tonight she had been included in the pre-ball dinner,

along with all of the Morpeth's family and closest friends. Including not only Gabriel, but the prime minister, Mr. Pitt. He had not been the prime minister when she had been active as a political hostess, but he was well-known to her all the same. William was one of his supporters.

She was extremely grateful that he was seated at the far end of the table near the earl. It was bad enough to have been on the receiving end of one of his condescending glares earlier as they had all assembled in the drawing room. To have been forced to make polite conversation with him throughout dinner—or worse, to have been publicly snubbed by him—would have been awful.

When dinner was over, the countess led the ladies out, leaving the men to their port. Imogen took George's arm and was led through the house to the main drawing room.

"Let's have a drink before the men join us," Lady Morpeth suggested. "I'm sure they're all enjoying their port, and frankly, I need a bit of fortification before I spend the next hour or so receiving guests."

George laughed and plucked the brandy decanter from the decorative commode which hid the earl's liquor supply.

"Anyone else?" she asked, filling a glass for Lady Morpeth.

A few of the braver ladies piped up, and George pulled out more glasses. Imogen accepted a glass and stared down the tabbies watching to see what she would do. She refused to be cowed.

If the countesses were drinking, then so too would she. The gossips could hardly label her as fast for doing so without also insulting their hostess. She sipped her brandy while George led her about the room, introducing her to the few women she was not already acquainted with. Some of them were less than friendly, but no one was willing to slight the Countess of Somercote, the future Marchioness of Tregaron, by cutting her bosom beau.

A maid brought in the tea things and those ladies not inclined to brandy or port were able to avail themselves of milder refreshment. China clinked, cups rattled in their saucers, a low buzz of conversation filled the room. Just before ten the earl arrived, proceeding the rest of the gentlemen, and then the Morpeths ushered everyone out of the drawing room and into the ballroom down on the ground floor.

Imogen went down on Viscount Layton's arm, a direct snub to many of the other women present, whose claims stood well-above her own. He seemed perfectly unaware of having committed any socialism, and chatted gaily with her all the way down the stairs. Once in the ballroom, he held onto her arm, and politely demanded the first set of dances.

"Not much of a dancer," he confessed, as they strolled about, admiring the decorations, nodding to their acquaintances. "But it looks bad if a man don't make at least a small effort."

Imogen laughed, loud enough to draw eyes to them, and the viscount smiled down at her. He was handsomer in powder and a formal wig. His eyes seemed brighter, his bearing somehow more dignified. As if he wore a suit of armor rather than one of spangled cut velvet.

Relieved to have been secured for the first set, Imogen soon found herself under siege. Her dances were rapidly snapped up by George's friends. Before the musicians had stuck up the first note, she had only two sets unclaimed, and was just a little uncertain that she would be able to dance all the dances she had promised. It would be exhausting.

The gentlemen could not have drawn their battle lines more clearly if they'd been wearing regimentals and sporting her name on a flag. She was theirs, and they would throw her in the teeth of the ton, and force society to accept her. She could only be flattered. Even George could not have forced them all to dance attendance on her in such a fashion.

The first set of country dances flowed into the next, and then the one after that, as she changed partners effortlessly, never being left alone for so much as a moment. Her partners even managed to make it all look completely natural, as though they weren't relentlessly guarding her. Eventually the countess caught her between sets, as she was being handed off from the countess's brother to Lord St. Audley.

"My lord," George said, quite loudly, "you might want to skip the first dance in the set and procure Miss Mowbray a drink. I don't think she's been off the dance floor since the dancing commenced. I'm sure she must be parched by now." Then she flitted off on the arm of an unknown officer.

Imogen smiled and assured the viscount that she would much rather dance. On the dance floor she was distracted from searching for Gabriel among the throng that packed the Morpeths' ballroom, and protected from any prolonged encounters with him, and whatever might ensue from there.

Gabriel watched George's little drama play out, gritting his teeth, trying to decide just how long he had to endure this farce of an evening. He'd watched his friends all dutifully paying court to Imogen; dancing with her, strolling with her between sets, making sure she was never alone.

They were like a large pack of dogs with one tender, juicy bone. He should be grateful. Whether or not they knew it, they were doing him a favor. But he wasn't. Jealousy flooded through him, leaving him resentful that they could all dance and flirt with her with impunity, while he was relegated to the sidelines. Left to watch her like some specter.

She was wearing some preposterous concoction that could only have been chosen by George. Blue watered silk covered by a slightly lighter colored netting, with small clumps of silver spangles decorating the bodice and hem. The dress had a bodice which barely managed to contain her, and showed off nearly as much of her shoulders as the infamous portrait which graced his bedchamber.

Gabriel slugged back the last of his drink and plucked another glass from a passing footman. That dress shouldn't have been allowed. Not on any woman, and certainly not on Imogen. Fashion be damned. More than one man was watching her with what could only be called lurid interest.

One poor sod had been so thoroughly distracted his wife had soundly boxed him on the ear, and another had tripped over his own feet while staring, spilling his glass of champagne all over Lady Jersey. Luckily for Imogen the lady's back had been turned, and she'd had no idea why the bumbling fool had done such a thing.

Gabriel was still brooding when St. Audley's set ended, and Alençon claimed Imogen for the supper dance. It was the final feather in her cap. Many of the people who would be willing to challenge George and Victoria over their championing such a black sheep, would bend to the duke's opinion. If Alençon approved, so would most of the toad eaters who aped him, which—as he was well aware—could prove useful when wielded purposefully.

With an irritated frown marring his features, Gabriel left the ballroom. He had been forbidden to go near her for now, and he'd be damned if he spent the entire night watching her like some moonling.

Chapter 29

We have only recently come face-to-face with the reality that nothing—not even adultery—can withstand the combined will of two or more peeresses . . . how else to explain Society's warm embrace of a certain fallen woman?

Tête-à-Tête, 10 December 1789

Two weeks later Gabriel was still at loose ends, sulking about his own home, or doing his best to make the days pass quickly by tiring himself at Angelo's fencing salle, or one of the other places in which the Corinthian set participated in their chosen pastimes. He'd fenced until his legs burned, until his sword arm shook with fatigue. He'd spent hours at Tattersalls looking over horses, and what seemed like days watching Mendoza practice for an upcoming match.

He had an afternoon appointment with his cousin Julian at Angelo's, but for now he was merely trying to kill the time between now and then. He poked his head into

Sandby's studio, and spent an absorbing half-hour studying the landscapes on display, then he wandered off to George's former abode.

The house was now simply known by its nickname from the days when George had lived there: The Top Heavy. He was admitted by the butler, and after divesting himself of his hat and gloves, he made his way up the stairs and entered the first floor drawing room.

The large room was nearly filled to capacity today. Men of all descriptions lounged about, drinking, reading, playing cards.

Gabriel helped himself to a whiskey and picked up a copy of *Philosophical Transactions* from the table beside him. *A Supplementary Letter on the Species of the Dog, Wolf and Jackel, Observations of the Class of Animals, called by Linnaeus, Amphibia, An Account of a Monster of the Human Species, Abstract of a Register of the Barometer, Thermometer, and Rain at Lyndon in Rutland.*

Good god. At least the first few looked promising. He flipped past the letter pertaining to dogs and the like and settled into Linnaeus' Amphibia, not so much reading it, as distracting himself with it. Before he'd waded through the second page the room erupted with a whoop, and he looked up to see George, a huge grin nearly splitting her face. She wasn't here nearly as much as the men would have liked, but she did still try to put in as many appearances as possible when she was in town.

She was instantly engulfed, all of them wanted to kiss her hand, give her a message from someone else, or report in on how their mutual friends were doing back on the continent.

She was in her element.

For several minutes she was almost lost to sight, and

then the group broke apart, and she swanned into the room, Imogen in tow. Gabriel felt his stomach drop, and his mouth go dry. In the hubbub, Imogen didn't even see him. She broke away from George and made her way to the unoccupied window seat.

Gabriel waited, the sound of the clock ticking on the mantle distinct even above the lively chatter filling the room. Then slipped over and sat down beside her. He immediately called her attention to a woman walking on the opposite side of the street.

"When George lived here we used to have what we called The Unofficial Ugly Hat Derby," he said, ignoring the excited thrumming of his body as her eyes met his and she made room for him beside her. "That monstrosity is a definite contender." Imogen smiled at him, and he felt compelled to add, "Possibly even a champion."

"A champion ugly hat?"

"Almost certainly, look, it even has fruit on it."

Imogen leaned closer to the window, trying to get a better look as the woman disappeared down the block. Fake fruit, and entire birds, were rather vulgar. Especially when displayed together.

"Cherries," he replied with certainty.

Imogen couldn't see them. The woman was now too far away. "She's gone round the corner." She rubbed at the spot her nose had left on the glass with her thumb.

"There'll be another entry along in a minute or two. There always is."

Imogen made herself a little more comfortable, keeping her attention firmly on the street below. She didn't need to look at Gabriel to be aware of him; she'd been aware of him from the moment she'd entered the room, and it had taken considerable willpower to not go directly to him.

His presence always acted upon her like a loadstone.

They sat together in a tension filled silence. Imogen scanning the street for any topic of distraction, Gabriel watching her. She could *feel* him watching her as surely as if he'd reached out and run a hand over her.

One of the men playing cards at the table nearest the window lit a cigarello and she sneezed.

"Shall we step out into the yard?"

"Yes, please." She sneezed again, and then sniffled, digging down through the layers of her petticoats and into her pocket for her handkerchief. Her hand slid over the cold metal of her vinaigrette and her face flamed.

They slipped out of the room, both of them giving the settee George was holding court upon a wide berth. She followed Gabriel down the stairs and out into the private yard that ran behind the house. It was well maintained, all shaped hedges and trim herbal borders. Starlings scattered from the stone birdbath at the garden's center as they neared it.

"Have you been here before?" he asked, breaking the silence.

"To the house? Yes, but not out into the yard. George likes to stop by at least once a week."

"So you've been enjoying the Little Season?"

"Immensely. I was afraid I wouldn't, but . . ." she trailed off, biting her lip, not sure how to put into the words all the reservations she'd been prey to. Not sure what there was to say . . . afraid something wholly inappropriate would bubble up.

"But George and my cousin have worked a miracle,

and you find yourself welcomed back into the hallowed halls of the ton?"

"I don't know if *welcomed* is quite the right word, but certainly tolerated."

"From what I've seen over the past weeks, I would think welcomed would be a mild term."

Imogen smiled, and tightened her grip on his arm. He was right. Mostly she had been welcomed back, if not with open arms, then with nothing worse than cool smiles. And she'd been enjoying herself. After years of telling herself she didn't really miss town life, she could now admit that she had missed it terribly. Missed what her life should have been.

"I'll allow you to use whatever term you like then. For I have been having a very fine time. And while I've not been greeted with rounds of hallelujahs by my old set, I find the one I'm part of now infinitely superior."

"Stodgy politicians no longer to your liking?" he asked with a conspiratorial grin.

Imogen glanced up at him curiously. Was that supposed to be a veiled reference to her former husband? If it was, she still agreed with it. "No, thank heavens. If looks could have killed I'd have expired on the spot the moment Mr. Pitt caught sight of me. So it's just as well I now prefer the sporting set."

"We are a good lot, aren't we?"

Unable not to laugh, Imogen readily agreed. They were indeed a good lot. They had no shame whatsoever, and if the consequences of their actions occasionally damned them, then so be it. Their own stood by them, and whatever indiscretions they might commit were eventually forgotten by the ton, displaced by fresher scandal.

Perhaps she'd been wrong about life with Gabriel

being a misery. He was accepted nearly everywhere, and she'd been warmly included in many things which only months ago she would have expected to have been forever barred from attending. And her brother had utterly failed to descend upon her and haul her away to the hulks waiting on the Thames. In fact, he'd written to say her mother's pearls had been found, as if that was supposed to mean something to her.

Maybe Gabriel had been right about their being able to marry without risking society's censure. She'd never be a political hostess again, but Gabriel didn't aspire to a seat in the House of Commons, so that needn't be a consideration.

He hadn't come near her in weeks, not even to pay a morning call, or stand up with her at a ball, but she was fairly certain he'd been under orders. The sudden cessation of all attentions had been too dramatic.

That small act alone had spoken volumes to her. He understood her dilemma; whether or not he'd liked it, or agreed with it, he understood.

Walking together in companionable silence through the back corner of the garden, he helped her down the steps to a small lower terrace with a high hedge screening it from the house. He dropped her arm and sat down on one of the benches there, then pulled her into his lap.

Without so much as a word he cupped the back of her head with one hand and set his mouth to hers, kissing her with all the pent up passion of the frustrating weeks they'd spent apart. He kissed her until her toes curled, and her breath was coming in ragged gasps; until she couldn't think at all, her whole concentration was simply upon him. His tongue and lips plundering her mouth in a decadent assault. When he broke away, he nudged her back from him so that she was still in his lap, but not right against his chest.

"So, nymph? Are you done torturing me?"

"Torturing *you*? You're the one kissing me, not the other way round." She leaned in to kiss him again, but he held her off.

He raised his brows questioningly, and she bit her lip again. Gabriel shifted her off his lap, placing her on the bench beside him. "I've asked you before, love. Are you ready to give me a different answer?"

Imogen smiled tremulously and nodded her head. If he was asking what she thought he was asking, then her answer was definitely yes.

"Is that a 'yes,' love?" She nodded again, and he looked at her more seriously still, his dark, foreign eyes holding hers in a steady gaze. "I want to hear you say it, Imogen. Will you marry me?"

"Oh, yes, Gabriel. Please?" Her smile grew larger, more impish. "But not here, not a big wedding in town. Just our friends?"

"The chapel at Winsham Court? When everyone has retired there for Christmas?"

"That would be perfect. Do you think Lady Glendower would agree to it?"

"I think she'd hunt us both down and skin us alive were we to do anything else."

Chapter 30

All of London is agog . . . word is the Duke of A—— has lost his prized filly in a game of cards. Can it be true?

Tête-à-Tête, 15 December 1789

" . . . nothing more than a whore. I was lucky to have found out before she presented me with a child I would have been duped into accepting as my heir."

The man's voice carried across the Lady Jersey's ballroom in the momentary silence created as the orchestra finished.

Imogen stiffened in his arms. Gabriel had no trouble recognizing her former husband's voice. The fool had a particularly nasal delivery. It had driven him crazy at Eton. Tonight it inspired him, much like the urge of a dog to shake a rat until dead.

Gabriel swallowed hard, his hand gripping Imogen's arm, squeezing until he was sure he must be bruising her. He was afraid to let go, sure she'd dash from the room, which would only make things worse. He'd hoped they would be married long before she was forced to confront Perrin. Before *he* was forced to confront the man.

No one in the room moved as Gabriel turned his head to face Perrin, who was staring directly at him, his face red, and his whole body tensed. Perrin knew exactly what he'd done.

Whether or not he'd meant to be overheard Gabriel didn't know, but he did know that Mr. William Perrin was now very, very afraid.

And he should be.

Gabriel hadn't fought a duel in years, but he'd never lost one, and that comment was far beyond the pale of what he could allow to pass.

Begin as you mean to go on. That was the only rule worth living by. If he let Perrin get by with insulting Imogen in such a way now, their lives truly would be miserable. He'd hound them incessantly. Drive them from the ton if he could. But if Gabriel stood up to him now, the matter would be settled.

Gabriel sensed more than saw his friends moving to stand behind him. Behind them. It was as though they stood in a boat, in a lock quickly filling, raising them to the next stage of their journey. George glittered in all her finery. Morpeth's shadow fell across them. Alençon stood at his shoulder, dangerous, radiating anger so strongly he could feel it wash over him.

Perrin's eyes got wider and wider as the ranks behind them swelled, becoming more and more formidable with each addition. The crowd stepped back, creating a clear path between them; perfectly aware that they didn't want to get caught between Brimstone and whatever fool had offended him.

A few men moved to stand behind Perrin, proving that

he had some friends willing to make a stand for him. Which was all Gabriel needed.

He couldn't challenge a man who couldn't so much as produce a second, but a man with friends at his side? That man was vulnerable to the form of counterattack Gabriel had in mind. To the kind he was a master of.

A few people tittered into the uncomfortable silence, but no one made a move to leave and go into dinner. A man coughed somewhere in the crowd. The crystals of the chandeliers tinkled overhead. Wax dripped onto the sleeve of his coat, marring the silk forever.

Gabriel dropped Imogen's arm, catching George's eye as he did so. He nodded as the countess stepped up to take his place, then he advanced slowly towards Perrin, his heels ringing smartly on the floor, every step a death knell . . .

But he wasn't going to kill the man. At least not here. Not now. He actually got halfway to his goal before Lord Jersey appeared in front of him, looking slightly panicked, his eyes searching out the crowd at Gabriel's back, silently begging for assistance.

"Mr. Angelstone?" He sounded as if he was going to be sick.

A hand gripped his shoulder, haulting his progress. Gabriel glanced back at his cousin's husband.

"Not here," the earl said flatly, eyes boring not into him but into Perrin.

A shudder ran though Gabriel. He jerked out of Morpeth's grasp. "Mr. Perrin made his insult publicly enough, and he'll damn well make his apology the same way."

Perrin puffed out his chest and glared back at him. A toad puffing up; its only defense. Was he really foolish enough to think he could brazen it out? Probably. He'd been fool enough to divorce Imogen, and that was a sign of lunacy.

"I'll say anything I want about that slut. I think I'm entitled to that after what she put me through."

Gabriel flicked his gaze up and down Perrin, his expression as insulting as he could make it. He wanted a fight. He wanted to kill him.

"I believe I am more than capable of making you regret uttering even the mildest slight against my future wife." He pitched his quiet threat to carry to the farthest reaches of the titillated crowd. "So you'll apologize to her, and then to me for putting me to the bother, and you'll do so now."

"Or what?"

Perrin clearly still did not understand the danger he stood in, or was simply unwilling to believe that he could be in any real danger. Gabriel smiled, letting his intention to kill the man leak from every pore.

"Or you'll name your seconds, and you'll make your apology in a much more public and humiliating fashion."

Perrin's nostrils flared, and his eyes narrowed, but he made no response. His hands shook visibly as he glanced behind him to see which of his friends were present.

He'd put himself between a rock and a hard place. Unable to back down, but clearly terrified of the situation he'd catapulted himself into. Gabriel took one deliberate step towards him, exalting as the bastard gave way.

"In fact," Gabriel added, baring his teeth in a wicked smile. "I think I prefer the option of exacting your apology, so much more satisfying; for me anyway. Morpeth?"

He glanced over and the earl nodded. A sea of grim faces surrounded them, frowns marring finely powdered skin. George looked as if she'd like to remove Perrin's head with her fan. Even Torrie wore an expression that he could only describe as bloodthirsty.

"Your second may make the arrangements with Lord Morpeth." Done, he turned his attention away from Perrin and strode back to where he'd left Imogen and George, relieved to see that his nymph was still there, George beside her, all their friends behind her.

Such a grand show of force. If there'd been any doubt as to where she stood it was over. When he reached them he paused and turned back to face Perrin. "Unless you come to your senses, in which case you may seek us out during supper."

Without another word, or so much as a backward glance, he claimed a white faced Imogen from George, and led her out of the room, their friends falling in behind them. An impenetrable wall of silk and velvet.

Imogen collapsed into the chair Gabriel placed her in, her gown crumpling around her. The seats around them overflowed with their friends. She simply wanted to leave, but when she'd tried to do so, George had shaken her head, and forced her to stand her ground.

The odd, hushed whispering conversations taking place set Imogen's teeth on edge. This was *exactly* what she'd been dreading all along. People were sneaking glances at her as they passed, and the occasional high pitched titter could only have been at her expense.

She fought back the urge to vomit, breathing slowly, deliberately. Gabriel reappeared with a selection of delicacies. A footman reached past her to fill their glasses with champagne.

"Drink up," Gabriel urged, eating a lobster patty

as though nothing were out of the ordinary. "You've earned it."

He was perfectly at his ease. Laughing beside her in grey striped silk, the curls of his wig negligently dangling over one shoulder. He was giving a masterful performance.

Imogen tossed back the entire glass. Gabriel handed her his, before waving the footman back over, and commandeering a bottle for the table. She drank the second glass in three gulps, and George filled it again.

Her stomach lurched in protest then settled. She had to make it clear to Gabriel that he was not to fight William. Anger churned, burning its way through her. "You're not—"

"Not going to discuss it here," the countess interrupted, cutting off whatever retort had sprung to Gabriel's lips. "We're all going to go on as if nothing happened. Eat. Drink. Dance, and then we can leave, and the two of you can fight about it all the way home, all night long, and into tomorrow if you care to, but not now."

Imogen swallowed her anger down, nearly choking. She took another gulp of champagne. Everyone was behaving as if this were a perfectly normal evening. It was tragedy masquerading as a farce. Couldn't they see that?

And they continued to pretend for the next several hours. She was paraded around the dance floor until the final notes of the evening wavered and dissipated. The crowd had hardly thinned. Everyone was watching them, curious, eager for another disaster. Another show.

Imogen shook her skirts out, smoothing them over her hoops. "Do they expect us to cap the evening by making love here and now?"

Gabriel chuckled and held out her evening cloak. "It

would certainly put the finishing touch on a rather unusual evening."

She hooked the clasp with shaking fingers. George grabbed him by the arm, hauling him back from her. "Not so much as a kiss on the steps, Brimstone."

Gabriel bit the inside of his cheek, amused despite himself, despite his nymph's obvious temper and the warning note in George's voice. Denied the prey he wanted, he was itching for a confrontation. Any confrontation.

He'd have loved to put on a show the ton would never forget, but Imogen had been tried almost past her limits. Better to get her home and into bed. She'd feel better in the morning, and so would he.

By morning he would know exactly where and when he'd get to extract Perrin's apology. Something which he was looking forward to with almost unholy glee.

Please let Perrin choose swords. Pistols would be too quick, too easy, too impersonal. Not nearly bloody enough . . .

When they arrived at Dauntry House George deserted them in the hall. "You don't need me in the middle of this."

Imogen stared dumbly about the hall, all emotion gone from her face. Poor thing. She looked numb. Done for. Gabriel tugged her into the salon and over to the chairs before the cold hearth. He gently pushed her down into one, then sank into the one opposite it, crossing one leg over the other and settling back into the embrace of the high-backed chair. He swept his wig from his head and tossed it onto the small table beside him.

"Well, love," he prompted.

"Don't even think about taking that tone with me." Her eyes flashed, the whites glowing in the dark room.

Gabriel didn't allow his lips to curl up into a smile. It took all the strength he had.

"Did you happen to notice that Perrin had made himself scarce by the time we returned from supper?" he asked offhandedly.

Imogen blinked. Clearly she hadn't noticed. She hadn't had the smallest idea that they'd already won the first battle.

When she didn't respond, Gabriel stretched out his leg and jiggled her knee with his foot. "Out with it. You were near bursting during supper."

Prodded out of her thoughts Imogen glared at him again. "You're not to fight him, Gabriel."

"Oddly enough, I'm going to."

"I won't have it," Imogen insisted, sitting up and leaning forward, her expression suddenly earnest. "Tonight was bad enough, but if you kill William—you'll—I'll—"

"You're right, love, tonight was awful, and if I don't meet your ex-husband it will be open season on us both." He held up a hand when she started to reply, and she fell silent, staring at him, her brows drawn together in a worried little frown. "And who said anything about killing him? There's no humiliation in that, or at least none he'd be around to suffer from, and that's what I'm after. That damn little popinjay isn't *ever* going to insult you again. When I'm done with him, no one will. And for that, I need him alive."

"But what if he kills you? I couldn't—"

Gabriel's laughter cut her off. He laughed until it turned into a fit of coughing and he had to stop to catch his breath.

"If you're not going to take this seriously . . ."

"Oh, Imogen, love," Gabriel replied, still smiling. It

really was so funny it hurt. "Perrin's never been in a duel, and from what I've heard, he's a terrible shot and an even worse fencer. By the time he has to stand across from me in some fog enshrouded field with the dew soaking through his boots, he's going to be shaking too badly to be any threat at all. My only worry is that his seconds will inform upon us in an effort to prevent the meeting."

"But you are going to shoot him? Or stab him or whatever it is you do with a sword."

"Like the cur he is, love. Like the cur he is."

"And if I asked you not to?"

"I'd advise you not to." Gabriel captured her gaze and held it. He had to make her understand. This wasn't something he could back down from. Not if they were to survive.

"But I am asking."

A dog barked in the distance. The watch called the hour from just outside the window. Gabriel watched her. Willing her to understand.

"Much as I hate to disappoint you, darling, that's not a request I can honor."

"Then neither is our engagement." Imogen tugged the betrothal ring he'd given her only a few days previously off her finger.

It was Gabriel's turn to glare. His eyes narrowed, and his nostrils flared. If she thought he was going to succumb to ploys such as this, she was mad.

He held out his hand and she dropped the ring into his palm. Without another word she fled the room in a flurry of silk and sobs.

Gabriel stared at the ring in his hand, clenched his fist around it. Blowing his breath out angrily he stood and thrust the ring into his pocket. His nymph had a knack for making things far more complicated than they needed to be. Perrin needed to learn a lesson. And unless the lesson was delivered, he'd feel free to torture them both for the rest of their lives. If left unchecked, he'd quickly turn them into exactly the social pariahs that Imogen feared to be.

Chapter 31

Nothing could have prepared us for the delicious sight of a certain Tory MP slinking from Lord and Lady J——'s soirée with his tail between his legs and his new wife railing like a fish wife.

Tête-à-Tête, 16 December 1789

At eleven the next morning, Imogen climbed into the small traveling coach usually reserved for the servants and threw herself back against the squabs. George handed in a basket of food.

"Are you sure, Imogen?" the countess asked, her brow puckered with concern.

Imogen nodded, unable to speak. She just wanted to get underway. If Gabriel caught her now, she wouldn't be able to go. With one last uneasy look, George stepped back and the footman threw up the steps and swung the coach door shut.

Imogen crumpled into the seat. She'd lain awake all night, trying to find a solution she could live with, and this was what she kept coming back to: escape. She wouldn't call it running away, though the phrase was apt. She pulled the carriage rug up over her lap and settled into the corner as the coach got underway with a lurch, metal banded wheels clattering loudly across the cobbles in the stillness of the morning.

Gabriel couldn't—wouldn't—see that fighting William would make everything worse. It would cause such an upsurge of gossip that she'd never be able to show her face again. The door to the ton had cracked open, but it was about to slam shut, right in her face. She'd either be the wanton who'd caused the death of a rising young politician or the slut who'd gotten her foreign lover killed.

Why couldn't Gabriel see that? Why do men so often seemed to think that violence would solve anything? Violence might be necessary to counter violence, but didn't seem all that effective for anything else.

A marriage between them would never work.

This was one case in which she was sad to have been proven right. All that was left was for her to get as far away from him as possible. And at the moment, that meant Scotland; to one of the estates belonging to the countess's brother. George had promised to send along her things, and not to tell Gabriel where she'd gone, though ringing that pledge out of her had been hard.

But once given George's word was sacrosanct. She wouldn't go back on her promise.

Imogen touched the countess's letter of introduction, flipped her book open so she could read the signature scrawled on the outside . . . Scotland.

Locks, heather, misty crags. It was not exile.

A tear slipped down her cheek, tracing a cold track down to her jaw. It wasn't. It was an adventure.

As her third best carriage disappeared round the corner, George blew her breath out with irritation and went back inside. If Imogen wanted to escape, there was nothing she could do about it, except provide a place to go, and a safe means of getting there.

Gabriel would have her head if she allowed Imogen to slip off to parts unknown. And much as she thought Imogen was making a mistake, it was her mistake to make. But just because George was going to let her make it, didn't mean she wasn't also going to do everything in her power to counter such a gaff.

Imogen was mad if she thought she was going to find a hiding place where Gabriel wouldn't be able to find her. Even if George didn't inform upon her—which she was going to very carefully skirt doing—it wouldn't take him that long to run her to ground. If he was quick about it, she wouldn't even get to Scotland. She had days and days on the road, and George had explicitly told her coachman to go as slowly as possible without letting on that he was doing so.

Far too pent up to stay home alone, the countess grabbed her coat and set off for The Top Heavy. The boys were doubtless already there, and she wanted to know what was going on. The duel couldn't have been fought this morning, but she was certain it would take place in the next day or two.

When she arrived, it was to find Morpeth and Bennett striding up the block deep in conversation. She waited for them on the steps, and then entered with them. Her former butler directed them to the second floor, to George's old private sitting room. Gabriel was already there, as were his cousin Julian and St. Audley.

Gabriel gave her a quick, appraising glance, before turning his attention to the earl. "Are we set?"

"We are," Morpeth replied, taking a seat. The earl's sitting down signaled everyone else to draw near and do the same. "It's for tomorrow."

"Weapons?"

"Time?"

"Where," everyone jumped in, their questions tumbling out in a rush.

"Breakfast plans?" George threw in, earning herself a glare from the earl.

"It's hardly your first duel," her husband said, shaking his head reprovingly. "Do try to contain yourself, you bloodthirsty wench."

"If I may?" Morpeth said, shooting them both a quelling glance. "Pistols. Seven . . . dawn being too early for Perrin. The green outside the Drunken Pelican, up in Hampstead. Breakfast reserved at the Pelican directly after, if that's acceptable to you, my queen?" he added with a smirk.

"Pistols?" George curled her lip. "Coward."

Gabriel smiled, looking thoroughly satisfied, and lounged back into his chair, crossing one leg over the other and swinging his foot. "It doesn't matter, Georgie. One will do as well as the other."

When Gabriel arrived at Morpeth's house the following morning, the city was just rumbling to life; drays hauling coal rattling through the dark streets, weaving through the fog past the occasional coach hauling home a late night reveler.

Gabriel made his way around the back of the house to the mews, where he found most of the party already assembled. He was obviously the last to arrive. He dismounted and handed over the case containing his pistols to the earl. He gave his gelding a firm slap on the haunch and the horse tossed his head, the soft rattle of his bit like a bell.

His friends milled about the stable yard, stamping their feet to ward off the cold. Gabriel checked his watch, and thrust the tortoiseshell bauble back into his pocket.

"Time to be on our way."

He had to consciously resist the urge to ask about his nymph. If there was anything he needed to know, he trusted George to tell him. She wasn't a secretive sort of woman. For now he needed to concentrate on the duel.

He had no concerns about his own safety; it was highly unlikely that his opponent would so much as graze him, but his own plan to wound Perrin without killing him would require greater skill than simply killing him outright. A simple torso shot was out of the question, too high a risk of hitting a vital organ. Which meant he was going to have to aim for an arm, or a leg.

If only he'd chosen swords. Cutting him to ribbons would have been so much more satisfying than putting a single bullet into him.

The sky was turning orange in the east, color cresting over the top of the trees as they arrived at the Drunken Pelican and turned their horses over to the ostler. Gabriel checked his watch again. Still only six-thirty. He flexed his shoulders and cracked his knuckles. There was no sign of the opponent or his seconds.

Perrin had better hurry up, it smelled like rain.

Inside the tap room they found the two surgeons. Gabriel spoke briefly to his, and paid him for his attendance. Bartleby was everything that was required in such a situation: reliable, highly skilled, and close as the grave.

Perrin's man on the other hand was huddled by the fire, imbibing heavily and muttering to himself in an aggrieved tone. Gabriel flicked his eyes over the man, and then looked questioningly at Bartleby, who rolled his eyes and shrugged.

At seven, when Perrin had still not put in an appearance, Gabriel and his friends stepped back outside to wait. Morpeth checked his watch and growled.

"This is ridiculous." Julian ground an errant weed in the cobbles under his boot heel.

"It does make one wonder if we're merely waiting for the constabulary," George said, craning her head and staring down the foggy road.

"It's certainly a thought," Gabriel agreed.

If Perrin didn't show, he'd be branded a coward, and publicly humiliated once word got out, but it would hardly be the satisfying outcome Gabriel was seeking. Such an outcome paled next to the visceral impact of losing a duel.

Another ten minutes passed before the sound of hooves caused everyone to watch the road. Eventually a carriage came into view, and upon entering the yard, it disgorged Perrin and four of his friends. Gabriel leaned insolently against the wall of the inn, chatting with his cousin and George while Morpeth approached the new arrivals.

"You're late," the earl snapped.

"Couldn't be helped," Lord Haversham replied, glancing guiltily at his boots.

"I'm sure. Shall we proceed?"

Haversham nodded and Morpeth motioned to Julian to bring the box of pistols over. "Do you wish to load for your principal, Haversham?" Morpeth asked.

"No, no," Haversham assured him. "Trust you to do it properly, Morpeth."

"Then I shall get to it, we're late enough as it is. Will you accompany me?" Morpeth turned without waiting for an answer, and went inside, Haversham trailing behind him.

Perrin and his three remaining friends stood in a tight knot, as far from Gabriel as they could, all of them patently ignoring everyone else in the yard. Gabriel glanced at them, prompting George to do so as well.

"Nervous as a hen with a fox outside the coop," she said with a smirk.

Gabriel gave a bark of laughter, and then chuckled anew as Perrin shied, his head snapping round, and then hastily turned back to his friends.

"You're a wicked, wicked woman, my dear."

George smiled and gave him a deep, formal curtsy. She stood up and placed one hand lightly on his arm. "You will be careful?"

"No such thing as careful in a duel, love. The only thing I got to choose was the distance."

"And the greater one you choose, the more to your advantage that would be." She clearly had a firm grasp on the inherent implications of someone of Gabriel's known skills facing a man such as Perrin.

"Ten paces." Gabriel shrugged, then twitched his coat so it lay more smoothly. "Gives him a chance of hitting me. A slight one anyway."

"And the number of shots?"

"Three, or until a serious wound is sustained by either party. It's all terribly standard. I guarantee he won't fire more than once though."

George made a face and tightened her grip on his arm. "I'm going to hold you to that."

Before he could reply, Morpeth and Haversham reappeared, flanked by the surgeons. Gabriel stripped out of his coat, tossing the expensive garment to George. "Hold that for me, my lady." George clutched it to her, smiling back at him wickedly.

Everyone set off across the wet grass, making for the large open green behind the inn. As they took their places, Perrin glanced nervously around, and rubbed his palms down the front of his thigh before choosing a pistol from the box Morpeth held.

Gabriel smiled and flexed his hand. God how he'd been looking forward to this.

The earl wandered almost lazily across the field, his long legs eating up the ten paces Haversham had marked out. He offered Gabriel the remaining pistol, and retreated to one side where the rest of the small audience was waiting.

"Gentlemen, at the count of three, you may fire when ready," Haversham announced loudly.

Morpeth counted off, and there was a thunderous report from Perrin's gun. Still breathing and completely whole Gabriel smiled and took careful aim. Perrin dropped to the grass, shrieking, both hands clasped to this thigh.

Gabriel glanced around, almost disinterestedly, looking to see if Perrin had managed to hit anything at all. He didn't think so. The bullet had certainly come nowhere near Gabriel himself. While he waited for the surgeon to make a pronouncement as to Perrin's fitness to continue, he savored the smell of sulfur in the air, the sweet scent of victory.

Perrin's somewhat soused surgeon was hustled to him by Haversham. After a few minutes, Lord Haversham approached Morpeth, then hastened back to his friend.

"Mr. Perrin is unable to continue," Morpeth announced in form. "Are you satisfied, Mr. Angelstone?"

"For the nonce." Without crossing to examine his handiwork, Gabriel turned and left the field. His friends fell into place behind him, and once they reached the private parlor they had reserved, everyone broke into congratulatory whoops.

"It would be beyond the pale to have cheered in front of Perrin, but oh, how I wanted to," George said, her eyes positively glowing as she took seat at the long table.

"You showed admirable restraint, witch," Somercote said with a grin, entering the room in Morpeth's wake.

"I've set Bartleby on them," Morpeth explained, as he piled his plate high with steak and eggs. "That sot Haversham engaged was next to useless."

Gabriel looked after shrugging himself back into his coat. "Did you tell Bartleby I'd foot the bill?"

Morpeth nodded, his smile growing wider.

"Well, that ought to stick in Perrin's craw," Gabriel added, picking up his coffee cup and inhaling the pungent scent with a sigh.

"I thought it was a nice touch," the earl admitted. "Dig the knife in a little deeper."

"Make him hunt you down to repay the dept," Julian cried with a laugh.

"Or better yet," Gabriel said with a thoroughly evil smile, "simply refuse to accept the money. Being beholden to me for such a debt ought to chaff."

A few minutes later a loud commotion could be heard from the tap room, followed by the sounds of a large group heading up the stairs. Apparently Perrin was going to live long enough to occupy one of the Pelican's rooms.

A ball to the leg wasn't likely to be life threatening, but one never knew. It could have hit an artery, or shattered the bone, or the wound could go septic. Right now he really didn't give a damn. If he had to take Imogen and flee the country so be it.

Chapter 32

Please let the rumors be true . . . a marriage between a man whose very existence is a scandal and a woman whose every action is an affront can only enliven all of our days.

Tête-à-Tête, 17 December 1789

As they mounted up and started back, George cut him out of the pack. "Gabe," she began, keeping her voice low.

He glanced over at her and stiffened, causing his horse to toss his head in protest. "I don't like that tone, Georgie. Why is it that whenever you sound like that I get shivers down my spine?"

George made a face, grimacing, and wrinkling up one side of her nose. "Because you know me?"

He raised his brows. Why was George stating the obvious? She was up to something, and that rarely boded well for any of them.

"Imogen left yesterday."

"And you were going to tell me this when?" The light

feeling fled, leading out his toes, draining away. Beetle shook his head again and Gabriel forced himself to loosen the reins.

"Well," she replied, without so much as a contrite look, "now."

"You couldn't have told me yesterday?"

She cocked her head, seemingly considering his question for a moment, while his hands itched to strangle her. "No, I don't think I could have. You had a duel to fight, and you couldn't have gone after her any sooner, so what would have been the point?"

Irritated beyond all belief, Gabriel gave her a squinty-eyed glare. "Are you going to tell me exactly where she went, and how she's getting there, or am I going to have to beat it out of you?"

"As if you'd dare," George replied with a laugh, which only got louder as he gnashed his teeth and half-heartedly swung at her with his crop. "I can't tell you where she's going. I promised not to, but I can tell you she's in my coach, the brown one, with the Somercote arms on the boot. And she's currently on the Great North Road. I can't imagine she's gotten all that far. I told Chandler to go *slowly.*"

Gabriel sucked in one cheek and bit it softly to keep from yelling at her. Irritating, interfering female. "I thought you were on my side, Georgie."

"Oh, I am on your side," she assured him, with her mischief-making smile beginning to peek out. The dimple in her cheek mocked him. "But this isn't about sides. It's about outcomes. And you and I both want the same outcome. Imogen does too, she just doesn't know it yet, or can't admit it."

Gabriel raised a brow. Lord save him from George

and her machinations. "So Imogen has cried off, returned my ring, and run away from town, secure in the conceit that I won't follow?"

George nodded, her grin growing wider. "I told your valet to have a bag packed. If you hurry, I imagine you should catch up to her by Peterborough. Newark at the latest."

"Thought of everything, haven't you?" Gabriel asked savagely.

"I rather think so," George replied, wholly unrepentant.

Imogen pulled the fur carriage rug tighter about her legs and rested her forehead against the window while she watched the scenery go past. She'd been on the road for four days, and they hadn't even reached Grantham yet.

The first day they'd barely made Stevenage before dark, and the second they'd been unable to procure a proper change of horses in Sandy, and had had to stop their journey there and wait. Then it had begun raining, turning the roads into a near impassable mire.

They'd become stuck twice before even reaching St. Neots, where she'd spent last night. She was hoping to reach Peterborough tonight. By now she would have normally expected to have been at least to Newark, if not beyond. At this rate it would take them a month to reach the Glenelg estate in northern Scotland.

If she'd been the kind of woman who saw signs and portends in such things she'd have told the Somercote's coachman to turn around and take her back to town. The coach hit another rut in the road and bounced her up off the seat. Grumbling, she rearranged herself for what felt like the thousandth time.

Lunch was a welcome distraction. After an hour in a small private parlor, warmed by a cheerful fire and several mugs of hot punch Imogen was feeling much more the thing. Her teeth had even stopped chattering by the time Chandler appeared at the door to urge her back into the carriage.

She hurriedly drank the last of her punch and pulled her gloves back on. Picking up her muff she stepped out of the parlor and moved quickly through the almost empty tap room. Only the determined and the desperate were traveling in such weather.

The earlier rain had diminished to a light drizzle, but even so, Imogen felt more than a bit guilty as she watched the coachman take his place on the box. She was freezing. How was he managing? There was no way she'd have been able to drive all day in such weather, even swathed in wool and coated in oilskin.

Shivering, she stepped out from under the eaves, preparing to climb back into the coach. A sudden commotion in the yard caught her attention as a steaming horse skidded to a stop, its rider already swinging out of the saddle, the skirts of his coat flying out.

An ostler claimed the animal and Imogen was left staring dumbly as Gabriel stormed across the muddy yard. Her heart gave a sickening lurch and her eyes felt suddenly hot. He was alive, and judging by his expression, he was very, very angry.

"Inside," he shouted with enough of an edge that her eyes opened wide and she fell back a step. "Chandler," he flung over his shoulder, "stable 'em." Then he turned, grabbed her by her arm, and dragged her back inside the inn.

The landlord appeared, confusion and concern bubbling over as Gabriel, his hand still locked about her upper arm, demanded a private parlor.

Imogen didn't bother to try and pull away. She didn't want to. That was the problem; when faced with him, all she could think of was getting closer. Her only hope had been in getting as far away from him as she could, and staying away from him.

At this exact moment her traitorous body was tingling from head to toe. A hot, wanton, totally inappropriate response to such a manhandling.

He was dripping wet, shaking with anger, and holding her so hard she was sure she'd be bruised tomorrow. Her heart was racing, and not with fear. Biting her lip she allowed him to drag her into the parlor she had just vacated.

Gabriel hauled Imogen into the room the frightened innkeep pointed to and kicked the door shut behind them with a resounding thump. Damn it all. He was wet to the skin, and suddenly so angry it was all he had been able to do not to beat her right there in the inn yard in front of God and everyone.

He'd thought he had himself under control until he'd ridden into the yard and caught sight of his nymph preparing to climb into her coach. The edge of his vision had tunneled out to black. His whole body had begun to shake. She hadn't even had the good sense to run. By the time he'd taken hold of her—a mistake that, he was well aware—his heart had been pounding so loudly he was practically deaf.

Once the door was shut, he dropped her arm, afraid to continue touching her. He stepped back slightly, prepared for recriminations, accusations, even violence. In the same situation, George would have broken his nose at the very least. She might have shot him.

Imogen swallowed hard, staring up at him, her eyes pricking with tears, a sea of blue shimmering beneath the rising water. Gabriel grimaced. Tears were something he had never been good at dealing with. She blinked, sending the first tear trailing down her cheek, then she launched herself at him, arms locking around his neck, lips finding his in a frenzied kiss.

Caught off guard Gabriel stumbled back until he came up against the buffet, Imogen clinging to him like a limpet. The room simply faded away. She was pulling him down to her, fierce, passionate.

He wrapped his arms around her, pressing her securely to his sodden chest, slanted his mouth over hers, meeting the thrust of her tongue with his own, devouring her as she offered herself up to him.

His hand shook as he gripped her waist, thumbs pressed hard against her stays. He hooked his fingers into her redingote.

A knock on the door interrupted them, and with a slightly guilty start Imogen's grip slackened and she slid down his chest. Gabriel kept one arm securely about her waist. If she was going to have second thoughts, he wanted to have a hold of her.

The door opened and the innkeep appeared, a steaming mug in his hands. He glanced worriedly at Imogen. "I thought, perhaps the gentleman, him being so wet and all, would welcome a hot arrack."

Gabriel's gaze flicked down to meet Imogen's. She smirked up at him. The landlord had obviously been afraid he was murdering her in here, and she was well aware of it.

God knew he'd felt like murder only moments ago.

"And so he would." Imogen pulled away from him

slightly and took the mug from the man with a soothing smile. "We'll be needing a room, too, since my husband so objects to my little jaunt without him."

The obviously relieved man bobbed his head and assured them that he'd have one ready momentarily so that the gentleman could change into something dry.

As he left, Imogen turned and handed Gabriel the mug, her expression impossible for him to read. Her eyes were still damp, her lashes tangled, but her mouth was soft, almost smiling. A dimple flashed in her cheek, so quickly he might have imagined it.

"I'm going to hold you to that you know?" He took the mug and gratefully swallowed a mouthful of the hot, sweet, rum-laced punch.

"I know." She caught her lower lip between her teeth. The swansdown of her tippet clung damply to her neck, trailed down over her chest in a bedraggled ruin.

"I'd look a fool if I didn't." He reached out and flipped the tippet off of her. "Can't fight a duel over one's fiancée, and then not marry her."

"No, that would be bad." Imogen nodded sagely.

"Very bad. Wouldn't be able to show my face in town ever again."

"Well, we can't have that . . . whatever would the ton have left to gossip about if they were deprived of your presence? And the shops in Bond Street. We must think of poor Mr. Manton. He'd go out of business. And Angelo's, why your business alone must account for—"

"Spiteful cat," he protested, laughing.

"I'm only agreeing with you."

"Seriously, my exasperating little nymph, I've got a special license in my bag, and tomorrow morning we're going to find the nearest vicar, and put it to good use."

"But Lady Glendower—"

"Will understand." He tugged her to him and kissed her again, his lips softly capturing hers in a brief, welcoming salute. "Not even going to ask about Perrin's fate?"

"I don't care." She slid her arms more securely about his neck and looked up at him, meeting his gaze squarely. "Are we fleeing to Italy after the ceremony? My bags are rather conveniently packed and ready you know."

Gabriel chuckled and kissed her again. "If it's Italy you want, love, Italy you shall have, but I think I'd prefer to live in England. We might be endlessly snubbed by Torrie, and we'll never cross the portals of Almack's, but I, for one, am prepared to live without warm lemonade and evenings spent performing endless country dances."

Imogen rested her check on his shoulder. "We've got to get you out of these clothes, Gabriel."

"I thought you'd never get to that."

She shook her head reprovingly at him. "I'm not going upstairs with you to make love in the middle of the afternoon, Gabriel."

"You think not?" He raised one brow in mock challenge. "What else do you propose we do for the rest of the day?"

Imogen glanced around the bare and rather cheerless little parlor, then with a wicked little grin she preceded him out of the room, calling for the landlord.

Epilogue

Corinthians, pugilists, and beaux everywhere are in alt. Their messiah is delivered, or so the steady flow of their ranks in the eastwardly direction of their queen would seem to indicate . . .

Tête-à-Tête, 18 May 1790

Gabriel adjusted his hold on George's new son and glanced across the room. His wife was curled up in the window seat beside George, both of them looking out over the gardens, speaking in tones low enough that only a soft murmur reached him. The baby made an incoherent sound of protest as he settled into the crook of Gabriel's arm, and both women glanced over their shoulders.

Gabriel shook his head at them and stood up, carrying the baby around the room with a soft bounce. He could understand Imogen mistrusting his skills, but George had seen him with his cousin's children often enough over the years to know better.

The walk failed to do its job and little Dysart Alan

Dauntry waved a small fist in the air, his small form swelling with outrage.

George yawned and turned to take him, arms already outstretched long before he reached her. The baby hiccupped and nestled into George like a puppy, clearly content now that he had achieved his goal. Gabriel grinned and stooped to kiss his wife on the back of the neck, the exposed skin too sweet to resist.

They'd attended the races at Epsom Downs last week, then immediately traveled up from London to be present for George's laying in—as had half their other friends—causing George to laugh and assign them all roles from the nativity.

He and Imogen had been proclaimed camels, while the Morpeths were sheep. Poor Bennett and Layton had been labeled asses. Probably because they were the ones most likely to hover over her. Only Alençon and Carr had come off well, being assigned the roles of angels. George refused to allow any of them to claim the roles of wise men, no matter what presents they might have brought. And no one spoke of the conspicuously absent St. Audley, at least after George brushed off his tardiness by calling him a star rising in the South.

"Want to go for a punt on the lake?" Gabriel whispered, trying not to let too wolfish an edge into his smile.

Imogen smiled back, extending her hand to be helped up off the seat. George made a disgusted sound in the back of her throat. "Do go and play for heaven's sake. There's no need to hover over me."

Gabriel gave a bark of laughter that made the baby jump. Imogen hushed him and pushed him from the room, one hand firmly set against his spine, propelling him forward.

Clearly the damp heat of the afternoon wasn't going to put her off a stroll down to the lake . . . and whatever else he might have in mind for her entertainment.